ROBIN FO
THE GINGER CAT MYSTERY

Robin Forsythe was born Robert Forsythe in 1879. His place of birth was Sialkot, in modern day Pakistan. His mother died when a younger brother was born two years later, and 'Robin' was brought up by an ayah until he was six, when he returned to the United Kingdom, and went to school in Glasgow and Northern Ireland. In his teens he had short stories and poetry published and went to London wanting to be a writer.

He married in 1909 and had a son the following year, later working as a clerk at Somerset House in London when he was arrested for theft and fraud in 1928. Sentenced to fifteen months, he began to write his first detective novel in prison.

On his release in 1929 Robin Forsythe published his debut, *Missing or Murdered*. It introduced Anthony 'Algernon' Vereker, an eccentric artist with an extraordinary flair for detective work. It was followed by four more detective novels in the Vereker series, ending with *The Spirit Murder Mystery* in 1936. All the novels are characterized by the sharp plotting and witty dialogue which epitomize the more effervescent side of golden age crime fiction.

Robin Forsythe died in 1937.

ROBIN FORSYTHE

THE GINGER CAT MYSTERY

With an introduction
by Curtis Evans

DEAN STREET PRESS

Published by Dean Street Press 2016

Introduction copyright © 2016 Curtis Evans

All Rights Reserved

Cover by DSP

First published in 1935 by The Bodley Head

ISBN 978 1 911095 16 3

www.deanstreetpress.co.uk

To

MY DEAR PAL, TERRY

AN IRISH SETTER

Robin Forsythe (1879-1937)
Crime in Fact and Fiction

Ingenious criminal schemes were the stock in trade of those
ever-so-bright men and women who devised the baffling puzzles
found in between-the-wars detective fiction. Yet although scores
of Golden Age mystery writers strove mightily to commit brilliant
crimes on paper, presumably few of them ever attempted to
commit them in fact. One author of classic crime fiction who
actually carried out a crafty real-life crime was Robin Forsythe.
Before commencing in 1929 his successful series of Algernon
Vereker detective novels, now reprinted in attractive new editions
by the enterprising Dean Street Press, Forsythe served in the
1920s as the mastermind behind England's Somerset House
stamp trafficking scandal.

Robin Forsythe was born Robert Forsythe—he later found it
prudent to slightly alter his Christian name—in Sialkot, Punjab
(then part of British India, today part of Pakistan) on 10 May
1879, the eldest son of distinguished British cavalryman John
"Jock" Forsythe and his wife Caroline. Born in 1838 to modestly
circumstanced parents in the Scottish village of Carmunnock,
outside Glasgow, John Forsythe in 1858 enlisted as a private in
the Ninth Queen's Royal Lancers and was sent to India, then in
the final throes of a bloody rebellion. Like the fictional Dr. John
H. Watson of Sherlock Holmes fame, Forsythe saw major martial
action in Afghanistan two decades later during the Second Anglo-
Afghan War (1878-1880), in his case at the December 1879 siege
of the Sherpur Cantonment, just outside Kabul, and the Battle of
Kandahar on 1 September 1880, for which service he received the
War Medal with two Clasps and the Bronze England and Ireland
until his retirement from the British army in 1893, four years after
having been made an Honorary Captain. The old solider was later
warmly commended, in a 1904 history of the Ninth Lancers, for
his "unbroken record of faithful, unfailing and devoted service."

His son Robin's departure from government service a quarter-century later would be rather less harmonious.

A year after John Forsythe's return to India from Afghanistan in 1880, his wife Caroline died in Ambala after having given birth to Robin's younger brother, Gilbert ("Gill"), and the two little boys were raised by an Indian ayah, or nanny. The family returned to England in 1885, when Robin was six years old, crossing over to Ireland five years later, when the Ninth Lancers were stationed at the Curragh Army Camp. On Captain Forsythe's retirement from the Lancers in 1893, he and his two sons settled in Scotland at his old home village, Carmunnock. Originally intended for the legal profession, Robin instead entered the civil service, although like E.R. Punshon, another clerk turned classic mystery writer recently reprinted by Dean Street Press, he dreamt of earning his bread through his pen by another, more imaginative, means: creative writing. As a young man Robin published poetry and short stories in newspapers and periodicals, yet not until after his release from prison in 1929 at the age of fifty would he finally realize his youthful hope of making his living as a fiction writer.

For the next several years Robin worked in Glasgow as an Inland Revenue Assistant of Excise. In 1909 he married Kate Margaret Havord, daughter of a guide roller in a Glasgow iron and steel mill, and by 1911 the couple resided, along with their one-year-old son John, in Godstone, Surrey, twenty miles from London, where Robin was employed as a Third Class Clerk in the Principal Probate Registry at Somerset House. Young John remained the Robin and Kate's only child when the couple separated a decade later. What problems led to the irretrievable breakdown of the marriage is not known, but Kate's daughter-in-law later characterized Kate as "very greedy" and speculated that her exactions upon her husband might have made "life difficult for Robin and given him a reason for his illegal acts."

Six years after his separation from Kate, Robin conceived and carried out, with the help of three additional Somerset

House clerks, a fraudulent enterprise resembling something out of the imaginative crime fiction of Arthur Conan Doyle, Golden Age thriller writer Edgar Wallace and post Golden Age lawyer-turned-author Michael Gilbert. Over a year-and-a-half period, the Somerset House conspirators removed high value judicature stamps from documents deposited with the Board of Inland Revenue, using acids to obliterate cancellation marks, and sold the stamps at half-cost to three solicitor's clerks, the latter of whom pocketed the difference in prices. Robin and his co-conspirators at Somerset House divided among themselves the proceeds from the illicit sales of the stamps, which totaled over 50,000 pounds (or roughly $75,000 US dollars) in modern value. Unhappily for the seven schemers, however, a government auditor became suspicious of nefarious activity at Somerset House, resulting in a 1927 undercover Scotland Yard investigation that, coupled with an intensive police laboratory examination of hundreds of suspect documents, fully exposed both the crime and its culprits.

Robin Forsythe and his co-conspirators were promptly arrested and at London's Old Bailey on 7 February 1928, the Common Serjeant--elderly Sir Henry Dickens, K.C., last surviving child of the great Victorian author Charles Dickens--passed sentence on the seven men, all of whom had plead guilty and thrown themselves on the mercy of the court. Sir Henry sentenced Robin to a term of fifteen months imprisonment, castigating him as a calculating rogue, according to the Glasgow Herald, the newspaper in which Robin had published his poetry as a young man, back when the world had seemed full of promise:

> It is an astounding position to find in an office like that of Somerset House that the Canker of dishonesty had bitten deep....You are the prime mover of this, and obviously you started it. For a year and a half you have continued it, and you have undoubtedly raised an atmosphere and influenced other people in that office.

Likely one of the "astounding" aspects of this case in the eyes of eminent pillars of society like Dickens was that Robin Forsythe and his criminal cohort to a man had appeared to be, before the fraud was exposed, quite upright individuals. With one exception Robin's co-conspirators were a generation younger than their ringleader and had done their duty, as the saying goes, in the Great War. One man had been a decorated lance corporal in the late affray, while another had served as a gunner in the Royal Field Artillery and a third had piloted biplanes as a 2nd lieutenant in the Royal Flying Corps. The affair disturbingly demonstrated to all and sundry that, just like in Golden Age crime fiction, people who seemed above suspicion could fall surprisingly hard for the glittering lure of ill-gotten gain.

Crime fiction offered the imaginative Robin Forsythe not only a means of livelihood after he was released in from prison in 1929, unemployed and seemingly unemployable, but also, one might surmise, a source of emotional solace and escape. Dorothy L. Sayers once explained that from the character of her privileged aristocratic amateur detective, Lord Peter Wimsey, she had devised and derived, at difficult times in her life, considerable vicarious satisfaction:

> When I was dissatisfied with my single unfurnished room, I tool a luxurious flat for him in Piccadilly. When my cheap rug got a hole in it, I ordered an Aubusson carpet. When I had no money to pay my bus fare, I presented him with a Daimler double-six, upholstered in a style of sober magnificence, and when I felt dull I let him drive it.

Between 1929 and 1937 Robin published eight successful crime novels, five of which were part of the Algernon Vereker mystery series for which the author was best known: *Missing or Murdered* (1929), *The Polo Ground Mystery* (1932), *The Pleasure Cruise Mystery* (1933), *The Ginger Cat Mystery* (1935) and *The Spirit Murder Mystery* (1936). The three remaining novels—*The Hounds of Justice* (1930), *The Poison Duel* (1934, under the pseudonym Peter Dingwall) and *Murder on Paradise Island* (1937)—were non-series works.

Like the other Robin Forsythe detective novels detailing the criminal investigations of Algernon Vereker, gentleman artist and amateur sleuth, *Missing or Murdered* was issued in England by The Bodley Head, publisher in the Twenties of mysteries by Agatha Christie and Annie Haynes, the latter another able writer revived by Dean Street Press. Christie had left The Bodley Head in 1926 and Annie Haynes had passed away early in 1929, leaving the publisher in need of promising new authors. Additionally, the American company Appleton-Century published two of the Algernon Vereker novels, *The Pleasure Cruise Mystery* and *The Ginger Cat Mystery*, in the United States (the latter book under the title *Murder at Marston Manor*) as part of its short-lived but memorably titled Tired Business Man's Library of adventure, detective and mystery novels, which were designed "to afford relaxation and entertainment" to industrious American escape fiction addicts during their off hours. Forsythe's fiction also enjoyed some success in France, where his first three detective novels were published, under the titles *La Disparition de Lord Bygrave* (The Disappearance of Lord Bygrave), *La Passion de Sadie Maberley* (The Passion of Sadie Maberley) and *Coups de feu a l'aube* (Gunshots at Dawn).

The Robin Forsythe mystery fiction drew favorable comment for their vivacity and ingenuity from such luminaries as Dorothy L. Sayers, Charles Williams and J.B. Priestley, the latter acutely observing that "Mr. Forsythe belongs to the new school of detective story writers which might be called the brilliant flippant school." Sayers pronounced of Forsythe's *The Ginger Cat Mystery* that "[t]he story is lively and the plot interesting," while Charles Williams, author and editor of Oxford University Press, heaped praise upon *The Polo Ground Mystery* as "a good story of one bullet, two wounds, two shots, and one dead man and three pistols before the end....It is really a maze, and the characters are not merely automata."

This second act in the career of Robin Forsythe proved sadly short-lived, however, for in 1937 the author passed away from kidney disease, still estranged from his wife and son, at the age of 57. In his later years he resided--along with his Irish Setter Terry, the "dear pal" to whom he dedicated *The Ginger Cat Mystery*--at a cottage in the village of Hartest, near Bury St. Edmunds, Suffolk. In addition to writing, Robin enjoyed gardening and dabbling in art, having become an able chalk sketch artist and water colorist. He also toured on ocean liners (under the name "Robin Forsythe"), thereby gaining experience that would serve him well in his novel *The Pleasure Cruise Mystery*. This book Robin dedicated to "Beatrice," while *Missing or Murdered* was dedicated to "Elizabeth" and *The Spirit Murder Mystery* to "Jean." Did Robin find solace as well in human companionship during his later years? Currently we can only speculate, but classic British crime fans who peruse the mysteries of Robin Forsythe should derive pleasure from spending time in the clever company of Algernon Vereker as he hunts down fictional malefactors—thus proving that, while crime may not pay, it most definitely can entertain.

Curtis Evans

Chapter One
Murder in Arcadia

The little village of Marston-le-Willows in West Suffolk had
suddenly become known to the inhabitants of Great Britain,
or more precisely to all those who read a daily or a Sunday
newspaper. A startling chain of events had caused this forced
emergence of Marston-le-Willows from its pastoral seclusion, its
almost mediaeval English passivity and quietude into the hustle
and noise of twentieth-century publicity. That chain of events
had culminated in a mysterious murder and apparently there are
few people who are not immediately interested in a mysterious
murder. It is said that even such exalted personages as prime
ministers, chancellors of the exchequer, law lords, headmasters
of famous schools and secretly a bishop or two are addicted to the
reading of fictional murders as an invigorating relaxation from
the terrible strain of their stupendous mental activities. Whatever
may be the truth in such matters, there's no denying the fact that
a murder made Marston-le-Willows notorious very much as a
murder made the village of Babbacombe notorious—one could
almost say historical. It might have been happier to achieve fame
like Giggleswick through an eclipse of the sun rather than through
the extinction of a human life, but that was not decreed by the
Fates. This fortuitous notoriety, however, had very little effect
on the slow, even tenor of life in Marston. John Rash, the baker,
round-faced, perennially cheerful and addicted temperately to
his pint of beer at fixed intervals during the day, baked in his
usual efficient manner in his old brick oven and could be seen
daily rocking along in his high-wheeled pony trap on a wider
round of his own while his boy delivered his bread in a narrower
circle by means of "push-bike" and basket. Walter Gammer, the
butcher, financially a shade more prosperous, distributed his
meat as punctually as ever by means of a small car, not only to
Marston inhabitants but to all the scattered cottages and houses

which stud the tortuous Suffolk roads for miles around the village. William Hunnibell, the newsagent, dropped his newspapers in farmhouse porches or thrust them through open cottage windows every morning, and if by any chance he saw a housewife, tried to persuade her to buy apples, pears, ice cream, tomatoes, herrings, kippers or haddocks which he brought along in his little governess cart as an extension of his commercial activities when the seasons and supplies permitted. Edgar Dobley, the carpenter and wheelwright, with that sharper intelligence which seems to distinguish his calling in a village, built his barrows, constructed his wagons, made and painted his ladders at a shilling a stave in his shop redolent of clean wood and resounding to the blows of a hammer or the tearing rip of a saw. The farmers were busy with their sugar beet, their wheat, barley, beans, their turkeys, fowls, cattle and black-faced Suffolk sheep. The sails of the windmills of the district still revolved as they had in the remote past, grinding corn now raised more generously under the fostering warmth of a wheat subsidy. The village boys, care-free and unconcerned, played football on the village green, using the village's two pumps as goal-posts at one end of the field and their discarded coats at the other. But tongues wagged more vigorously in Marston, if tongues can ever be said to wag to the slow, high-pitched, singing Suffolk dialect. They wagged, too, in a way peculiar to the rural areas of the county. A topic is broached, an idea is born and communicated and further conversation consists of a repetition of that idea. Behind this repetition, however, may lurk a significant intonation, an almost imperceptible but informative wink, a slow, cautious, illuminating smile, for your countryman is naturally guarded in his speech in a village where gossip can easily be brought home to its source and the network of relationship is embarrassingly involved and comprehensive. There is, moreover, an inborn desire to live at peace which seems a reflection of the gentle lines of the landscape, of low horizons blurred by the hazy blue of distant woods, of the wide contented skies.

The cause of the trouble that burst so unexpectedly on Marston-le-Willows had its source in Marston Manor. Some years previously, old Squire Chevington had died. His estate, which had been held by the Chevington family for centuries, had been broken up and sold and the family seat of Marston Manor had been bought by a Mr. John Cornell. John Cornell, though a Suffolk-born man, had gone up to London in his teens to fill a very minor post in the offices of the well-known firm of Ince and Colt, general merchants, merchant bankers and bill discounters of Mincing Lane. Slowly but steadily he worked his way up to the position of senior partner and at the age of sixty retired with a considerable fortune to spend the remainder of his days in the peace and seclusion of his own county. His rise to affluence had been the outcome rather of bucolic shrewdness, unwavering pertinacity and relentless thrift than of any gift of financial brilliance, and perhaps this is an indirect compliment in days when financial brilliance frequently connotes a questionable rapidity in the acquisition of wealth. Those who knew him and liked his rather simple and frank nature, wondered at times how he had attained his fortune and position and generally agreed that his success was in a great measure due to the tact, lively wit and business acumen of his wife, Clara. Three years prior to her husband's retirement Clara Cornell died, leaving her own modest fortune to her son Frank, the sole offspring of her marriage, who was then twenty-one years old and intended for the Bar. On the death of his wife an extraordinary change came over John Cornell. He appeared all at once to renew his youth and pass once more through a romantic phase characteristic of adolescence. Formerly very austere and old-fashioned in his garb, wearing clothes almost as a uniform emphasizing the seriousness, the conservatism, the stability of his business, he now began to indulge in brighter materials and a livelier cut. His sombre neckwear burst into striped and chromatic gaiety; his gloves tripped lightly from brown or dark grey to chamois; his prim white handkerchiefs lapsed into the

voluptuousness of spotted foulards. Even when playing his very
occasional game of golf he had always worn grey flannels and
a Harris jacket of particularly subdued colour. These he now
discarded for snuff-coloured plus-fours, a jumper of conspicuous
design and vivid hue and startled his older friends by wearing a
yellow beret cocked at a ludicrously pert angle on his large and
shining bald head. Previously always parsimonious, he now began
to spend almost lavishly. Though he had seldom frequented
places of amusement and then only with an air of boredom, as
if he were fulfilling a necessary but uncongenial social duty to
please his wife, he now appeared regularly at the opera in spite
of the fact that he secretly thought most operas artificial foreign
rubbish. He became a stalwart first-nighter at theatres and was
frequently seen at a fashionable night club dancing and deporting
himself with the zest and agility of a man of half his age. When
he travelled he now travelled by air; he rented a costly villa on
the Riviera during the season, bought a sumptuous houseboat
on the upper reaches of the Thames and, having sold his old
moderate-priced saloon car, acquired a luxury liner of the road.
The houseboat, the name of which he had altered from "Mayfly" to
"Mayfly But Can't," soon became the week-end resort of a crowd of
young and fashionable people, friends of his son, who all treated
him with that affectionate tolerance which youth now grants to
moneyed age and experience. John Cornell soon became generally
popular and, though he made his son Frank the excuse for this
bright rejuvenescence (the jolly-pal rather than pompous-father
attitude), it was abundantly clear to all that the hearty old man
was thoroughly enjoying himself and having what is colloquially
termed "a high old time." His frozen sedateness seemed to have
thawed miraculously in the autumn sunshine of his years and
with the sudden realization that he was no longer attached to the
dominant personality of his shrewish wife. There was nothing
vicious about this late burgeoning of John Cornell; it was the
expression of a healthy virility still capable of a whole-hearted

pleasure in living. Its true significance, however, was disclosed by its culmination in a second marriage.

Among his son's many friends, for Frank Cornell had a genius for collecting friends of the most diverse temperaments, was a beautiful, sophisticated, at times rather wistful, young woman, Josephine Rivron, who became a regular guest at all John Cornell's week-end houseboat parties during the summer following his wife's death. It was at first thought by everyone that she was to be Frank Cornell's wife and some averred that he actually proposed to her but was refused. The news that she was engaged to the father therefore came as something startling and eruptive to all the family's relatives, friends and acquaintances. The engagement was the source of considerable malicious gossip and to the cynical it seemed clear that the young lady was in an unseemly hurry to lay hands on the loaded Cornell coffers. To marry the son was, so to speak, merely marrying a reversion. Josephine Rivron was naturally told by a candid friend all that was being said about her, but it failed to disturb her remarkable equanimity and exactly a year after their first meeting she became John Cornell's wife. Shortly afterwards John Cornell retired from business, bought Marston Manor and began to live the life of a country gentleman. The marriage was to all outward appearances eminently happy. John Cornell's effulgence dimmed to a natural glow and he settled down to enjoy his leisure, his wife's charming company and his country mansion.

During all the years of his unbending attachment to business, in moments of idle rumination John Cornell had looked forward to this time of retirement. At the core of his dreaming was a garden and flowers and an ineffable peace: it was a secret passion of which he was almost ashamed. He would have a magnificent garden and magnificent flowers, stupendous blooms like those he saw exhibited by commercial horticulturists at flower shows. The time had come to make his dream come true and he was daily to be seen in consultation with Braber, his gardener, planning the accomplishment of that dream. Josephine his wife was equally absorbed in Marston Manor for she had discovered an outlet for her domestic activities in the general adaptation of the old house to modern requirements, a moulding of a mediaeval skeleton to what she called "the amenities of up-to-date living." With the help of the local doctor, Stanley Redgrave, who was versed in the lore of the English manor, she was accomplishing this task with a fine regard for its ancient beauty and in the process had become very friendly with her "medical adviser." Then some years after their arrival at Marston, John Cornell suddenly fell ill. He had apparently been in robust health and there had been no warning symptoms of disease to herald the approach of a swift departure from life. His illness began with a violent headache, persistent vomiting and repeated convulsions. A period of wild delirium was swiftly followed by profound coma and within a week he was dead. Doctor Redgrave, who attended him throughout his brief illness, certified that death was due to pneumonia, and John Cornell was buried in the churchyard of All Saints', Marston-le-Willows. Josephine, his wife, was for a time prostrate with grief, and Marston-le-Willows sincerely mourned his loss for more material reasons.

A short obituary notice in a few of the London papers and half a column of kindly eulogy in the *West Suffolk Post* was all the publicity that was granted to the passing of John Cornell for the time being. It was as much as any man of his status could expect from a world mechanically industrial, not given overmuch to sentiment, and too preoccupied with the strenuousness of living to be arrested by any perplexing meditation on the mystery of death. But the passing of John Cornell was not going to be such an ordinary occurrence as it had first appeared. Six months after his burial something mysterious occurred in Marston-le-Willows, something that might be called in an increasingly trite phrase "a major phenomenon." It was the first of the chain of startling events that made the name of Marston-le-Willows as well-known as that of Brighton. Perhaps an excerpt from the *West Suffolk*

Post of the 15th of August will give an adequate description of the occurrence. It ran:

EXHUMATION BY LAMPLIGHT
Marston-le-Willows. Sunday.

The body of John Cornell, the well-known London merchant and banker, who died suddenly at his home, Marston Manor, last February, was exhumed here early this morning with great secrecy, following representations made to the Home Office.

Policemen were posted at the gates of the cemetery to prevent the presence of unauthorized persons while the work of exhumation was carried out by lamplight.

A post-mortem was held this afternoon at which Doctors Redgrave and Lake represented the financier's wife. Dr. McAndrew, the famous pathologist, conducted the post-mortem and certain organs were removed from the body for examination by the Home Office Analyst. The inquest was adjourned pending his report.

In spite of the great secrecy referred to by the *West Suffolk Post*, before nightfall on that memorable Sunday in August all Marston-le-Willows knew that the body of John Cornell had been exhumed, that the representations had been made to the Home Office by David Cornell, his blind brother who lived in a bungalow in the Manor grounds, and that it was suspected that the deceased had been poisoned. The days that intervened between the exhumation and the resumed inquest were days of intense, suppressed excitement. The outward calm of the village and its inhabitants seemed unreal, almost ominous, in conjunction with their inward and hidden tension. There was only one topic of conversation, but that topic was discussed in guarded whispers by one intimate friend with another. Even in the tap-room of "The Dog and Partridge" the subject was generally avoided by the handful of regular customers and if it happened to be touched on by some rash spirit, the landlord, Abner Borham, would display a childlike ignorance of the whole business. The only villager who blurted out what he thought was old Harry Weddup, the thatcher, but he was the licensed *enfant terrible* of Marston. He openly declared it was his opinion that the young wife had got rid of her aged husband by poison so that she could marry someone young and lusty like herself and enjoy the old man's money. Putting the matter in terms of horseflesh, he thought it was perfectly natural for a fresh young mare to get tired of a worn-out old hack who hadn't as much as a whinny left in him. He would say that on her behalf but it was all he could say. It was a damnable thing to poison the old man and she would certainly be found out, like Mrs. Maybrick, and pay "the dire penalty." Serve her right, too. At this point, Harry Weddup (he had drawn his old age pension and drunk an extra pint or two) delivered a long lecture on the evil of old men hankering after and marrying young women. "Noo wine bust old bottles," he declared, and if those gents got poisoned in the end it served them right, too. After this impartial dispensation of justice he fell into silence so that his words of wisdom might sink into the understanding of his somewhat facetious listeners.

The day of the resumed inquest, though opening with tremendous excitement, may be said to have ended in a weak anti-climax. The squib had hissed itself out instead of detonating. The *West Suffolk Post*'s report was as follows:

DRAMATIC PROTEST AT INQUEST
WIFE'S PAINFUL ORDEAL
NO POISON

Marston-le-Willows. Friday.

The resumed inquest of Mr. John Cornell, who died in February last and whose body was exhumed at midnight on August 15th, was held here to-day. The inquest had been

opened and adjourned for an examination of the organs
by the Home Office Analyst. Dr. McAndrew, the famous
pathologist, had conducted the post-mortem examination.

The first sensation occurred when the coroner asked
those not connected with the case to leave the court.

Dr. McAndrew, the first witness, then handed the
coroner several pages of typewritten matter which the
coroner read to the jury. He said he was present when the
coffin was opened.

The coroner was then handed the Home Office
Analyst's report which read, "I have examined all the
samples submitted to me and can find no trace of poison."

After a brief consultation with the coroner, the foreman
of the jury announced that they were satisfied that Mr.
Cornell's death was due to natural causes.

Mr. Godbold, on behalf of Mrs. Cornell, then made a
dramatic protest against the exhumation, pointing out the
suffering which the whole proceeding had inflicted on his
client and that it was a disgrace that proceedings of such a
grave nature should be started on the mere idle suspicion
of a relative of the deceased. On the conclusion of his
remarks, Mrs. Cornell the dead man's widow, broke down
and was assisted from the court by her medical adviser.

No poison! So this was the mild sequel to a week of the tensest
expectancy. Though the inhabitants of Marston-le-Willows
said they were glad for the young lady's sake that such had
been the verdict, they were really secretly disappointed. Their
disappointment was an impersonal affair and had nothing to
do with the protagonists in the drama. In their annoyance they
thoroughly agreed that Mr. Godbold was perfectly justified
in making his protest against the exhumation and some very
unpleasant things were said about Mr. David Cornell, John
Cornell's blind brother, who had been the prime mover in the

whole unsavoury business. Prior to the verdict of the coroner's jury they had said that David Cornell was perfectly justified in seeing that the mystery of his brother's sudden death should be thoroughly investigated. Harry Weddup firmly declared his belief that the old man was poisoned by a "secret pisin" and that the doctor from London hadn't been able to detect the method. All Londoners were fools more or less but it was hardly fair to blame him. How could anyone be expected to detect a "secret pisin"? There the matter ended and Marston-le-Willows was lapsing into its normal quietude once more when another and more startling event occurred.

Exactly a week after the final inquest on John Cornell his son Frank was found lying dead on the half-landing of a staircase leading to the first storey of Marston Manor. He had been shot through the right eye and the bullet had come to rest at the back of his skull. The discovery was made by one of the maids who was taking up morning tea to the young man's bedroom. She fainted and let the tray crash to the floor. Making a swift recovery, she at once roused her mistress who after a lapse of a few minutes sufficiently recovered from her shock to telephone the police. The local sergeant and a constable soon appeared on the scene and after a brief examination the sergeant at once summoned Dr. Redgrave and informed the police at Bury St. Edmunds. Later in the day, the Deputy Chief Constable and a superintendent arrived at Marston Manor. After a very careful investigation and a thorough search for the weapon which could not be found, they concluded that the dead man had been murdered. The assistance of Scotland Yard was promptly asked for and Chief Inspector Heather with Detective-Sergeant Goss arrived from London by car and took charge of the case.

Chapter Two
Anthony Vereker Wakes Up

Anthony Vereker, known to his friends as Algernon unabbreviated, returned to his flat in Fenton Street, W., with a large parcel in his right hand and several unmanageable rolls of paper under his left arm. He had forgotten to take his latchkey with him and, having pressed the bell-push of the door, stood listening for the measured tread of his manservant, Albert. Instead of Albert's military slow march he heard rapid footsteps hastening along the corridor from the direction of his studio and next moment the door was pulled unceremoniously open by his friend Manuel Ricardo.

"Hello, Ricky, you here! You're a great stranger. I haven't seen you for some months. Where have you been and what have you been up to?"

"The story's too long to retail on a doormat, Algernon. Come in and make yourself at home in your own flat."

"Been waiting long for me?"

"I've been here over an hour but good whisky shortens even the longest wait. I've helped myself. I told your man Albert he could go and get me the evening newspapers and that he needn't hurry back. I assured him I'd be in when you returned."

"That was good of you. Gives the old boy a chance of a breather."

"Never thought of that. To tell the truth, I never can enjoy myself in your flat when Albert's about. He makes all sorts of ridiculous excuses to enter your studio and looks reproachfully at your decanter every time he comes in. Besides, I've been busy as well. I'm at work on a thriller; they've got a temporary ascendancy over the love serial just now."

"Why not use some of my cases as material?" asked Vereker.

"Too pedestrian, Algernon. Your business is detection. Nearly as dull as being a policeman on point duty. You mustn't confuse the thriller with a detective story. The latter amuses people by making them think they're thinking, the thriller by doing its damnedest to prevent them thinking at all. You're laden like a pack mule and I deduce you've been in Jermyn Street."

"Yes. I simply can't pass an artist's colourman's. His shop has the same pull for me as a cocktail bar has for you."

"*Chacun à son goût*, which I once brilliantly translated at school as 'each one to his favourite drop.' But you can't be thinking of settling down to paint with this mysterious shooting affair at Marston Manor eating up the columns of the daily Press?"

"I'm tired of crime and seek some other relaxation, Ricky. Do you remember those lines of Gerard Manley Hopkins?

'I have desired to go
Where springs not fail
To fields where flies no sharp and sided hail
And a few lilies blow.'

That's just how I feel at the moment. I'm mentally stale. Can you prescribe?"

With these words Vereker flung down his parcels on his studio table and sank wearily into an easy chair.

"I think I diagnose your malady correctly, Algernon. You've got a touch of the disease called 'rustic bunk' which is prevalent just now. It's not new. Horace suffered from it when he twittered complacently about his Sabine farm. The disease is more rampant in this industrial age and is aggravated by all art, especially poetry. Your chief symptom is a desire for rest and quiet, thatched cottages and buttercups."

"You're right there. I crave for rest and silence."

"I thought so. Now listen to this:

'All day long the wheels turn,
All day long the roaring of wheels, the rasping
Weave their imprisoned lattices of noise...
Only a little beyond the factory walls
Silence is a flawless bowl of crystal

Brimming, brimming with who can say beforehand?
Who can returning even remember what
Beautiful secret? Only a little beyond
These hateful walls, the birds among the branches
Secretly come and go.'"

"You've a delightful memory, Ricky. Now suggest a remedy for the malady. I must try and wrench myself out of this despondent mood."

"Six months in the second division is the best cure. The alternative is to go and rusticate where you can't have a hot bath every morning, where woman is brawn served up ugly, and a whist drive is the last thing in thrills. Go with Mr. Yeats to Innisfree or where Mr. Davies said, 'for I could sit down here alone and count the oak trees one by one!' I've never tried it, but counting oaks one by one must be an excellent sedative. Better still, go to Marston-le-Willows and get busy on your game of detection. I see by the Stop Press news to-night that your friend and rival has gone. 'Scotland Yard called in. Inspector Heather takes charge. Suffolk police show an example to the rest of England by promptly asking for expert assistance.'"

Vereker, whose eyes were closed and who seemed on the point of falling asleep, suddenly started up in his chair.

"You're not pulling my leg, Ricky?" he asked.

"There's no fun in that, Algernon; it's much too easy. Now take my advice. Don't give Heather a long start. You require a change, mental and physical. Life is movement; therefore, put a jerk into it; pack your bag and set off to-night. If the excitement of sleuthing doesn't cure you of your touch of 'rustic bunk,' silly Suffolk will."

Vereker glanced at the clock on the mantelpiece and asked, "Do you know anything about how to get there, Ricky?"

"Yes, I know all about it. Marston-le-Willows is this side of Bury St. Edmunds. I remember Bury particularly because it's a magical place. It's as romantic as Baghdad and as somnolent as a hot summer's day. I met Cicely Minto there. You remember Cicely's smile?"

"Very distinctly; a perfect screen grimace. They say monkeys can't smile and I sometimes think it a pity that some women can. But I don't want any of your romantic history. Tell me how to get to Marston."

"I'm sorry you didn't like Cicely. As for getting to Marston, that's a simple matter. Take a motor-coach from King's Cross. You're down there in three and a half hours. Lovely country, comfortable ride, no changing and there's a delightful pub half-way. I was nearly left behind there once; the barmaid was so good!"

"Yes," said Vereker slowly as if speaking to himself, "I think I'll go. I ought really to be busy with my painting but I'm feeling disgruntled with art. I'm getting a temperature; first signs of the old detective fever."

"Give art a rest, Algernon. The more a man gets preoccupied with ideals the farther he gets away from life. I always think your interest in crime's a perfect antidote to painting. You take leave of the abstraction of beauty and rub shoulders with the terrible, sordid motives that drive men to murder. You must go to Marston, dip your fingers in blood, gaze fearlessly on the worst of human passions, wallow in the satanic, gorge yourself with ghastliness. You'll come back to your work refreshed. It's a natural reaction, just as a saint is never so saintly as on the day after he has thoroughly sinned."

"Do you know when the motor-coach starts?"

"Six o'clock. You'll be in Marston at nine-thirty. That gives you half an hour to fill up before closing time. If I remember well, the inn's called 'The Dog and Partridge.' I'm really glad you've made up your mind. May I stay here till you return?"

"Of course, Ricky. Albert will look after you and I may want you to do some spade work up here as you've done on former occasions. Can I count on your being here in an emergency?"

"I shall be as fixed as the pole star. I'm absolutely broke and must settle down to work. It's a tragedy that a man of genius should have to write for money, but as old Doctor Johnson said, he's a fool who writes for anything else. That's one of the drawbacks of fame; you can't spend it."

"I'm glad you're going to be busy; it'll do you good and you can retrench while you're here. I hope there's no young lady in the offing at the moment?"

"None whatever, *mon brave*. Romance is in abeyance; I've spanked Cupid and put him to bed. I've finished with Clara or rather she gave me up for a man called Monty Willis."

"He was good-looking, I suppose," said Vereker lighting a cigarette.

"Don't be spiteful, Algernon. No, Monty's as ugly as the average co-respondent and as dreary as a bigamist. Worse still, he wears a bowler hat with brown shoes! In any case, Clara and I could never get on together. She was always trying to explain me to myself in terms of psycho-analysis and I don't like major operations on my human soul."

"Then I can count on you. I'll tell Albert to pack my bag when he returns."

"And give me the key of your cellarette. I'm trying to build up a new cocktail. I'm concocting it expressly for use at my uncle's little clerical gatherings. It's a bland little *bijou* and I'm provisionally calling it 'Gracious Spirit,' but that's sure to be considered in bad taste and I may alter it to 'Jubilate.'"

Vereker rose from his chair. "I've just got time to run up and see Geordie Stewart of the *Daily Report*," he said. "On these occasions it's always useful to be the *Daily Report*'s special correspondent without portfolio, so to speak. In case Albert doesn't turn up, Ricky, will you pack a bag for me?"

"It'll be ready for you on your return, Algernon. I think I can lay my hands on everything you'll need. You must leave me a few safety-razor blades."

"Good. Don't forget my Colt automatic. *Au revoir*."

Chapter Three
Getting into Harness

At five minutes to six, Anthony Vereker strode into the large up-to-date motor-coach station at King's Cross. He was accompanied by Ricardo who was carrying his case and had come to see him off. Passing through the waiting-room, he bought three evening papers at the bookstall, filled his raincoat pocket with his favourite brand of cigarette in case supplies were unobtainable in the wilds of Suffolk, and taking leave of his friend jumped into the coach. Settling himself comfortably in his seat, he opened an attaché case and extracted from it a newspaper-cutting book in which he had methodically pasted all the extracts from *The Times* and the *Daily Telegraph* bearing on the recent and mysterious happenings at Marston Manor. These he read carefully until he had thoroughly memorized all the details of the affair that had so far been made public. At nine-thirty almost to the minute the coach drew up at The Dog and Partridge Inn at Marston-le-Willows. Gathering up his belongings, Vereker alighted and strolled into the front entrance, the door of which was wide open for the autumn night was sultry and windless. Half a dozen villagers were seated at a long deal table, smoking, drinking and talking in the wide brick-floored passage which served as an extra room. A tall, lean man in well-worn breeches and gaiters, coatless and with his shirtsleeves rolled up to his elbows, stood leaning against the wall of the passage near the deal table. He had been listening to the conversation and though not of the company, occasionally broke in on their talk with some remark of his own. On Vereker's entry he straightened himself slowly from his relaxed pose and asked, "Yes, sir?"

Satisfied that he was Abner Borham, the landlord, whose name was above the door of the inn, Vereker at once asked if he could have a room. After some hesitation the innkeeper replied that he thought so, but that he would first see his wife. He disappeared and returning a few minutes later said that he had a room but it was not a very nice room for a gentleman. If the gentleman didn't mind being a bit rough and ready the room was vacant and they'd do their utmost to make him comfortable. Three things he could guarantee; "a clean and comfortable bed, good, plain food and sound ale."

"That's all I want, Mr. Borham. If you'll show me the room I'll leave my baggage up there and then if you can manage it I'd like something to eat."

"There's plenty of food, sir, if you don't mind a cold meal."

"I like a cold meal at night."

"Then we can manage all right, sir," replied the landlord, and reverting to his ordinary Suffolk intonation and dialect he summoned his wife.

"Look after things, Emily, while I take the gentleman up to his room," he said to that lady on her appearance and, picking up Vereker's case and attaché case, he led the way upstairs.

After showing Vereker his small, oddly-furnished but spotlessly clean room, he asked, "Any idea how long you're going to stay, sir?"

"I've been sent down on the Marston Manor case by the *Daily Report*. I shall be here till the police have cleared it up. That's as definite as I can be. Have you any other guests at the moment?"

"The detective-inspector from Scotland Yard and a detective-sergeant."

"Ah, Detective-Inspector Heather and Sergeant Goss. Are they in by any chance?"

"The sergeant's gone over to Bury and won't be back to-night. The inspector's just come in and is in his room having a wash and brush up before his supper."

"That's excellent. I'll have my supper along with him."

"I think he wants to be alone, sir. He was very particular on that point."

"You needn't worry about that, Mr. Borham. We're old friends and he won't be the least surprised to find me here."

"Very good, sir. It will be less trouble for us. Everything will be ready in about ten minutes in the little private room second on the right at the foot of the stairs."

After the refreshing effects of a basin of clear rain water, Vereker descended to the room the landlord had indicated and finding a table laid for two, seated himself and waited for the arrival of Heather. A few minutes later, the inspector walked in carefully carrying two brimming pint mugs of beer. Without any greeting he handed one of these mugs to Vereker.

"I thought you'd be thirsty after your journey, Mr. Vereker," he remarked and raising his own mug added, "Here's luck to us both and may the best man win."

"You were expecting me, Heather?" asked Vereker smiling. "I thought I was going to surprise you."

"I was just wondering whether the Stop Press news to-night would bring you down here when I heard your voice talking to the landlord. I saw you in Regent Street about a fortnight ago. You were looking as miserable as a man who'd been jilted by his best girl or one whose wife had presented him with twins when he was out of a job. I knew you were busy on your picture painting; it always gives you a sort of drunk and disorderly look. This morning I met Mr. Ricardo just after I had learned that I was to take charge of the Marston business. We had a little bet that you'd be on it. Remembering that haunted look on your face, I bet him a sovereign that you wouldn't and he took me on. I always lose my bets, so I was dead certain you'd turn up."

"I wondered why he was so eager I should have a change," remarked Vereker, "but let's tackle this cold beef and salad and discuss matters."

"You've read up the case in the papers, Mr. Vereker?"

"Yes, I think I know all that's been divulged in the Press, but as you know that's not much of a foundation to build on. What do you make of the exhumation business that preceded the murder of young Cornell? Has it any connection?"

Heather munched silently for a few minutes before replying. "It's early days yet," he said at length, "and that was naturally one of the first questions I asked myself. But as you know, I stick to hard facts while you generally let your imagination run riot. I'd like to bet you've got some fantastic notion that they're connected."

"I had an intuition that they were, that's all."

"Well, it's a bad beginning. The road to error is paved with bright intuitions, Mr. Vereker. If I were you I'd keep intuitions for your art. You know that the Home Office analyst found no poison in the samples submitted to him for examination?"

"Yes, yes, I read all about that, but I can't do without my intuitions. I was born with a big share of what the scholastics called *habitus principiorum*."

"I don't know what that means but at the back of your mind you've a doubt about the correctness of the analyst's conclusion."

"Well, even a Home Office analyst is human. The body was buried in February and exhumed in August. All sorts of things can happen in that time. I always have a lively suspicion about the effects of decomposition on the human body and on poisons. Then the said analyst merely stated that he had found no poison in the samples he had examined. This is a very non-committal and guarded statement. In the circumstances it was all he could possibly say. But as you'll remember, Heather, if Crippen hadn't buried his wife's body in lime, it's almost certain that it would have been impossible definitely to state the cause of her death. The lime prevented the decomposition of the hyoscine."

"Yes, I remember that point clearly, Mr. Vereker. But as no poison was found in the case of John Cornell, I'm assuming temporarily that he wasn't poisoned. *Prima facie* he died a natural death and it was only the suspicious mind of his brother that caused all the bother about exhumation. Now I'll go further and say you've an intuition that Mrs. Cornell being a young and beautiful woman married to an old man had fallen in love with someone of her own age."

"The possibility certainly struck me," agreed Vereker laughing as he helped himself to more salad.

"Well, as far as I can gather from the little conversation I've had with the villagers here, your intuition's correct," replied Heather with his slow smile.

"That's one up for intuition!" said Vereker and asked, "Who is the gentleman?"

"The village doctor is a handsome bachelor. Mrs. Cornell and he are as thick as thieves, so you've got a line on the first part of your mystery right away. Who could poison the old man more cleverly than a doctor?"

"This is serious," commented Vereker quietly.

"Very serious, Mr. Vereker. Could you manage another pint?"

"Not for me, thanks, Heather."

"The beer's first rate here. It's a good omen. All my failures have been coupled with inferior brews. Sound liquor brings out the best in a man. But to proceed. We must extend your romance to the killing of young Cornell."

"A natural step. What were the terms of John Cornell's will?"

"We've got to look into that."

"I daresay the widow has been provided for and the son inherited the greater part of the estate. There'll be a proviso should he predecease his stepmother and leave no family that the money will revert to her."

At this suggestion Heather burst into loud laughter. "So you've now got a line on the killer of Frank Cornell. The stepmother is the culprit. Pack up your bag and go back to London and I'll take out a warrant for her arrest."

"By Jove, Heather, your wits grow nimbler with every case. I hadn't jumped to that conclusion. It's feasible."

"Everything's feasible in this world, Mr. Vereker. What I don't like in this case is the absence of clues. That's where your fictional detective scores. What with cigarette ends, maker's name on the butts, handkerchiefs, buttons, scent, finger-prints, footprints in snow and elsewhere, stones out of rings, his job is comparatively simple. Even if the murderer hasn't left a tangible clue, there'll be a tiny but necessary gap in the time-table. The one clue he never gets is a laundry mark because that would entail pages of hunting for a laundry. You can't spend an hour reading about a hunt for a laundry; it's not what you'd call a blood sport."

"No revolver even in our case!" agreed Vereker with a simulation of depression. "It's a bad look-out."

"No revolver yet, but we're going to make a thorough search. I've got a squad of assistants. The lily pool in the formal garden hasn't been properly dragged. The house will have to be ransacked and the garden and grounds overhauled systematically."

"It would be glorious, Heather, if detection wasn't such a prosaic job at times. It reminds me of archaeological excavation. Days, sometimes weeks, of digging before one thrilling little find."

"It often reminds me of sea fishing, one of my hobbies," agreed Heather bringing out a short briar pipe and filling it with strong tobacco. "You figure you'll get a bucket of lovely whiting and you come home with an unpleasant-looking tope and a case of empty beer bottles."

"Who were in the house on the night of the tragedy, Heather?"

"Mrs. Cornell and her stepson Frank; a young man called Roland Carstairs who was a great friend of the dead man. They were at college together. A pretty and very modern young lady, Valerie Mayo, and her mother. Miss Mayo is stage-struck. She was the young man's fiancée. They had just become engaged and she was on a visit to see her young man's stepmother and get her bearings, so to speak, with regard to the family and, more important, the property. I saw her to-day when I called at the Manor. Very dignified, rather cocksure, and gives you the impression that she had her head screwed on all right and keeps her hand on her tram fare."

For some moments Vereker was lost in thought, puffing quietly at his cigarette. "What a pity there's no such thing as pure romance, Heather! Love, like religion, can't escape the economic argument. Before the nicest marriage there's generally a settlement and after the most spiritual sermon, the plush offertory bag!"

"Well, I can't shed tears on the subject, Mr. Vereker. Even as it is, life's not half-bad and perhaps some day, ahem! under a Liberal government, all things'll be added unto us."

"How many servants in the house, Heather?" asked Vereker reverting to the subject uppermost in his mind.

"A butler; old Mr. Cornell's valet who was being retained by the son till he got another job; a cook and three housemaids. These all live in the Manor itself. The gardener and chauffeur have cottages in the village and there's a boy who helps the gardener and does odd jobs for the house."

"They've not been questioned yet?"

"Not by me. I'll also question the family and friends, but you'll help me greatly if you can worm your way in somehow and pump them in your most plausible manner. There's always a barrier between the gentry and the most aristocratic and handsome detective-inspector. I can manage servants rather well. They never take me seriously. Something to do with my phiz, I suppose."

"It's that playful little moustache, Heather, and you simply ooze good nature."

"In any case it's always the same. When I was questioning the cook in the Armadale case, I asked her quite seriously if she was married. She blushed, looked coy and replied, 'Lor', Inspector, you are a speed hog!' What can a man do in such a predicament? On the spur of the moment I nearly proposed. It was a narrow shave," said the inspector with humorous smugness.

"It ought to have been literally, Heather. But what are you going to do to-morrow?"

"I'm going to examine the scene of the crime more closely. You'd better come along and nose round. We can compare notes later and I can correct your intuitions with deductions from mere facts."

"Good. But there's one point, Heather, that puzzles me right away about the killing of Frank Cornell. From the Press reports I gather that one of the maids discovered the body. She was taking up morning tea to the young man's bedroom at eight o'clock. She found the body fully dressed. Is that correct?"

"Yes."

"Doctor Redgrave, I believe, was at once called in. Did he express any opinion as to when the shot was fired?"

"He gave it as his opinion that the man had been dead eight or nine hours."

"If the doctor's correct, Cornell must have been shot about midnight or, say, one o'clock?"

"That's so."

"What was he wearing? Evening kit?"

"No, a tweed lounge suit. He must have gone up to his room after dinner and changed."

"When did he go up to his bedroom?"

"About eleven o'clock."

"No one heard the shot?"

"Apparently not, but that's a point that I must go into farther. Questioning people's often like squeezing a lemon. If you put on a bit of extra pressure you get the extra drop of juice you want. The rest of the house went to bed roughly about the same time and it's not likely everyone was asleep when the shot was fired."

"Very peculiar," remarked Vereker reflectively. "He went up to bed at eleven and was shot somewhere about midnight. He had changed into a tweed suit and ordinary walking shoes. It's quite out of order. He ought to have been found in his pyjamas and dressing-gown and red morocco slippers."

"And in his fiancée's bedroom to make the story interesting," remarked Heather quietly. "Still you shan't be cheated of your romance, Mr. Vereker. I forgot to tell you a most important point. The house is haunted."

"Since the arrival of Scotland Yard, I suppose," commented Vereker glancing up at the inspector to see if he were joking.

"No, it's one of the hundred per cent. ghost-haunted houses of old England," assured Heather earnestly. "I know you have a weakness for the supernatural and I treasured this bit of news till the last."

"I keep an open mind on everything psychic, Heather. There's too much evidence by reputable witnesses for any man to say off-hand that it's nonsense."

"Tommy rot!" exclaimed the inspector emphatically.

"It's no use trying to convince you, Heather. Belief is much more a matter of temperament than of truth. You belong to the nineteenth century and the mechanistic school of thought. You won't have haunted houses in spite of Mannington Hall, Holland House, Glamis castle, Corby Castle, Bisham Abbey, Grachur Manse, Cawood Castle and innumerable other spook-ridden places. But we'll discuss this matter when we've finished with the Marston Manor affair. I'll say good night. I'm tired and we've a big day in front of us."

"I've got the local police reports to run through and I think I can manage another..."

"Pint," concluded Vereker.

"Pipe," corrected Heather solemnly.

Chapter Four
Scratching Around

When Vereker got into bed that night he tried in vain to fall asleep. At first his mind, running on the last topic discussed with Heather, busied itself with ghosts and haunted houses. If apparitions were actually what Heather called "tommy rot," the persistence of human belief in them was almost miraculous. The old-world room in which he found himself with its carved oak central beam, black with age, its uneven, creaking floor, faded carpet and hangings, its faint smell of musty lavender, its intense silence so different from the noise of his London flat, even the feeble candle which had lighted him to bed were favourable for the growth of eerie musing and strange, unquiet dreams. In his mind's eye, too, was the brief glimpse he had caught towards the close of his journey of Marston Manor in the bright moonlight, its chimneys and roofs just visible through the sombre belt of trees that almost completely screened it from the road. That such a peaceful, old-world seat should be the scene of a murder seemed at first incongruous; on second thoughts he realized that the haunts of ancient peace had generally been the haunts of ancient strife. The very architecture of such manors echoed the words, defence against assault, even if they had not primarily been built for such. As he mused, the very setting by some curious association of ideas seemed to throw a fantastic glamour over the crime that had so recently been committed there. The harsh brutality of the act softened under the romantic power of lapsed time; it seemed to be thrust back into the past, gathering from the mediaeval structure some essence of the long bygone, of the irrevocable, and losing the sharp horror of recency.

As he looked forward to his work on the morrow his excitement increased and he grew more wakeful. The virus of detection was beginning to work with its old feverishness in his blood. The feelings of lassitude and dejection which he had experienced of late were fast vanishing under the stimulus of the approaching hunt. For some time he tossed restlessly in spite of the enveloping comfort of the feather bed, his mind flitting with nervous alertness from one idea to another. Then he suddenly sat up, lit his candle and from the pocket of his jacket, thrown over the back of a chair beside his bed, produced a well-thumbed volume of Emerson. This was his habitual sleeping draught, a certain remedy for a feverish mood of wakefulness. He opened the book and began to read the lecture on literary ethics. The amazing perception, the inexhaustible flow of bright analogy, the astonishing sequence of associated ideas and apt imagery, the poetry and plasticity of expression at once caught him in their hypnotic web and tore him away from preoccupation in his own affairs. At length he yawned, closed his book, blew out the candle and his mind sweeping from the Emersonian empyrean sank softly to earth and restful slumber.

The bright morning sun pouring in at the open window wakened him. It had dispelled a soft autumn mist which covered the lush grass of the meadows in a silvery sheen of heavy dew. He glanced at his watch, jumped out of bed and almost immediately afterwards a knock sounded on his door announcing the deposit of a can of hot water. A quarter of an hour later he entered the small private room in which he had had a meal the previous night. He found to his surprise that Heather had already breakfasted and gone out. He had left a message for Vereker saying that he would be at Marston Manor at about eleven o'clock. Vereker ate a leisurely meal, glanced through the pages of the *East Anglian Times*, and was about to rise from the table when the landlord entered the room.

"Good morning, sir. Sleep well?" he asked pleasantly.

"Soundly. The room is an excellent one and the bed most comfortable."

"Had sufficient breakfast, sir?"

"Made a splendid meal, thanks."

The conversation lapsed into silence and the landlord was about to depart when Vereker asked, "What do you think of this business up at the Manor, Mr. Borham?"

"A shocking affair, sir; one hardly likes to speak about it."

"I've always found a village inn a kind of central news exchange. You'll have heard all that the village has to say about it?"

"Well, yes, sir. Customers will talk and I can't help hearing what's said. Not that I take all the yarns for gospel. Some men talk sense and others a lot of rubbish. There's old Harry Weddup, the thatcher, for instance. If what he says was to be taken seriously, he'd get locked up in no time. A spell of silence might do him a heap of good, too."

"Did Mr. Frank Cornell ever visit the inn?"

"Oh, yes, sir. If he happened to be staying up at the Manor, he never missed a day. A first-rate customer."

"What sort of man was he?"

"Very pleasant young gentleman. Fond of drink and company and free with his money. I'll miss him for one and so will some of my regulars. When he was in the mood it was drinks all round and it's surprising how many customers would arrive when drinks were going free. The news travelled almost as quick as wireless."

"Rather a rapid young man?" asked Vereker.

"I wouldn't say that, sir. He was brisk, full of life and liked a joke. He was a great favourite with the young ladies, I'm told. You haven't heard how he won first prize for Victoria plums at the flower show last year?"

"No."

"Well, he put in his entry just like one of the villagers for the best dozen plums. Now Jim Pettitt has the best Victoria plum tree in the district and had won the prize last three years in succession. Got a notion that it was almost his by right. Mr. Frank beat him and Jim Pettitt lodged a complaint. Well, the young gent confessed to the committee he had stolen Into Pettitt's garden one afternoon just before the show while Jim was at work and his wife over at Bury market. He pinched what he reckoned was the best dozen plums and beat the old man with his own fruit. He did it for a barney and then doubled the prize money to quieten old Jim down. Most of us knew beforehand what he was up to and I can tell you it was the best joke we've had in Marston for years. You'd think so, too, if you knew Jim Pettitt."

The innkeeper's long face burst into genial smiles at the memory. "He was a bit of a lad, I must say," he added, "but he'd have settled down all right when he'd got married. Needed a woman who could boss him. That's what he needed."

"He was engaged to be married, I hear," remarked Vereker.

"Yes, to a young lady from London. She was going on the stage, so they say. Not the kind I'd marry, but there—that's all over now!"

"Of course there are as good women on the stage as off, Mr. Borham," suggested Vereker.

"I daresay, sir, but we all expected he would marry his cousin, Miss Stella Cornell. They were very fond of one another, so everyone said, but perhaps they saw too much of one another."

"Were they engaged?" asked Vereker.

"No, it never came to that, more's the pity. Now, Miss Stella's as good a young lady as ever trod ground. Not a child in the village but loves her and the help she has given to those who needed it badly will never be known. She is always doing something for the village—women's institute, amateur theatricals, church work and all that. A great favourite with us all is Miss Stella. I don't know what parson would do without her."

"Whose daughter is she?"

"She's the daughter of Mr. David Cornell, old John Cornell's blind brother. Old Mr. John built his brother a bungalow in the Manor grounds and settled a comfortable little income on him, so they say. Mr. David's wife's dead and he lives there alone with his daughter."

"I suppose she keeps house for him," remarked Vereker.

"Yes. They have one maid, Mary Lister, daughter of Jack Lister, the Marston carrier. A very capable girl she is, too."

"Has Mr. Cornell been blind from birth?"

"Oh, no, sir. He lost his sight in 1917 at the front during the war. I think he was in the canteen service or something of that sort. A German shell blew up the canteen and Mr. David went up with it. When he recovered consciousness he found he was blind. At first there was some hope he would get back his sight but he never did. I've never met the gentleman though I've often seen him walking through the village. By all accounts he's as fine a man as anyone could wish to meet. He always says he wouldn't have minded being wounded in the front line, but it was hard luck to get hit when hiding behind the canteen groceries."

"What was he before the war?"

"He'd tried his hand at all sorts of things and was farming when the war broke out. He never could make things pay. Had no money sense. Lots of men have no money sense and if you haven't got it you're always in trouble. They say he always wanted to be a composer of music but never had the time to go in for it properly. Now he's better off than ever he was and spends most of his time at his music. His daughter writes it all down for him. Some say it's good and some say it ain't got no toon in it."

"What does the village think of Mrs. Cornell, John Cornell's wife?"

"Everyone speaks well of her, sir, but she has never taken any interest in the village. Nobody knows much about her. Very reserved lady who keeps herself to herself."

"I suppose there was some gossip over the exhumation of her husband's body? It was an extraordinary event for Marston village."

"A lot of nasty tittle-tattle among those who're always ready to think bad of anyone. I must say the lady wasn't wise to be seen so much about with young Doctor Redgrave. People will talk when a good-looking young married woman gets friendly with a handsome bachelor even if there's nothing wrong behind the scenes. I was glad the gossips got a suck-in when nothing came out of the business. Some of them was real disappointed if I'm not mistaken. As for myself, I think Doctor Redgrave's a straight man and mighty clever at his job. My missus always swears he saved her life when she nearly went under with the 'flu and pneumonia two years ago this winter. But all the ladies swear by him and good looks is a great help when you're mixing up medicines," smiled the innkeeper shrewdly.

At this point the voice of Mrs. Borham calling sharply from the tap-room for her husband brought the conversation to an abrupt end. Abner Borham excused himself and hurried away at a pace quite unusual for him for he almost ran, and Vereker rose and went up to his room. Glancing at his watch he found it was half-past nine. He had an hour to spare before meeting Heather at the Manor. Slipping on a rainproof coat, for the morning sky promised light showers, he left the inn and made his way leisurely towards his destination.

A quarter of an hour's walk brought him to the wide entrance gates of the Manor. A small lodge and a diminutive garden flanked it on the side nearer the village. He was about to walk up the drive but as he had some time on hand, changed his mind and continued his way along the high road with the idea of getting a view of the house as he had seen it the previous night from the motor-coach. He came to the point from which he had caught that first romantic glimpse of Marston Manor in the moonlight and was surprised to see that almost the whole frontage of the building was visible by day from the highway and running at an angle to it so as to face the south. The morning was warm and sunny and in the wide sweep of meadow which divided the Manor from the road, black and white cattle grazed lazily or sought the shade of the magnificent forest oaks scattered at wide intervals about the parkland. Strolling along farther, Vereker came to a second entrance gate about half a mile distant from the first. He opened this gate, entered, and was proceeding up the drive when in an adjoining paddock there came to view a modern bungalow with white roughcast walls and a green-tiled roof.

"That'll be Mr. David Cornell's place," he thought and wandered off the drive through a belt of rhododendrons to the hedge dividing the Manor grounds from the adjoining paddock. From the brief description of the man which he had elicited from the innkeeper, Vereker was already interested in Mr. David Cornell. The fact that he was a musician, an artist and ineffectual in business, unconsciously deepened this interest. All the arts spoke the language of beauty; music sang it. The tragedy of the man's blindness, too, evoked in Vereker the sympathy which any human suffering at once evoked in him. Finding a gap in the dividing hedge, he forced his way through, entered the paddock, and walked slowly in the direction of the bungalow. As he approached there suddenly came to view a garden which was a sheer blaze of colour. Bordering a wide crazy pavement, the nasturtiums ran like a cordon of fire; through them, gladioli thrust their fountains of scarlet upwards and higher still in the floral sky dahlias burst like rockets in starry showers. As Vereker stood, his eyes delighted with this vivid mass of colouring, his quick ear caught the sound of footsteps behind him. He turned sharply and came face to face with a young woman of about twenty-six years of age who had evidently been making her way to the bungalow and was approaching him. Her face, which was pale and serious, at once broke into a pleasing smile.

"You look as if you'd lost your bearings. Can I help you?" she asked.

"No, thanks. I was making my way leisurely up to the Manor and noticing the bungalow came into the paddock to have a look at it. I hope I'm not trespassing," replied Vereker, feeling that even the truth seemed to limp badly as an explanation of his curiosity.

"Oh, no, not at all," she said affably. "I was just admiring the garden when you came up. I'm rather proud of it," she continued.

"The dahlias have been a great success. Of course, the year has been exceptionally fine."

"You're Miss Cornell, I presume?" asked Vereker.

"Quite correct. You seem to know all about us," she remarked, her dark brows arching in a quizzical expression.

"I'm afraid it's a newspaper correspondent's privilege to be inquisitive—almost impertinent at times," apologized Vereker.

"You've come about this horrible affair at my aunt's place," she said, a frown suddenly clouding her face. "I don't envy you your job."

"No, I daresay you don't, but the matter's quite an impersonal thing with me. I'm already very much interested. I certainly wouldn't look at it in that light if I were intimately concerned."

"No, I suppose not," she remarked slowly as if her thoughts were not in her words. "Is there anybody you want particularly to see at the Manor?"

"Well, I've an appointment there with Inspector Heather of Scotland Yard at eleven o'clock," replied Vereker, glancing at his watch.

"He has been up there all the morning. I've just been through the ordeal of what I believe is called a searching police interrogatory. It's been quite an experience. I didn't think famous detectives could be so affable. Wisdom of the serpent with the gentleness of the dove, I suppose," she remarked thoughtfully as she tapped an elegant shoe with her light walking-stick.

"I hope you were on your guard," suggested Vereker pleasantly.

"I was dreadfully nervous," she replied with sudden seriousness. "I can't explain why and I'm sure I should have broken down if the inspector hadn't immediately put me at ease. The whole affair has upset us all terribly and I was—I was very fond of my cousin Frank."

Her large dark eyes suddenly grew moist with imminent tears and to save the situation from further embarrassment she exclaimed, "But I mustn't detain you. It's nearly eleven o'clock.

With these words she passed on and Vereker, turning on his heel, extracted a loose cigarette from his pocket and lit it.

"First character in the tragedy in order of appearance," he soliloquized and made his way back to the approach to Marston Manor.

He found Heather engaged in what he called "scratching around," a phrase which came natural to him for he kept fowls and was deeply interested in everything connected with them.

"You stole a march on me this morning, Inspector," remarked Vereker as he joined him.

"Gathering facts is so much slower than getting intuitions that I reckon we now start about fair," replied Heather.

"Managed to gather any important ones?" asked Vereker.

They were standing together in the spacious rectangular entrance hall of the mansion at the foot of a wide staircase facing the front door.

"Come upstairs," said Heather quietly, "and see what you make of things. I'm afraid this is going to be a difficult problem. There's nothing much to lay hold of."

They ascended about a dozen steps to what is generally called by house agents a "half-landing" with a wide window. On this half-landing, close to the window, was a pedestal flower-stand bearing a large pot from which dropped in an orange cascade a mass of wax-like begonia flowers. To the left as one turned to ascend the remaining steps to the first storey corridor, was a door.

"What room's this?" asked Vereker casually and to his surprise the inspector approached him on tip-toe with a serious face.

"Music room," he replied in an almost inaudible whisper. "It's—it's haunted! Contains pickled ghosts!"

Vereker, smiling at the inspector's little joke, turned the handle of the door only to find that it was locked.

"Never mind that room for the moment. Do you see this?" asked the inspector pointing to an inverted flower-pot on the polished oak of the floor and to other pots on the steps of the second flight to the right of the door.

"Ah!" exclaimed Vereker, "you've made a discovery. Bloodstains, I suppose?"

"Yes, rather important. Have a good look at them."

Vereker went down on his knees, produced a magnifying glass from his pocket, lifted a pot and examined the floor closely.

"How on earth did you twig them? They're hardly visible to the naked eye," he said.

Heather immediately flashed an electric torch on the floor.

"Is that better?" he asked.

"Excellent! I can see this one fairly clearly now," replied Vereker.

"Just so. First instruction for beginners: when searching for dried bloodstains on polished floors or furniture use artificial light. The stains show up more clearly. But you're keeping the important part of that clue to yourself, Mr. Vereker."

"No. I was just going to ask you where the body was found."

"On the landing at the top of this flight of steps. I'll let you see the photographs that have been taken later."

At this piece of information Vereker turned and was about to descend the first half-flight of steps.

"No, you needn't go down," said the inspector, "I've examined every inch of that first half-flight and there's no further stain to be found."

"None in the main hall?" asked Vereker.

"Not a drop. As far as I can see, he must have been holding his handkerchief to the wound for he certainly ascended the stairs after being shot."

"You inferred that from the shape of the drops of blood on the steps; they splashed forward in the direction of his ascent."

"Mr. Vereker, you're becoming as orthodox as a policeman," remarked Heather with a smile. "You'll have to give up the amateur status and lose that popular halo you wear with such grace."

"Now, now, Heather, you can't hoodwink me. You're just talking to side-track me. Here's where my knowledge of psychology has you beaten. Confess now that you're hiding the fact that the entrance hall floor was washed by one of the maids on the morning of the discovery of the murder, yes, and washed unfortunately before the police arrived and gave instructions that there must be no further cleaning of the house till further orders."

"You've guessed right; it was a bright shot, Mr. Vereker. The hall lino, which is an imitation of a red-tiled floor, is washed every morning first thing. The maid carried out her duties as usual yesterday morning. Priceless clues may have vanished and our work doubled by the accident for it was an accident in a way. These little things are sent to try us, I suppose."

"By Jove, but that's really tragic!" soliloquized Vereker with an ironic smile and ascended the second half-flight of steps on to the first-storey corridor landing.

"Here's where the body lay," said Heather, "and that dark stain on the carpet is where a pool of blood flowed from the wound."

"He ran up the stairs and collapsed here. Let me see the photographs you've got tucked away in your pocket, Heather."

Heather chuckled and extracting some photographic prints from a note-case handed them to Vereker. The latter immediately switched on an electric light at the head of the stairs for, owing to the length of the corridor, the natural lighting was bad. He carefully examined the prints and handed them back to the inspector without comment.

"What d'you make of it, Mr. Vereker?" asked the officer seriously.

"Strange that he's lying on his back, Heather. Can you explain?"

"He fell forward and turned over or he may have turned in falling, for he was bearing to his left towards his bedroom and would be slightly off his dead balance."

"That's possible, I suppose, but it strikes me as peculiar, very peculiar and most unlikely. But tell me, Heather, what was the man doing in a lounge suit at that time of night? He had dressed for dinner, went to bed at eleven and was dead at twelve or one o'clock in a complete change of clothes. He must have gone out. Could he let himself in?"

"Only if he had let himself out. If he had gone out before closing time he'd have left instructions with one of the servants for the front door to be left unlocked. You haven't examined the front door yet?"

"No. Anything peculiar?"

"The lock is inside the door. Nearly all the locks in the house are these old-fashioned exposed affairs. Then when the front door—it is in reality a double door with glass panes—is closed, a pair of folding shutters are drawn out from the wall on each side and are made secure with an iron fastening bar."

"Then he didn't go out, after all?"

"Apparently not, but we mustn't jump to conclusions just yet, Mr. Vereker. The butler locked up and bolted all the doors and unlocked and unbolted them in the morning. He says he found every door leading out of the house locked and bolted as he had left them the night before. Of course, Mr. Frank Cornell may have opened one of these doors again to go out and then locked and bolted it on his return, but the butler is certain he didn't."

"You've accepted the butler's words as true?"

"The man looked as if he were speaking the truth and for the time being we'll say his statement is correct. We must begin somewhere and somehow."

"And the windows?"

"He says he personally examined all the windows and doors immediately he found Mr. Frank had changed into a lounge suit, because he himself inferred that the young man had been out or at least intended to go out."

"Temporarily we'll say he didn't go out, but he must have gone downstairs for some purpose after he had changed, otherwise there wouldn't have been those blood splashes on the half-landing and second flight of steps. This is working itself up into a first-class mystery, Heather. Where's his bedroom?"

"First door on your left."

"Let's have a good look at it. I may pick up some information there."

"Before we leave the staircase, Mr. Vereker, there's one important thing I must tell you. I was going to hide it, but feel it wouldn't be quite fair. The young gentleman had taken his shoes off and dropped them on the half-landing in his ascent. The shoelaces hadn't been untied."

"I was on the point of asking you why his shoes had been taken off before the police photographed the body," remarked Vereker smiling. "I suppose we must infer he was creeping up the stairs in his socks to avoid disturbing the sleeping household. The tied shoelaces is a curious point and needs thinking over. Anything else you're concealing so as to favour your own chances?"

"Nothing unfair," said Heather with a smile. "I mustn't bottle-feed you or you'll get lazy."

With these words he glanced at his watch and said he must keep an appointment with the Deputy Chief Constable. "Mrs. Cornell, Mrs. and Miss Mayo are lunching with Dr. Redgrave. They won't be back till late. Mr. Carstairs has gone over to the village. I've told the servants in the house that you're my assistant, so you'll be able to scratch round on your own while I'm over at Bury. We'll discuss matters in the 'Dog and Partridge' when I return."

"That's splendid, Heather, I like scratching round on my own. It's the same when I'm painting. I always become self-conscious if there's anyone looking over my shoulder; paralyses all my faculties."

"On my way I'll call at Dr. Redgrave's surgery where the body lies. He has extracted the bullet and I'll pick it up. I'll ask him to let you see the body if you think it worth while."

"It may not be necessary, Heather. You're not hiding the fact that you've found the ejected cartridge shell if the weapon was an automatic?"

"No trace of a shell. It may have been an ordinary revolver," replied the inspector.

"I shall want to see the bullet, Heather."

"You shall, Mr. Vereker. I hope the beer's good in Bury."

"Wasn't it one of your sayings, Heather, that there's no such thing as bad beer, but that some kinds are better than others?"

"Possibly. I always forget my best wisecracks. Someone ought to record them for posterity."

"Before you go will you tell me where the dead man's shoes are?"

"You'll find them in his dressing-room. They're a heavy pair of brown brogues. You can't make any mistake."

"Thanks. I'll see you on your return to the Inn."

Chapter Five
The Haunted Room

On Heather's departure, Vereker descended the stairs to the entrance hall and carefully examined the front door. He then wandered into the drawing-room and noticed that its wide open doors led on to a lawn which ran to a dense belt of trees forming a woodland screen against northerly winds. Here again, when the glass doors were closed, wooden shutters could be drawn and fastened by strong iron bars and catches as in the entrance hall. This room was furnished with a few choice antique pieces, an old bureau, an upright grand piano and two china cabinets full of valuable odds and ends of china and old English glass. On the walls hung two or three examples of early English water-colour and some Delft plates. A buhl cabinet on which stood an old ornate French clock, a settee and three or four comfortable chairs completed the contents, giving the room an air of spacious comfort. For some time Vereker was lost in his examination of the watercolours and then suddenly remembering that this occupation was irrelevant to his work, strode out of the room, crossed the hall and entered the dining-room. After a similar survey of this room he returned to the hall and slowly ascended the stairs, carefully examining every step as he went.

"Not a vestige of a clue," he remarked as he once more stood on the half-landing. "Heather is terribly thorough."

After a further scrutiny of the bloodstain on the polished wood of the half-landing he quickly mounted the stair and stood in the long corridor of the first floor. He walked along this corridor to the window at one end and looked out. Fifteen feet below him were a gravel "surround" a few feet wide and the lawn on to which the drawing-room doors opened. He pushed up the window, leaned out and looked around. The scene was almost magically peaceful. The warm autumn sunlight was reflected from a thousand glittering foliage points twinkling under the stir of a soft breeze. The leaves of a holly tree close to the window were turquoise blue where their glossy surfaces mirrored the now cloudless sky. Evidently satisfied, he quickly closed the window and retraced his steps slowly down the corridor to the door of the room which Heather had indicated as Frank Cornell's. He was about to enter this room when the door opened and a manservant emerged. The latter's face expressed surprise and suspicion in rapid succession and then he asked almost apologetically, "Are you Mr. Vereker, sir?"

"Yes, I was just having a look round the house. I think the inspector told you I would be here."

"That's so, sir, but it had quite gone out of my mind for the moment. We have strict orders to allow no unauthorized people to hang about the place. My name's Tapp, sir. I was old Mr. Cornell's valet and was kept on by young Mr. Cornell till I could find a place."

"This was young Mr. Cornell's room, I believe," said Vereker indicating that apartment with a glance and a nod.

"That's so, sir."

"I'm just going to have a look in, Tapp. You might come with me. I may want to ask you some questions," said Vereker and turning the handle of the door walked in. "Nothing has been touched, Tapp, since Mr. Cornell's death?"

"No, sir. I happened to hear footsteps about and just glanced in to see that everything was all right. I didn't notice you in the corridor."

"I see," said Vereker and observing a suit of dress clothes flung untidily across the bed asked, "You were in attendance when Mr. Frank dressed for dinner that Sunday night?"

"I laid out everything for him as usual but that was all."

"When did you see him last?"

"About six. Dinner was at seven."

"You didn't see him alive again?"

"No, sir. As a matter of fact, he was a very independent young gentleman. He often told me he didn't want a valet fussing round him as he was quite capable of looking after himself, but that I could stay on as his valet till I got another job so long as I kept out of his way. It wasn't very satisfactory for me considering all things, but jobs are hard to get nowadays."

"You knew nothing about his intention of changing into a lounge suit as if he was going to go out that night?"

"Nothing at all, sir."

"As far as you know he didn't go out?" asked Vereker with sudden earnestness.

"To all appearances he didn't. Crowley, the butler, locked up as usual and no one can let themselves in after that unless he gives orders for one of the doors to be left open. Still, I wouldn't be positive."

"Why did he change his clothes, I wonder?" remarked Vereker almost to himself.

"Possibly changed his mind after he'd changed his clothes," suggested Tapp helpfully and after a period of hesitation added, "It wasn't the first time, either."

"You mean he sometimes changed from evening dress into a lounge suit after dinner?"

"Not so frequently of late, but at one time nearly every night. When I was looking after old Mr. Cornell, I used to keep an eye on

Mr. Frank's clothes and shoes. Nearly every morning I used to find he'd changed because he left the lounge suit on a chair where I used to find it next morning. More often it was on the floor, for he was a very untidy young gentleman."

"Which lounge suit did he wear?"

"He has four or five, sir, all in the wardrobe. It might be any one of them according to his fancy."

"Which pair of shoes did he wear the night he was killed?" asked Vereker, glancing at several pairs arranged on a boot rack.

"A pair of heavy brown brogues. They're there under that chair, sir. The inspector put them there."

Vereker at once crossed the room to the chair and picked up the pair of shoes. After a brief glance at them he laid them down again, a curious look of satisfaction on his lean face. He then made a closer survey of the room; opened the window, looked out and shut it again. He examined the catch and was about to move away from the window when his eye caught sight of three parallel scratches on the paint of one of the jambs. Pulling out his magnifying glass, he scrutinized these scratches and measured them with a small steel tape. At the same time he began to hum the waltz from *Faust*, a sure sign that he was mildly excited. Turning away from the window he picked up Frank Cornell's brown brogues once more and turned them over to look at the soles and heels. Instantly his humming ceased and his brow was furrowed in thought. He replaced the shoes and turned to Tapp, who was watching him as closely as a cat watches a mouse.

"You're sure these are the shoes Mr. Frank Cornell wore on that Sunday night, Tapp?"

"Certain, sir," replied the valet.

"That's very interesting," continued Vereker enigmatically and walked round the room. He looked critically at the pictures on the wall, noted the two shot-guns, a twelve-bore and a sixteen, which stood on the right side of the wardrobe and a bag of golf clubs on the left. At sight of the golf clubs Vereker at once crossed the room and pulling out the driver addressed an imaginary ball. Replacing the club, he repeated the pantomime with a brassie and a putter. Then he turned to the dress suit on the bed and looked at it critically.

"How old was Mr. Frank Cornell, Tapp?" he asked.

"Twenty-three last birthday, sir."

"A small, light man?"

"About five foot six, I should say, and not more than nine stone weight at the most."

Without further remark Vereker turned to the mantelpiece on which stood four photographs in silver frames. They were of four young women of about Frank Cornell's own age. The one farthest on the left Vereker recognized as Miss Stella Cornell to whom he had spoken that morning in the paddock near the bungalow. The one on the extreme right was taken in theatrical costume and remembering that Frank Cornell's fiancée was an aspirant to the stage he picked up the photo and looked carefully at it.

"This is Miss Valerie Mayo, I suppose?" he asked, turning to Tapp.

"Yes, sir."

"Do you know who these two ladies in the centre are, Tapp?"

"No, sir," replied Tapp after looking at them. "Must have been two of Mr. Frank's latest friends. Except for the photo of Miss Stella, who's his cousin, I think he changed the others every time he came down from London."

"A gay Lothario, eh?" exclaimed Vereker.

"If that means a bit of a lad, sir, I should say yes."

"Strange how these small men have a tremendous capacity for affection. Did you find him an easy master to get on with, Tapp?"

"Yes, sir, one of the easiest. No one could help liking him. He was always ready for a joke and a laugh and simply threw his money away. That's why he was such a favourite with the ladies. He was young and he'd have learned better if he had lived."

"Have you any idea who killed him, Tapp?" asked Vereker, suddenly turning round and looking the man straight in the eyes.

The unexpected question seemed to throw Tapp off his guard. His face, which Vereker had already noticed was not a particularly open one, at once assumed a shifty and apprehensive look.

"I know nothing about the business, sir," he said after a moment's hesitation.

"Of course not. If you did, you'd have informed the police inspector. But you've thought about the matter like everyone else, I should say, and I naturally presumed you'd have formed some kind of theory."

"Not in my line, sir. When the young gentleman was found dead, I thought it must be suicide and I says to myself that's what comes of getting into debt with drink and young women. Seeing they can't find the pistol it must be murder, I suppose."

"How do you know Mr. Frank Cornell was in debt, Tapp?" asked Vereker quietly.

"Well, sir, he said as much to me himself. When he was looking very down in the mouth only a few days ago I asked him if he was feeling unwell. 'No, Tapp, not what you'd call unwell,' he said and asked me, 'Have you ever been up to the eyes in debt, Tapp?' 'No, sir, thank God,' I said and he replied, 'Well, never get up to the eyes in debt. It's worse than feeling unwell; it's more like frizzling in hell—in a supercharged hell,' was the words, to be accurate."

For some moments there was silence while Vereker stood lost in thought and then, as if waking from a day-dream, he said, "Is the music room always locked, Tapp?"

"Always, sir. Occasionally Mrs. Cornell has it dusted and aired, but that's very seldom."

"Do you know why it's kept locked?"

"Supposed to be haunted, sir. Mr. John Cornell was a keen spiritualist and it was his orders that it was to be kept locked."

"Anyone ever seen the ghost?"

"Only Mrs. Cornell. Not long ago she went into the room after dark to look for some music and came out in hysterics. She said when she opened the door the piano suddenly began to play very softly. She looked up and saw a young woman in her wedding dress sitting at the instrument."

"Very romantic," remarked Vereker smiling. "I wonder how many ghosts wander about in their wedding dresses. Their name must be legion. As it's broad daylight and I'm not easily scared, I think I'll have a good look at the music room. Who keeps the key?"

"The butler, sir. Shall I get it for you?"

"Thanks. I'll wait for you on the half-landing."

Tapp having disappeared, Vereker promptly opened the bedroom wardrobe and swiftly examined every lounge suit it contained one by one. In the midst of this operation he suddenly uttered an exclamation of surprise and, picking off some almost invisible object from one of the garments, inserted it in his pocket book between a sheet of folded notepaper. Satisfied that nothing more was to be learned here, he replaced the suits in the wardrobe and proceeded leisurely down the half-flight of stairs to the small landing off which the music room opened. Examining the door, he noticed the large, old-fashioned keyhole of the lock, and taking a lead pencil from his pocket pushed it through as if to remove some obstruction. Then bending down he peered into the room, noting the fairly wide angle of vision the aperture permitted. He stood erect once more and was musing as to what type of story had given rise to the Marston ghost, when Crawley, the old butler, appeared at the foot of the stairs and ascended as quickly as his stiff limbs would allow. In his hand he held two keys, a large, old-fashioned one and a smaller, modern one. On reaching the half-landing, he apologized to Vereker for keeping him waiting.

"Had to search for the keys, sir," he explained. "Mrs. Cornell used them last and forgot to give them back direct to me. Instead of putting them on the usual nail she left them on one of the shelves of my pantry."

"When did she use them last, Crawley?" asked Vereker casually.

"Just the other day. In fact, the very night Mr. Frank was killed, sir. It was some time after dinner she asked for them and said that Doctor Redgrave who was dining at the house that night was going to try his luck with the Manor ghost. He had never seen a spook before and was anxious to see one."

"Did she replace the keys that night?"

"No, sir. After locking up the other doors, I remembered the music room keys and glanced to see if they had been put back. They weren't there and not wishing to trouble madam about the matter I let it slip."

"You tried the music room door before you turned in?" asked Vereker.

"Certainly, sir. It was locked all right and that's one of the reasons I didn't bother madam about the keys that night."

"Didn't Inspector Heather look into the room to-day?" asked Vereker with a shade of surprise.

"That I couldn't say, sir. He went round the house with madam this morning, and if he did, she must have come for the keys and put them back herself. I was over in Marston village all morning about arrangements for the young master's funeral."

"What did you do about the keys last night? Did you notice they hadn't been replaced on their nail?"

"Bless you, sir, I wasn't worrying about keys last night. I had other things to think about and didn't get to bed till the early hours. The whole house is so upset that I don't know half the time what I'm doing. My memory, too, is getting shocking bad and it's about time I packed up with service."

"You'd be sorry to leave Mrs. Cornell, wouldn't you?" asked Vereker.

"Yes, sir, in some ways. She's a very nice lady and very good to her servants. Never grumbles but she's firm and will have everything done properly. We all get on very well with madam, but there's no entertaining here like real gentry entertain. You couldn't say we had a wine cellar, leastways not what I'd call a wine cellar. Just a few bottles of this and that for occasions. People nowadays don't seem to know how to live and enjoy themselves decent. This is a dull place. No horses, no dogs, no huntin', no nothing!"

With these remarks and a lugubrious air Crawley inserted the larger key in the music room door, turned it and flung the door open.

"Do you believe in spirits, Crawley?" asked Vereker as he looked round the gloomy, low-ceilinged room.

"If they're good, a drop now and then don't do you no harm, but there's nothing to compare with good wine, sir," replied the butler, his mind evidently still pursuing its former train of thought.

"I mean ghosts, Crawley," said Vereker with a broad smile.

"Beg pardon, sir, I thought you was referring to refreshments. Ghosts? Bless my soul, I've lived with ghosts all my life, sir. Last two places I was in both had ghosts hauntin' them."

"Ever see one, Crawley?"

"Not a ghost of a one, sir, if you'll pardon the joke. I won't say there isn't no such thing, as some do, but with me seeing's believing and I've not seen one yet. Don't particular want to, neither. There's plenty to do with the living without troubling about them that's dead and gone."

"By the way, Crawley, what's this other key?" asked Vereker as he extracted from the music room door its larger key and another one dangling to it on a small circle of cord.

"For the door leading down into the garden, sir," replied the butler.

"I see," remarked Vereker and crossed the room to the door the butler had indicated.

This was a modern door. It opened on to a winding flight of stone steps which led down to the gravel path running through the spacious gardens at the back of the house.

"Were this door and steps here when you came to the Manor, Crawley?" asked Vereker.

"No, sir. That was one of Mr. John Cornell's improvements. Although the room was never used much, Mr. David Cornell used to come and sit here at the piano for hours with Miss Stella. He used to let himself in from the garden by that door. But he said he didn't like the feel of the room. Although he can't see, he said he was sure it was a haunted room, so Mr. John bought him a piano for the bungalow and he hasn't been in the house for over a year now."

"Has he still got the keys to the doors?" asked Vereker immediately.

"Not that I know of, sir. There was some argument about those duplicate keys. Mr. David said he returned them to Mr. John, and I know for certain they were in my key cupboard for a while. Then they went missing. We never found them and didn't trouble any more about them."

"I suppose he used to come here and compose," remarked Vereker.

"That's what he called it, sir. I don't know nothing about music, but all that twiddling about on the keys don't seem music to me. I like a good song like 'John Peel' and that one which starts with 'In cellar cool.' But he's a proper musician, I must say. I once came in here when he was working and he asked me what he could play for me. I asked him if he knew 'My dear old Dutch' and he simply played it right away, I was glad he couldn't see that day because he played it so beautiful the tears were running down my cheeks before he'd finished. I'd lost my old missus just five years before to the very day."

Crawley heaved a sigh and added, "Yes, sir, he's a proper musician all right."

During Crawley's reminiscence Vereker's restless eyes had been busy. A chintz-covered settee in a bay window overlooking the garden had particularly attracted him and, bending over it, he had looked at it with the most minute attention. Finally he picked from the chintz cover with a small pair of steel forceps some almost invisible object and carefully put it away in his note-case between a folded sheet of paper beside the one he had discovered on Frank Cornell's lounge suit. Then on hands and knees he examined the carpet close to the settee with his magnifying glass. Satisfied with the scrutiny, he rose once more to his feet.

"When was this room last cleaned out, Crawley?" he asked.

"The morning of the very day Mr. Frank was killed, sir. It was done properly, too. All the chair covers taken off and replaced with new ones, carpet vacuum cleaned, paint all washed and the chimney swept. It was all finished by lunch time."

"It hasn't been used at all since?" asked Vereker with surprise.

"No, sir, I don't think a soul has been in the room except Doctor Redgrave who looked in the other night to see if he could see the ghost. If you ask me, sir, he simply wanted to have a quiet chat with madam and wasn't bothering about no ghost."

"Thanks, Crawley. Don't let me keep you off your work if you're busy," suggested Vereker, who noticed that the butler had just glanced at his watch.

"I was going to suggest, sir, that if you didn't want me, I had a particular job I'd like to get on with. Mr. Carstairs is going to be in for lunch at one o'clock. If there's anything you'd wish will you please ring."

"I thought everyone had gone over to Doctor Redgrave's for lunch," remarked Vereker.

"Only the ladies, sir. Mr. Carstairs said he'd be here all afternoon in case there was any urgent inquiries by the police and Mrs. Cornell was glad there was someone to take charge in her absence."

With these words Crawley departed and Vereker began a very systematic and thorough search of the room. He lifted up the top of the grand piano, thrust his hands into the interstices of chairs and settee, peered behind pictures, and even probed up the chimney. He then unlocked the door leading down to the garden by the stone steps and immediately a look of surprise came over his face. Something important had caught his highly alert and observant senses. As he stood ready to step out he again turned the key forwards and backwards. This moved the bolt of the lock with such unexpected ease and silence that he promptly looked closely at the bolt and found that it had been recently oiled. Quickly bending down, he smelled the bolt and then brought his hand down with an ecstatic slap on his knee.

"By Jove, this is excellent," he exclaimed. "There's simply no mistaking the pleasant, sweetish odour of 'Three in One' oil."

Descending the flight of stone steps, he wandered round a portion of the garden and carefully examined the gravel path that ran contiguous with the walls of the house. Finding nothing to arrest his attention, he returned, re-entered the music room, and locked the door once more. He had just satisfied himself that for the time being there was nothing else to be learned in this quarter of the house and was about to explore the rooms leading off the first-floor corridor, when he heard footsteps ascending the stairs and a few seconds afterwards a tall young man entered the room. He had an earnest, shrewd face with a firm mouth and chin and walked with that gait which unmistakably discloses a full measure of self-confidence.

"You are Mr. Vereker?" he asked bluntly.

"I am," replied Vereker as briefly.

"My name's Carstairs," he continued with an added inflection of amiability as if he felt his address had been too curt and wished to apologize for it. "Mrs. Cornell has asked me to take charge here for her while police investigations are being carried out. If there's anything I can do for you, please let me know."

"Thanks, I'm very much obliged. Can you tell me if there's a cat in the house?" asked Vereker.

For a moment an unpleasant look of aggression lit Mr. Carstairs' eye. He thought that the visitor was being impertinently facetious. Seeing that Vereker was in earnest he replied, "As far as I know, only one black cat which is an excellent mouser. Mrs. Cornell adores him."

Silence ensued and was at length broken by Carstairs.

"What are you doing about lunch to-day?" It's nearly one o'clock," he said glancing at his watch.

"I shall see what 'The Dog and Partridge' can do about it in half an hour's time. These country inns often surprise one quite pleasantly in the matter of a good meal."

"If you'd care to lunch with me, I'd be quite glad," continued Carstairs. "It's dull eating by one's self and I might be helpful to you with regard to your work in this dreadful business."

"If it would be no trouble," replied Vereker, feeling that he certainly would like to hear Mr. Carstairs' views on the murder of Frank Cornell. Frank Cornell and he had been friends since they were at school together and he probably knew the dead man more intimately even than his own family.

"No trouble at all. I'll just see Crawley at once," he said and disappeared down the stairs.

Chapter Six
Mr. Carstairs' Story

In spite of a certain aggressive confidence in himself and a peculiar habit of assuming an impressive air when about to speak, Mr. Roland Carstairs made on the whole a favourable impression on Vereker. He was very direct and if opinionated certainly wasted no time in irrelevant subtleties or beating about the bush. Moreover, he showed himself intensely interested in the technicalities of detection and evinced a wholehearted eagerness to get at the truth about the mysterious murder of his friend, Frank Cornell. He was anxious to discuss every point of the case with utmost freedom and give Vereker any information he could. Having measured up his man with swift insight, Vereker lost no time in taking advantage or the occasion to add to his knowledge of the whole strange affair.

"You were a great friend of Mr. Frank Cornell?" he asked after the first stiffness of conversation had thawed into geniality.

"We were at school together, went up to Oxford together and had more or less kept in touch ever since, Mr. Vereker. In a friendship between two men you will generally find that one of the two is the dominant character. He doesn't consciously assume this superiority, he doesn't intrude it unpleasantly on the other; it's the consequence of the rather obscure thing we call personality. Now in our friendship I was the dominant partner. I was a couple of years older, but I don't think age had anything to do with it. His was the more brilliant and supple mind and in spite of a certain boyishness of behaviour, Frank was undeniably clever. My outlook, however, had a quality which his lacked and the only word I can find to express it is, rigidity. It's not an intellectual asset, it's a thing of temperament. I acted as a moral brake on his rather amoral recklessness. Often our differences came to the point of my giving him a jolly stern lecture on his general conduct. Now, he had the astuteness and courage to see and admit that I was right and even when I'd lost my wool and said bitter and brutal things to him, he'd wind up by being repentant in his jocular way. He often used to heal a tiff with, 'Never mind, Roly, I'll take your advice and try and act on it in future. You see you were born with just those qualities that make you a splendid unit of a shining social herd. I've got to break myself in and form those qualities. It's a hell of a hard job, my boy. A feckless Frank can't be hammered into a righteous Roly in the twinkling of an eye.'"

"You did your best to keep him straight," suggested Vereker, secretly amused at the hint of priggishness that peeped out of Carstairs' conversation.

"Yes, I did my very best because I was genuinely fond of him. I knew he thought I was a self-righteous old stick and used to laugh at me, but I never allow myself to be intimidated by ridicule in doing what I think's my duty."

"That requires a good deal of moral courage," said Vereker and noted that his companion was secretly gratified by the compliment. It at once removed his initial attitude of reserve and he became more informative than ever.

"I look at life in this way," he continued as he sipped his wine with delicate precision. "Human beings are diverse and it's no use saying a man's worthless if his character differs from your own. But we've got to jog along together happily and everyone must conform to a certain social code. If your propensities bump against that fairly elastic code, you've simply got to clip the wings of your propensities. If you seek complete personal liberty you're asking for humming birds. It can't be done, Mr. Vereker."

"But suppose the social code isn't based on biological necessities," said Vereker, faintly roused to an argumentative mood.

"Biological necessities be damned," returned Carstairs firmly. "It's the modern scientific way of saying we must follow Nature's laws. Subversive rubbish! Nature is haphazard and pure opportunism. Lust, cruelty, greed, rape, theft, war are all natural. No, no, it won't do. Now Frank and I were absolutely dissimilar. He was too fond of drink, of gambling, of philandering. He always had his snout turned towards the path that leads to social disaster. I didn't think he was depraved on that account. I simply thought he was a fool and tried to show him that he was."

"He was badly in debt, I believe," remarked Vereker.

"He was always getting badly into debt. His father rescued him on several occasions. I've helped him, too, according to my means. But his father took him the wrong way. He stormed and raved at the poor fellow instead of trying to reason with him. That only put Frank's back up and he could be as obstinate as a pig. Old Cornell had threatened to cut him off with a shilling so frequently that Frank used to say the bobs were mounting up to quite a respectable legacy."

"Did his father give him an adequate allowance?" asked Vereker.

"Five hundred a year but what's the use of five hundred a year to a man who thinks in champagne, horses and costly presents for pretty young women. It's an ample allowance for any sensible fellow, I admit, and he ought to have lived down to it while he was studying for his profession."

"He was intended for the bar," suggested Vereker.

"Yes, but reading for the bar was merely a camouflage with Frank for living in chambers and having a floodlight time of it."

"He'd have settled down all right after marriage, perhaps."

"Perhaps!" repeated Carstairs ironically. "If he'd married the right sort of woman. Once upon a time he was really in love with his cousin Stella and she with him. It would have made an admirable marriage—unless you think biologically. Stella's one of the best women that ever breathed: that is, of course, in my opinion. But old Cornell was dead against it and so was Stella's father. They both forbade their children to enter into such a union. Old Cornell wanted Frank to make a better match, connect up with a good county family. David Cornell thought his daughter too good for what he called 'that drunken little profligate.' In the end the lovers cooled off."

"What about Miss Valerie Mayo?" asked Vereker.

"Yes, John Cornell thought his son might do worse. She comes of good family and is fairly wealthy as wealth goes nowadays, but I can't stand the woman myself. It was none of my business but strictly between ourselves I think she was the last person Frank ought to have married, had he lived. Over-sexed, cocktail-sipping blonde with an hysterical desire for limelight! Her very phrase, 'I'm just crazy about Frank,' was enough for me. In my opinion she's simply just crazy and nothing else. No genuine feelings, just a sticky mess of screen heroics, inordinate vanity and gingered sexual appetite. She'd have suited Frank till he tired of her physically and then there would have been the inevitable divorce. And she'd have thought such a deplorable climax fashionably smart if it attracted sufficient publicity!"

"A very modern young lady," commented Vereker.

"I don't agree with you," contradicted Carstairs emphatically. "Modernity has nothing to do with it. The type has always existed. At certain periods of human history she lived her real life secretly and conformed to public opinion openly. Human nature doesn't alter but its mental plumage is pagan or puritan according to what is called the swing of the pendulum. We're rather pagan at the moment."

"You think Miss Mayo was genuinely in love with Frank Cornell?" asked Vereker.

"Oh, yes, in her own way. She does nothing by halves. Everything is 'most frightfully' or 'just too perfectly.' You know the kind of ecstatic being. Her love for Frank would be a 'body and soul' business or nothing."

"Was he tiring of this intense young lady?" asked Vereker.

"I don't think so. The type appealed to him strongly. Her hyperbole awoke something sympathetic in his own genuine recklessness."

"You were in the house on the fatal evening?" asked Vereker.

"Oh, yes. At dinner there were Mrs. Cornell, Doctor Redgrave, Mrs. and Miss Mayo, Frank Cornell and myself. After dinner we went to the drawing-room where Miss Mayo played and sang and, to give her her due, she can be most entertaining. She is anxious for a stage career and certainly has ability. Then someone suggested bridge, but it never materialized and finally Dr. Redgrave was persuaded by Mrs. Cornell to do some of his conjuring tricks for our amusement. At that sort of thing he's amazingly clever, quite up to professional standard, I should say. Personality here again counts almost as much as conjuring skill."

"And then?" asked Vereker trying to shepherd his informer away from any irrelevancy.

"We just talked. When it was dark, the conversation turned on the Manor ghost and Miss Mayo, probably picturing herself as the future mistress of the Manor, said it was frightfully thrilling to have a house with an authentic ghost. Redgrave listened attentively to Mrs. Cornell's story of the lady at the piano in her wedding dress, his disbelief in the apparition well hidden by his admiration for the narrator."

"The doctor admires Mrs. Cornell?" asked Vereker.

"They're absolutely infatuated with one another and can't hide it," replied Carstairs bluntly. "Anyhow, at the conclusion of the story, Redgrave expressed a desire to see the ghost and Mrs. Cornell said she'd get the keys to the music room. They disappeared together to satisfy the doctor's yearning after the psychic. An hour later, about ten o'clock, Mrs. Cornell returned alone."

"Was she looking quite normal?" interrupted Vereker quickly.

"Well, yes, on the whole. There might have been a trace of tears in her eyes. At the time I thought she had been crying."

"No news about the ghost?"

"No. Redgrave had been disappointed. As it was getting late and he had to make a call on a patient on his way home, he left without returning to the drawing-room. Mrs. Cornell made his apologies for him."

"This friendship with the doctor commenced some time ago, in fact prior to the death of Mrs. Cornell's husband?" asked Vereker.

"Yes. Apart from any moral standpoint, and as far as I know there has been nothing immoral in their relations. It's a very foolish thing for a handsome young doctor who is a bachelor to entertain any kind of friendship, however platonic, with a married woman. It's simply asking for trouble. When the married woman is young and beautiful and her husband very many years her senior the situation is doubly hazardous."

"Did old John Cornell know anything about it?"

"Frank told me he knew all about it and that, when someone who was anxious about the matter informed him, he angrily retorted that he'd trust Redgrave with his life as well as his wife, adding that when he objected to the friendship it would be time enough for those whom it didn't concern to worry."

"What did Frank Cornell think of the business?"

"He was wholly indifferent. Up to a very recent date he liked Redgrave and was also on excellent terms with Jo. Jo, by the way, is short for Josephine, Mrs. Cornell's name and Frank always called her by that abbreviation. He never could screw himself up to using the word mother to a woman not very much older than himself."

"After Mrs. Cornell returned to the drawing-room, what happened?" asked Vereker.

"As the Manor ghost had been so disobliging, conversation petered out and at ten-thirty the ladies said good night and retired. Frank and I sat smoking till eleven and then turned in."

"You never saw him alive again?"

"No."

"Strange! Your bedroom is next door to the one he occupied."

"That's so."

"You didn't hear him leave his room?"

"When I get into bed I simply shut my ears to all the incidental noises that occur in a house at night. I couldn't have been between the sheets ten minutes before I was sound asleep. In any case the walls of the old place are so thick and sound-proof that the occupant of one room can't hear even loud conversation in the next. I tried this out since the tragedy just to satisfy my curiosity."

"It's a wonder no one heard the pistol shot!" exclaimed Vereker.

"I don't think so. It's only in the popular detective story that half the house are awake and some of them on the prowl at the moment of a tragedy. Old Mrs. Mayo, who is a light sleeper and highly nervous, said at one o'clock she heard a noise as if I had taken off and flung one of my shoes with a bang on the floor. She occupied the room next to mine on the side nearer the corridor window. She said, like the nervous man in the old story, she lay awake half an hour anxiously waiting for the sound of the other shoe but it failed to happen and she fell asleep without hearing any further noise."

"Which was Miss Mayo's bedroom?"

"The one opposite her mother's and Mrs. Cornell's is the one next to Mrs. Mayo's at the end of the corridor."

"Would you hear anyone passing your door in walking along the corridor?" asked Vereker.

"Oh, yes, if you're awake and particularly listening. I hear the maid passing my door as she takes round the morning tea and hot water."

"Have you any theory as to who shot your friend?" asked Vereker bluntly.

"It's dangerous to express any theory on such a dreadful affair even if you have one," replied Carstairs guardedly. "I might in turn ask you what's your explanation of the crime. As a detective you must have formulated a theory from the facts you've gathered."

"I haven't got as far as that yet," said Vereker cautiously, "but the time will doubtless come. Just now you hinted that Frank Cornell's relations with his stepmother and Doctor Redgrave had not been altogether cordial. What caused the friction?"

"That's a very curious story and one that I don't feel I ought to divulge in the nature of the circumstances. Apart from my friendship with Frank the affair was no concern of mine," replied Carstairs and lit another cigarette.

"It might throw some light on the business and help me in my investigation. If the story assists in the slightest way in bringing the murderer to justice, I think you can feel you're doing the right thing in divulging it. As his friend you might even say it was your duty. What do you think?"

"I'm listening to the voice of the charmer and he's charming ever so wisely," remarked Carstairs and for some minutes sat in meditative silence. At length he suddenly drew himself together as if he had made a difficult and momentous decision. "Perhaps you're right, Vereker," he said with animation, "but I should like to make one or two preliminary remarks. In the first place I'm not sure whether the story I'm about to tell you has any bearing whatever on the subsequent murder of my friend. I have my own ideas which I shan't express, but you can draw your own inferences from my remarks. Secondly, whatever happens this must be a secret between ourselves. The facts may help you and they may not, but whatever you do you mustn't disclose that I told you. Do you agree to the terms?"

"I give you my word of honour," replied Vereker sincerely.

"That's enough for me. I know I can rely on you," said Carstairs, and having poured out coffee, passed Vereker his cigar-case. He then moved his chair round to the other side of the table so that he could speak more intimately.

"Of course you've heard all about the exhumation of John Cornell's body?" he asked.

"Yes, I've read all about that and naturally wondered whether it had any connection with the shooting of Frank Cornell."

"A natural question for a detective to ask, I should say. I've been wondering, too, but let me explain. You know all about the exhumation, the examination by the Home Office analyst, his report and the verdict of the coroner's jury. Doctor Redgrave gave pneumonia as the cause of old John Cornell's death and he may have made that statement in all sincerity. We must keep an open mind and make no charges we can't substantiate. But behind the scenes is a very strange story. John Cornell was in perfect health only a few days prior to his sudden death. His illness began with a headache, persistent vomiting and convulsions. For a day or so he was wildly delirious, then fell into a profound coma and died within a week. Now these symptoms are probably the symptoms of pneumonia and as everyone knows pneumonia is a deadly business, especially with a man of his advanced years. He was buried and nothing more was said or thought about the matter for the time being. Six months later came the bombshell of the exhumation. This was due to representations made by his blind brother, David Cornell, to the Home Office which was compelled to take action in the matter. A very curious set of circumstances led to this action on David Cornell's part. In the first place, though he was never very friendly with his brother's young wife, he was never openly hostile, though he freely expressed his opinion to his brother and to all and sundry that he thought it was a very imprudent marriage for a man of his years to contract. Like most of us he thought the young woman was making a *mariage de convenance* or, to put it bluntly, was after the old boy's moneybags. From Jo's subsequent behaviour we were most of us, I speak especially for myself, inclined to think we had judged the young lady very harshly. She was an affectionate and good wife to John Cornell. Some time after their arrival at Marston, Dr. Redgrave appeared on the scene and soon he and Mrs. Cornell became very friendly. This friendship arose out of Redgrave's interest in her domestic improvements in the Manor. He's a man of great refinement with a special knowledge of what we may call the growth of the English house. He had been here in Marston some years before the Cornells bought the place and always had a great love for the beautiful old building. But he's a very handsome and charming man as well, and it wasn't long before Jo showed openly that she had conceived a great admiration for him as a man apart from any qualifications he might have on theories of house renovation. He, in turn, undoubtedly began to admire Jo as a woman. I can quite understand all this. Redgrave ought at this point to have looked at things dispassionately and from a worldly point of view. But as someone has said, love's not an affair of the intellect and instead of avoiding any risks of a scandal he stuck obstinately to his friendship. Sometimes the very best women and men can do this and do it successfully, but the sudden death of John Cornell coming at a period when it was clear that his wife and Dr. Redgrave were in love was, to put it in any way you like, a difficult thing for the world to swallow without some kind of suspicious comment. The whole affair might have ended there quite harmlessly if I hadn't unfortunately come on the scene."

For some minutes Carstairs sat in lugubrious silence.

"Yes, I was the *deus ex machina* that indirectly caused all the trouble," he said at length. "All my life I've been dogged by this unhappy fate of causing trouble—sometimes quite unintentionally. In that respect I must have been born under some malignant star, but I'm not going to excuse myself. It has happened and can't be helped now. To return to the subject, old Cornell's sudden death gave rise to a certain amount of secret suspicion among those acquainted with the circumstances. Passion has always been one of the most powerful motives for murder and even if there was not one iota of foundation for suspicion in this case, it was almost certain to arise in some minds. I knew nothing of Redgrave and not very much about Jo, and though I'm not prone to suspicion, old Cornell's death struck me as strange, especially when Frank told me of the symptoms. However, we discussed the subject and then in a repentant mood dismissed it as unworthy of ourselves. For a time neither of us referred to it again. Then last July, Frank asked me down to the Manor as his guest. I accepted the invitation and came. I sometimes wish I'd never set eyes on the place, but it's no use indulging in these idle regrets. I came and ran up against George Tapp who had been John Cornell's valet for over a year."

"To interrupt you for a minute, Carstairs, may I ask how John Cornell left his money?" suddenly questioned Vereker.

"Jo, of course, had been well provided for by a marriage settlement, but she benefited again very considerably by her husband's death. Frank was the residuary legatee and became a wealthy man. Old David Cornell got an addition to his yearly income and Stella received a legacy of five thousand pounds clear of death duties."

"Was any proviso made about Frank predeceasing his stepmother?" asked Vereker.

"Yes. Old John Cornell, knowing his son's ability to spend recklessly, took care to leave his money in the hands of trustees. Frank could only squander the interest on the capital and I believe some of his creditors have garnished him. In case of his death the whole of the capital reverted without any reservations to his stepmother, Jo."

"And now for the life of me, I can't guess what part George Tapp could play in your story," said Vereker.

"I'm going to tell you about George Tapp. He's one of Nature's saturnine jokes. About a year previous to his death, John Cornell lost his old valet and was looking for another. He was making inquiries to this end when Doctor Redgrave suddenly discovered the right man for him. He told Jo that he knew the very man for the job and Jo told John Cornell. To cut the story short, Tapp arrived and was the perfect valet. John Cornell was essentially a kindly man and he liked George Tapp immensely. He almost treated Tapp as a companion. Everything went well until I arrived at Marston Manor on my first visit after Frank had become its owner. Tapp was now Frank's valet and a very good one, too. But I had met Tapp before in very peculiar and distressing circumstances. At the time, my mother and I and my sister had a very nice house at Richmond. It was not a magnificent place for we weren't what you call wealthy, but it suited us admirably and was very comfortable. We had been in Richmond only a year when a very serious epidemic of disease broke out. Its victims were generally people of mature years and the young. Both my mother and my sister caught this epidemic and died. At first it was thought to be a kind of influenza germ, but after a very careful investigation by medical experts it was found to be cerebro-spinal fever, or meningitis, a most deadly infectious disease. Now it's a peculiarity of this disease that an epidemic is generally caused by what is called a germ-carrier, and after considerable trouble and difficulty the germ-carrier was tracked down. That man was poor George Tapp. He was a milk roundsman in our district and I knew him well by sight. Formerly he had been a gentleman's valet, but after the war he came back to look for another job as his master had been killed in the battle of the Somme. Being a countryman and knowing all about the sale of milk, for he had taken round milk as a boy in his native village, he took the job in Richmond as a stop gap until he could return to valeting."

"Did Tapp know he was a germ-carrier when the medical inquiry tracked him down?" asked Vereker, deeply interested in this strange story.

"He said he didn't and from what I know of Tapp, I should say he was speaking the truth. The trouble about a germ-carrier is that ostensibly he is in perfect health. It is most difficult to recognize a healthy carrier as a potential danger to his fellows and so far all 'cures' of the carrier state have been unsuccessful. It's a problem that the State in conjunction with the medical profession will have to face soon and boldly, and it's one of the most difficult of problems. You can't lock up and segregate a decent man for being a carrier through no fault of his own."

"But what has this germ-carrier business of Tapp's to do with Cornell's death from pneumonia?" asked Vereker pointedly.

"A very pertinent question, Vereker. Cerebro-spinal fever can be very easily mistaken for the so-called cerebral type of pneumonia. Unless the ordinary medical practitioner was acquainted with the former, the mistake would be a pardonable one."

"Redgrave, you think, made that mistake?" asked Vereker.

"That's not for me to say definitely but old Cornell's symptoms were the very symptoms of meningitis. The epidemic which caused the deaths of my mother and sister naturally gave me a morbid interest in everything pertaining to the disease. Knowing the symptoms, in conjunction with Tapp's presence in the house and close attendance on his master, I'm certain in my own mind that John Cornell died of cerebro-spinal fever."

"How is the infection transmitted?" asked Vereker now suppressing with difficulty the excitement he was feeling.

"The germs, it appears, are in the carrier's nose and throat secretions and are transmitted by coughing, sneezing and spitting, or even by handkerchiefs, spoons, or other fomites."

"I suppose a medical man could make a culture?"

"Quite easily, but the germ is a very delicate one and particularly sensitive to cold."

"This is all very interesting, Carstairs. As a layman you seem to have a good knowledge of the subject, but if Redgrave introduced Tapp into the Cornell household, he cannot possibly have known the man was a germ-carrier."

"We're now treading on extremely dangerous ground, Vereker, and I'm going to be very guarded. It's quite possible that Redgrave was ignorant of the fact. When I told Frank in great secrecy about George Tapp's unhappy affliction, and that I was fairly certain that indirectly his presence in the house had caused his father's death, he simply lost all sense of proportion. Always a bit imaginative and suspicious, for his light reading consisted solely of the rubbish we now put under the generic name of 'thriller,' he immediately saw in the matter a subtle and fiendish plot on the part of Redgrave to get rid of his father so that he could marry Jo. His very words to me were, 'It looks to me, Roly, that it's simply a case of murder by natural death.' When I pointed out to him the terrible nature of the charge and that such a means of killing would also endanger his life and Jo's, he replied with a certain amount of truth that neither he nor Jo nor any of the servants was of a susceptible age to catch the infection. He began to inquire secretly into the history of George Tapp and found that my story was correct. Moreover, he found that Redgrave had a practice in Richmond at the time and must have been cognizant of the whole affair of the epidemic and Tapp's connection with it. The one thing he couldn't discover was how Redgrave got in touch with Tapp for the purpose of introducing him into the Cornell household. At first he was going openly to tax Redgrave with the business, but on my earnest pleading refrained from such a reckless course. But he couldn't keep the matter entirely to himself and once in a vindictive mood, he'd possibly been drinking, hinted to Stella that Redgrave was directly responsible for his father's death. He didn't explain to her how or give her any details. She, in turn, confided in her father what Frank had said, and the blind brother, who knew all about the indiscreet friendship between Jo and Redgrave, at once began to suspect that his brother had been subtly poisoned. This suspicion preyed on his mind to such an extent that without making definite charges he communicated with the Home Office. The whole sorry business of the exhumation resulted from his action. Redgrave was naturally terribly upset. The accusing finger of the public was silently pointing at him and if not at him at Jo, with whom he was now passionately in love. You can imagine the distress of a medical man in such a predicament; it was sufficient to wreck his career and ruin his life. The relations between Redgrave, Jo and David Cornell became very strained to put it in the mildest way. The matter unfortunately didn't rest there. One day Redgrave, who now openly made love to Jo and had taken up the attitude of her protector, took upon himself the duty of lecturing Frank on his behaviour in the village where he was rapidly acquiring the reputation of a roysterer and spendthrift. Jo was fond of Frank and had probably instigated Redgrave to this action for Frank's benefit. Now Frank could stand a lecture from his father or from me, but he resented Redgrave's interference in his affairs very strongly. He told Redgrave curtly to mind his own damned business. Some weeks later when the doctor had dined at the house, Frank, in one of his freakish, vindictive moods, introduced the subject of cerebro-spinal fever and remarked that he was sure that his father had died of that affliction and not of pneumonia. In a mood of assumed banter he also said that he was certain George Tapp, the valet, was a germ-carrier. Redgrave apparently took this all in good part, but he was never friendly with Frank Cornell again. Moreover, a curious change came over the doctor. He lost his usual urbanity and charming manner, became silent and morose, and it was clear to many of his friends that something was preying on his mind. Personally, I feel sure he guessed that Frank Cornell was harbouring a suspicion that he had carried out a devilishly subtle scheme for getting rid of John Cornell so that he could marry Jo. Perhaps he was also afraid that Frank would tell Jo the nature of his suspicions and poison her mind. Outwardly, however, he kept on terms of polite friendliness with Frank. Then, to conclude my story, Frank was murdered, and on Inspector Heather and you devolves the task of discovering who shot him."

"And still you have no secret theory as to who murdered your friend?" asked Vereker pointedly.

"To tell you the honest truth, Vereker, I haven't the vaguest idea. From your question I guess you think I suspect Redgrave of the crime or at least of being an instigator to the crime. The nature of my story and my knowledge of this secret affair might bias my mind in that direction. That's only natural. I might at the same time suspect Jo. If she became aware of Frank's suspicion it might work her up to the point of committing such an act to save the reputation of the man with whom she is passionately in love. The broadcasting of such a suspicion would naturally be a terrible thing for both of them, and even if they took legal action which is intricate and difficult, the suspicion would still persist. A cat may have nine lives but suspicion has ninety-nine."

"This is a most amazing business," declared Vereker seriously, "and I'm very grateful to you for confiding your story in me, Carstairs. My job's to unearth the slayer of your friend and a full knowledge of all the circumstances is essential to success. I'm afraid it's going to be a most delicate and difficult task—much more so than I anticipated."

"Perhaps I oughtn't to have told you," said Carstairs. "It may give your mind an unfair bias, but I've thought the matter out very fully and dispassionately. I was going to tell Inspector Heather, but couldn't just screw up my courage to the point. Now I've got rid of a big load off my chest I feel happier. In whatever way you look at it, I felt I owed a duty to my old friend Frank to tell you this and I've done that duty."

Vereker thanked him again and rose from his chair.

"I'd like to have a general look round the house before I go," he said.

"I'll show you round the whole shoot," replied Carstairs
and together they visited every room on the first floor corridor,
finishing up with Mrs. Cornell's bedroom. This was a spacious
room, delightfully furnished, its whole tone of colour being a soft
pink. On the dressing-table besides the usual brushes, combs,
cosmetics and knickknacks, stood a portrait in a silver frame.
Carstairs picked it up and handed it to Vereker.

"Doctor Redgrave," he said.

Vereker looked carefully at the portrait. It was that of a man
of about thirty-five years of age. The eyes were particularly fine,
the eyebrows well-marked, the mouth and chin firm but not
aggressive. A certain lightness and softness in the formation of the
lips declared a gentle, perhaps artistic side to his nature. The hair
was thick and naturally waved across a broad, intellectual skull.

"Looks more like a film hero than a leech," commented
Carstairs as he stood watching Vereker's intent gaze.

"He's a very handsome man," replied Vereker. "I can
understand any young and romantic woman falling for him, as the
Americans characteristically put it."

"And you won't be disappointed when you meet him in the
flesh," continued Carstairs.

Leaving Mrs. Cornell's room they rapidly made a round of
the servants' wing, climbed to two attics which were only used
as storerooms, and thence returned to the ground floor. Vereker
took leave of Carstairs and having returned the keys of the music
room to Crawley, the butler, he left the house by a side entrance
and wandered into the gardens lying in its rear. Here the borders
were a blaze of autumn flowers and he wandered along the trimly-
kept gravel paths, now gazing at some particularly fine mass of
colouring, now lost in his own thoughts, his head bent and his eyes
fixed on the ground he was traversing. At the farthermost limit
of this walled garden he came to a lily pool with its soft, white
waxen blooms floating with fairy-like grace on its placid surface.
Here and there between the gaps of the large flat leaves could be

seen the sudden flash of a goldfish as its glittering scales caught the light. Beside this pool, on a pavement of irregular flagstones, stood an oak garden seat. Tired after his morning's work, he sank lazily on to it and drew from his pocket a notebook and pencil. In this book he carefully jotted down every observation of significance he had made during his survey and roughly sketched a plan of the ground floor and first floor of the house. Returning his notebook to his pocket, he thrust his hands into his trousers pockets, stretched his legs, and was lost in thought over the incidents of the morning and the story which Roland Carstairs had told him. He felt that he must weigh this strange tale very carefully in the balance and not allow it to colour his thoughts or affect his judgment. It had, if it were true, a tendency to throw grave suspicion on the character of Doctor Redgrave and on the disinterestedness of his motives. It incorporated in this web of suspicion the woman with whom he was ostensibly in love and who was as obviously in love with him. Before crediting it he must satisfy himself as to the character of the man who had told it. On the surface Carstairs was a sincere and truthful man, possibly actuated by his devotion to his dead friend, but he must probe beneath this apparently satisfactory first impression. Carstairs had been eager to tell the story in spite of his hesitancy to begin. In some particulars it was a fantastic tale and displayed glaring weaknesses. Might it not be intended to throw him off the true scent? If so, what was Carstairs' motive? The phrase used by Frank Cornell ran in his mind with baleful significance—"murder by natural death." He recalled a recent case which had occurred in New York where a doctor was accused of murder by the injection of pneumonia germs. Science was daily increasing the powers of those devoted to the detection of crime: it was also putting in the hands of the criminal fiendish and deadly weapons to carry out his sinister machinations. In the present instance, if the germ-carrier had been introduced into the Cornell household with the secret intention of communicating a most deadly disease, the further complication had been added that the crime had been committed by indirect means and by a method which was almost impossible to bring home to the perpetrator. It was sufficient that Tapp should be in daily attendance on the victim, handle his clothes or articles he himself touched in the thousand and one actions of his daily life. Those susceptible to affection were either the very young or the aged, a fact which in this case practically narrowed the field of incidence to the desired victim. For the present he must keep an open mind and a very alert eye on Mr. Roland Carstairs. The latter's attitude of absolute fairness in the matter might in itself be the ruse of a subtle trickster to deceive. He must investigate every ramification of the strange affair with utmost impartiality and look at it from every angle of view.

Vereker was thus deep in speculation when a green wooden door in the north wall of the enclosed garden opened and Miss Stella Cornell entered. At once Vereker realized that this entrance to the Manor grounds was the nearest to the bungalow and afterwards he discovered that it led by a field path through a belt of woodland and across a meadow to David Cornell's residence. At first unseen himself, he watched the approaching young woman with idle interest. As she came nearer, he could see that her pale face was set and her brow furrowed. It was evident that the mysterious death of her cousin had left its mark on her. She stopped for a moment beside an orchid dahlia, tossed her head in a petulant gesture as if dismissing an unpleasant train of thought, and cupped one of the blooms in her hand. After a few moments' admiration she turned, glanced across the formal garden to the lily pool, and at once noticed that the seat beside it was occupied. For a second she hesitated as if uncertain who the lounger might be and then with an air of recognition hastened her step towards him. Vereker, whose eyes had never left her for a moment and who had admired the graceful poise of her slim body as she had bent over the dahlia flower, rose at once from his seat and raised his hat.

Chapter Seven
A Heart Bowed Down

Good afternoon, Mr. Vereker," said Miss Cornell pleasantly as she came up, "for I presume you're the Mr. Vereker that Inspector Heather told us to expect this morning."

"Quite correct, Miss Cornell," replied Vereker. "I was just admiring the goldfish in the lily pool and having a siesta before returning to the village."

"That sounds like a tactful fib to begin with," she said with a smile. "You were looking terribly serious. I thought you must be concocting a sensational column for the *Daily Report* when I remembered that the inspector said you were a very keen amateur sleuth. Aren't you a special correspondent after all?"

"Officially I am. As for being a detective, that's merely an unofficial business, a secret passion. You see, I must have some excuse for being on the scene. Scotland Yard wouldn't tolerate interference by amateurs and if I wasn't a Press correspondent apart from being a very old friend of the inspector's, I'd have been told long ago to run away and play."

"I see, and have you solved the mystery, Mr. Vereker?" she asked banteringly.

"Just solved it and I'm going to take out a warrant for your arrest," replied Vereker. The words uttered with mock gravity caused Miss Cornell's face to turn pale and then almost as suddenly to flush with embarrassment.

"You gave me a horrible fright," she said as she swiftly regained her composure. "You said the words so seriously that I was almost going to plead guilty right away. You oughtn't to make such grim jokes."

"I'm very sorry and apologize humbly," said Vereker. "Won't you take a seat? It's delightful to sit here in the warm sun."

"I was just going up to the Manor to see Mr. Carstairs. He asked me to have tea with him, but it's early yet so I'll stay here for a while. By the way, Mr. Vereker, do you know anything about music?"

"I used to play 'God save the King' on a tin whistle with some *brio* when I was younger," said Vereker taking a good look at Miss Stella Cornell's face as she sat down on the seat beside him and presented a three-quarter view. It was a serious beautiful face, pale with the pallor of health. Her hair in glossy black waves swept over her shapely ears and reflected blue in the high lights. Her eyes were large, dark brown and slumbrous; her mouth small, delicately formed and firm, the upper lip being a trifle too short to be perfect. Her figure was slim but delightfully proportioned, the broad shoulders and well-formed arms and limbs denoting considerable strength.

"And I suppose you were also a virtuoso on the Jew's harp, the ocarina and the tambourine. Be serious, Mr. Vereker. Are you interested in music?"

"Passionately fond of it but I'm out of date. I don't understand its recent developments. I'm not musically educated."

"Why not educate yourself? You can't appreciate the finest things in any art without some serious study. The average man, for instance, doesn't understand the quality of line in a really beautiful drawing."

"Quite true, Miss Cornell. I suppose music, like graphic or literary art, has advanced from the simple and generally romantic to the intellectual and subtly abstract. But why do you ask?"

"For a very simple reason. My father's a very keen musician and composer. I think his work's really good but, of course, I'm biased. He's a lonely man and blind. If you'd pay us a visit while you're here and talk music to him it would be doing him a very real kindness. When he heard you were the correspondent of the *Daily Report*, he at once said, 'I wonder if he's interested in music.' I was then ordered to pump you tactfully and ask you to drop in. Will you do so? I'd be very grateful to you if you would."

"You ask so persuasively I can't refuse," said Vereker. "I'll talk music with him but I'm afraid before many minutes he'll put me down as an awful dud on the subject and diplomatically get rid of me. Anyhow it'll be a pleasing change from thinking about crime."

"Oh, yes, this terrible business," said Miss Cornell and the expression of her whole face changed as a sunny landscape changes under the shadow of a heavy cloud. "Have you got very far in your investigation?"

"No. I'm afraid in this case I'm really up against it! So far there's very little to work on. Actual clues are remarkable by their absence and those that have come to light seem to lead nowhere. In the circumstances one has to rely on what one can gather in questioning everyone who is likely to shed even the faintest light on the mystery, in learning all about the dead man, all the ins and outs of the family and household, and then trusting to intuition rather than matter-of-fact deduction."

"If you'd like to ask me any questions, Mr. Vereker, do so. I won't mind a bit," suggested Miss Cornell with friendly alacrity.

"That's very good of you. I'll try and not be impertinent. If I am, you must just say so."

"First of all let me say I wasn't in the house on the night of Frank's death so that I may not be very helpful, but I'll do my best."

"When did you see your cousin last, Miss Cornell?" asked Vereker at once.

"About a week before his death. I was invited to the Manor to meet his fiancée, Miss Mayo."

"You weren't one of the dinner party on the night?"

"No. I'd been asked to go by Jo, that is, Mrs. Cornell, but I refused. In the first place I didn't want to see Miss Mayo again and I didn't like to leave father all by himself. Not that he would have minded much; he likes being alone at times, but that night he wanted me to write down some music for him. He was in the mood at the time so I made it an excuse for dodging the dinner."

"Did you sit up late?"

"Not late for us. We both went to bed at about eleven o'clock. We're rather night owls at the bungalow."

"Why were you anxious to avoid Miss Mayo?" asked Vereker pointedly.

For a few seconds Miss Cornell hesitated, blushed becomingly, and then replied, "Now that question is very personal but there's no reason why I shouldn't answer it. It may sound like taking you into my confidence, but if you haven't heard my story you're bound to hear it sooner or later, so I may as well tell you first-hand."

"If you'd rather not tell it to a perfect stranger, don't hesitate, Miss Cornell," suggested Vereker.

"Well, it's nothing very terrible. You see, Frank and I had known one another since we were children and later we grew very fond of one another. Secretly we became engaged—not formally but just between our two selves. When our parents heard about it, for we gave them a hint as to the state of affairs, neither his nor mine would hear of it. The reasons were simple enough. Frank's father was determined that he should make a brilliant match and I was scarcely in that category. Besides I was a cousin. My own father thought I'd rue my choice for the rest of my life, for he thought Frank was leading a very fast life."

"Was he?" asked Vereker bluntly.

"No, I don't think so. Frank was full of life and fun. He drank perhaps rather more than was good for him, but I'm sure it was just a youthful phase. Many good men have done exactly the same. I was, of course, told that he mixed with questionable women but I couldn't believe it. In any case, he was really good at heart and a most generous, kindly man. That was more to me than all the material astuteness and hardness that usually mark successful men. You see, I loved him..." Miss Cornell's voice broke with sudden emotion.

"I can quite understand your point of view," said Vereker to cover her momentary embarrassment. "Why didn't you both ignore your parents' wishes?"

"We decided to wait and see. We thought that they might relent. It was a fatal mistake."

"They continued to be adamant, I suppose," commented Vereker. "It's an easy role when you're dealing with other people's destinies."

"Well, we waited too long. Frank went up to London to read for the Bar and we became separated. He was susceptible to the attractions of a pretty woman and he ran across Valerie Mayo. It wasn't long before I noticed a change in his attitude to me. He was just as amiable and jovial and all that but he avoided any approach to our old intimacy. I knew then that he had fallen in love. I tried to blind myself to the truth for I hadn't changed..."

"You were faithful to the last?" interrupted asked Vereker casually.

"Yes. Not that I think faithfulness to the last the virtue some people think it. It's entirely a matter of temperament. If I had met someone who appealed to me more than Frank did, I might have changed. I don't think I would; I was probably born that way, but it's no use discussing the point. The faithful-for-ever lover is probably one whose early teaching has formed something in him stronger than his instincts. I don't know. In any case, Frank changed; it was in his nature."

"You took the matter very much to heart?" asked Vereker sympathetically.

"Oh, please don't speak about it. It was too terrible for words. In time I might have got over it, but now..."

"Tell me, Miss Cornell," said Vereker quickly for he saw that she was on the point of breaking down altogether, "when your parents forbade your marriage, did you continue to see one another?"

"Yes, we met secretly," said Miss Cornell and her eyes wandered with a curious wistfulness round the formal garden.

"Possibly on this very seat," remarked Vereker who had been intently watching her.

"Yes," agreed Miss Cornell starting suddenly, almost with an expression of alarm. "How on earth did you guess that?"

"Just a wild shot," replied Vereker cautiously, for her eyes had told him her secret.

"So you now see why I didn't particularly wish to meet Miss Mayo again, Mr. Vereker," she said reverting to the origin of her frank confession. "It was simply to avoid very acute suffering. Even my pride couldn't rise to putting a hypocritical face on it and pretending I didn't care."

"What is your candid opinion of Miss Mayo?"

"I haven't got one. I don't know her. The little I saw of her I didn't like, but that was probably a very natural prejudice. Frank was passionately in love with her."

"What does Mrs. Cornell think of her?"

"I don't think Jo admires the type, but Jo moves in a curiously detached orbit of her own. She saw that her stepson was bent on marrying the young lady and she accepted that as she would accept an eclipse of the moon—something that interested her up to a point but really had no bearing on her own affairs."

"She's self-centred?" asked Vereker.

"Oh, no, I wouldn't say that. I think she's perfectly adorable. No one can help liking her, but she has an almost angelic calm and is a terrible fatalist. What is to be, is to be, forms a big lump of her philosophy. When you meet her I'm sure she'll make a big impression on you."

"She has evidently made one on Doctor Redgrave, if there's any truth in village gossip," commented Vereker expectantly.

"Gossip can say what it likes now, Mr. Vereker. She's a free woman, but don't let that make you think Jo wasn't absolutely honourable prior to her husband's death. There never was a greater stickler for principles. She told me she was very fond of Doctor Redgrave long ago, but she would never permit even a shadow of intimacy. She had married John Cornell because his character appealed to her quite apart from anything in the nature of love.

She admired him immensely. He was persistent, forceful, and old enough to be a very satisfactory intellectual companion. She had never met a man she could love without all sorts of reservations."

"Now she has met that man, d'you think he'll make her the ideal husband?"

"I don't know. Doctor Redgrave's a very charming man, very handsome, but I'm never at ease with him. He's so much cleverer than I am that he makes me feel my mental inferiority. Also, he has at times a way of smiling at my remarks as if he saw through and through me and was amused at what he saw. I suppose there's something in me that strikes him as ludicrous and no one really enjoys being laughed at even in his very gentle way."

"He believes in ghosts," said Vereker almost as if his thoughts were running on two planes.

"What makes you think that?" asked Miss Cornell suddenly.

"Of course you know all about the Marston Manor ghost?" suggested Vereker with his eyes furtively watching her expression.

"We've all heard about her majesty," replied Miss Cornell and her eyelids fell for a second with a curious air of amused hesitancy.

"You haven't seen the lady in her wedding dress?" asked Vereker.

"No. But what makes you think Doctor Redgrave believes in ghosts?"

"Mrs. Cornell, I'm told, has seen the apparition and on the night of Frank Cornell's death she took Doctor Redgrave to the music room so that he could have a chance of seeing it."

"And you think he believes Jo's story?" asked Miss Cornell, a hint of a smile curling her short upper lip.

"It looks like it. In any case he didn't succeed and the only result was that Mrs. Cornell mislaid the keys to the music room and the butler had a job to find them when I wanted to have a look round this morning."

"You've looked round the room?" asked Miss Cornell, glancing at him shrewdly.

"I searched every inch of it."

"What were you looking for?"

"A pistol or revolver, of course. We haven't found the weapon yet."

"Oh, I see. But why on earth look in the music room?" asked Miss Cornell with suddenly roused curiosity.

"Well, you have to look everywhere in such an important search."

"Of course, but the music room door is always kept locked."

"I know and the butler has charge of the keys. But in my investigation this morning I learned a very curious thing. Once upon a time there were duplicate keys to the music room and not long ago they were missing and no one seems to know anything about them," continued Vereker.

"Father used to have the duplicate keys when he regularly used the music room. He returned them to Uncle John when uncle bought him a piano for the bungalow and he has never to my knowledge been in the Manor since."

"You have no idea what became of them subsequently?" asked Vereker.

"Not the slightest. Crawley ought to know where they are," replied Miss Cornell looking Vereker straight in the eyes.

"He doesn't," said Vereker feeling that the question had been too pointed and trying to meet her direct gaze with equal frankness.

"But do you think there's any connection between the music room and the person who shot Frank?" asked Miss Cornell seriously.

"At the moment I see none," replied Vereker guardedly, "but if his enemy wasn't in the house he must have entered and withdrawn by some door or window. In the circumstances we have to consider every possible contingency. I have an idea that the entry was made by the music room."

"I hadn't thought of that. It seems very clever to me who knows nothing about detection how you decided that."

"I may be wrong," suggested Vereker.

"Of course you may," she agreed with a nervous little laugh. "Well, I'm glad I'm not a detective. It would give me a perpetual headache to think of every possible contingency," and glancing at her wrist-watch added, "It's quarter-past four and I must leave you, Mr. Vereker. I promised Mr. Carstairs that I'd be up at the Manor at four. Poor Roly, I'm afraid I treat him very shabbily and he's always so patient with me."

"You seem very sorry for the gentleman," remarked Vereker jocularly as he noted the sympathetic tone of her voice.

"Yes, I am, but that's more of my personal history and I'm not going to tell you anything about it," replied Miss Cornell. "By the way, you won't forget to call at the bungalow and talk music to father when you can spare the time."

"I'll look him up the first opportunity I get," said Vereker and asked, "Can you give me the name of a good hairdresser in Bury, Miss Cornell? There's not one in Marston village as far as I can see."

Miss Cornell promptly gave him an address which Vereker jotted down in his notebook.

"That's the place I always go to," she said, "and I'm sure there's a gentleman's department. In any case there are several good hairdressers in the town. You'll have no difficulty in finding one. When you call at the bungalow I shall probably be in, too. Don't be afraid to ask me any further questions. I want to help you all I can. *Au revoir.*"

With these words she rose from the garden seat and walked quickly towards the house. On her departure Vereker immediately let himself out of the garden by the door in the north wall through which Miss Cornell had entered. He soon discovered that there was a beaten path which, passing through a narrow belt of woodland, led to the bungalow and thence on to the main Bury road. He reached this main road by leaving the bungalow on his right. A few minutes later he was walking towards Marston at a leisurely pace when a bus overtook him. Seeing that its destination was Bury, he boarded it and reached the town about half an hour later. There he went to the address Miss Cornell had given him, had his hair cut, got into a long conversation with the barber about the Marston murder, and journeyed back to The Dog and Partridge Inn. Inspector Heather had not yet returned and Vereker repaired to his room. Opening his suitcase he produced a microscope and setting it up on his dressing-table in a good light, commenced a minute examination of certain objects which he had collected during his afternoon's work. As he examined these objects his face showed traces of suppressed excitement.

"Rather important!" he soliloquized. "In fact the evidence may prove vital!"

He was busy on this operation when he suddenly heard the booming voice of the inspector talking to the landlord below. Leaving his instrument on the dressing-table, he washed and descended to the little room on the ground floor for his evening meal.

Chapter Eight
The Big Two Confer

You're back early, Mr. Vereker," said the inspector as he sat down to the table.

"I returned about six o'clock."

"You've been over to Bury to get your hair cut," said the inspector. "I was thinking it was time you shed your artist's thatch and began to look respectable like a detective. What have you been doing up in your room for the last hour and a half?"

"Playing about with a microscope. You see, Heather, I can't hand over odd jobs to experts as you do."

"I often think it's a pity I didn't mug up microscopy myself," said the inspector. "It's difficult sometimes to let the expert know just what you're after. Not being a detective, he frequently doesn't know the points to look for and misses the things the 'tec would grab with both eyes. What have you been examining?"

"We'll come to that later, Heather. I now propose a conference, one of our usual ones. You must give the findings of the hundred per cent. detective and I'll give the results of my amateurish fumbling. D'you feel like it?"

"I'm in the very mood," replied Heather putting a large fat hand lovingly round his pewter mug. "Let's begin at the beginning. First point for discussion—where was Frank Cornell shot?"

"In the right eye," replied Vereker.

"No, don't start fooling or I'll shut up shop and send for more beer. Where, in what place, at what spot in Marston Manor, was the young man?"

"Either on the half-landing or in the music room, seems to be the answer, Heather. I'm at present banking on the half-landing. The big objection to that theory lies in another question. I gather that the bullet entered his right eye and came to rest to the left of the occipital bone. Here's where your knowledge of pistol shot wounds comes in. Would death be almost instantaneous, or could Cornell have staggered up the stairs to the corridor landing with a bullet in his brain?"

"The point you raise is a difficult one. Most people would at once say he couldn't have run up those steps, but it's impossible to be definite in such a matter. In one case well known to all criminologists a man had a knife stuck up to the hilt in his brain. He walked a couple of miles to a doctor who yanked it out. The man recovered and his is not an isolated case. He must have been what we call hard-headed. Therefore in our case a sound expert would be very cautious in making a definite statement. Of course your question raises the point of how Cornell got up those steps if he was killed almost instantaneously."

"Good, Heather. Did the murderer carry him up? You remember the body was lying on its back. If the murderer had dragged the body up the second flight he would naturally turn it over on its back on account of the feet. It was an unusual position. I expected to find him lying on his face."

"That's possible, but why should he drag the body upstairs?"

"To hide the fact that he was shot near or in the music room. He may have intended to drag the body up to the body's bedroom."

"You've got music room on the brain, Mr. Vereker," remarked the inspector, but a slow smile spread over his face and he added, "Yet it's a cute suggestion. What made you first think the murderer had dragged the body upstairs?"

"Cornell's shoes. A man can walk upstairs quietly enough in his shoes if we leave bibulous jokes out of our consideration. But he can't be dragged upstairs without their bumping noisily on every step. The shoelaces hadn't been untied which shows that the shoes had been pulled off in a hurry in the dark."

"He could have pulled them off himself in that fashion," remarked the inspector. "I wear my shoes fairly large and easy and in a hurry I often force them off without untying the laces. But you've got your theory and you're going to make details fit it comfortably. You've some idea about that music room, I see. Out with it like an honest man."

"Yes, Heather. I've a strong suspicion that the murderer entered by the music room and left by it or was in the house and left by that outer door. In your inquiries you'll have found that a duplicate set of keys to the music room doors is missing. It went missing some time ago."

"Does your ghost come into the business?" asked Heather filling his pipe carefully.

"Ghosts are handy things at times and one may have had a finger in this pie, but we'll leave ghosts alone for the moment and go over the ground carefully. In the first place, it's pretty certain Cornell never left the house that night in spite of his changing his clothes and putting on ordinary walking shoes. He may have had the intention but he never carried it out."

"That's sound," interrupted the inspector. "Sunday was a wet, dirty night and his shoes are just as clean as when they left Tapp's hands. But to spoil your little theory of the body being dragged upstairs, it's possible Cornell took off his shoes himself and dropped them to defend himself when the murderer, we'll say, opened the music room door and fired at him. Your idea that he dragged the body up to the corridor was born firstly, because you think the murderer wished to conceal the fact that he entered the house by the music room or had anything to do with the music room; secondly, because it's not likely that a man with a bullet in his brain could reach the corridor on his own feet. Am I correct?"

"True, oh, Inspector, you follow me very adroitly," replied Vereker smiling at the officer's acumen.

"Your theory implies another very important idea, Mr. Vereker," continued Heather. "It says indirectly that the murder was committed by someone outside the house."

"Steady on, Heather, don't jump to wild conclusions. Still, the absence of a weapon points that way, too. If anyone in the house fired that shot, the pistol would probably have been hidden in the house or flung away somewhere in the grounds. Knowing your thoroughness in searching, I feel sure it was not hidden in the house. What about the grounds?"

"My squad have gone fairly thoroughly over the grounds but that job's not finished yet. There's a belt of woodland to search and the lily pool to be dragged again. It's not in the house. We've even examined the nails in every floorboard to make sure that none has been lifted. Nails driven into floorboards have their heads below the board surface and can't be extracted without leaving tell-tale marks on the boards."

"Well, I'll take it for granted the pistol's not in the house. It's certainly not in the music room. I have poked behind every picture and felt in the crannies of every chair and settee. I even searched the grand piano. Now, Heather, you've seen the body and got the doctor's evidence. How about the wound? What course did the bullet take?"

"Almost dead straight—only a very slight angle from the eye to the back of the head."

"Then the man could hardly have been on the stairs above him or below him. At least, it's improbable. It looks as if he was either a taller man or about the same height and met him face to face."

"I wouldn't count too much on that. If the man was shorter than Cornell, he might have been on a step above him, if taller, on a step below. Let it pass then," said Vereker, "but you can now fish out the bullet for my inspection."

Heather produced a matchbox and handed it to his friend. "You'll find the pellet inside," he said.

Vereker opened the box and taking out the bullet from its wrapping of cotton wool held it on his palm and examined it meticulously under his magnifying glass.

"By Jove, that's very strange!" he exclaimed almost involuntarily.

"What's strange?" asked Heather, who had been watching him intently.

"The remark wasn't meant for you, but there's a very deep scratch or groove on the nickel case of the bullet. Did it hit the orbital bone in its passage, Heather?"

"No," replied Heather quietly. "It's a strange mark. Not been done by the rifling of the pistol, I should say offhand. I wish to heaven we could find the weapon!"

Vereker then pulled an ordinary lead pencil from his pocket and adjusted the base of the bullet to the blunt end. "Not quite a quarter of an inch in diameter," he said. "22-calibre pistol and from the material of the bullet—an automatic at that."

"I see you're borrowing our methods, Mr. Vereker. The end of a lead pencil's a very useful little measure. The pistol is evidently what they call a vest-pocket automatic."

"A very difficult weapon to shoot with, I should say. Was the murderer a deadly shot or was it just luck?"

"That's the question!" exclaimed Heather with just a suspicion of excitement. "You're getting hot. To add a little romance to the business, it's a weapon a woman would favour. Easily carried in a handbag and would be used more to frighten than to kill. A weapon of defence, say, against an amorous tramp, or a comforter during a Ripper scare. They're commoner in America than in England."

"This is getting exciting, Heather. By the way, who was the last person in the house to see Frank Cornell before he retired?"

"At first I thought it was young Carstairs," replied Heather, "but after some hesitation his fiancée admitted that probably she saw him after that. She was very coy about it and actually blushed when she confessed."

"What made her hang back on the point?" asked Vereker, glancing up at the inspector's face.

"A very delicate matter, a very delicate matter, Mr. Vereker. The young lady knocked at his bedroom door and said she wanted to kiss her darling good night. She said he hadn't changed into his lounge suit when she saw him."

"That all! Very disappointing story, Heather. Now has any woman in the house ever had or seen a vest-pocket automatic pistol?"

"I wasn't going to let you know that," said Heather, "but I'll play fair. When I saw Mrs. Cornell this morning she said she wanted to do everything in her power to help me. Coming from a beautiful young woman, I was duly appreciative and asked her if she'd accompany me round the house. It wasn't long before I tactfully questioned her about pistols. I knew there had been a bit of a scare in the neighbourhood a couple of years ago. A tramp had assaulted a young woman about two miles out of Marston village and I wondered if Mrs. Cornell had bought one at the time. 'Now that you mention it, Mr. Inspector,' she said, looking lovelier than ever, 'my husband bought me a vest-pocket automatic a long while ago, but it was of no use to me. I think I could manage any man, tramp or otherwise, but I couldn't fire a pistol to save my life or honour for that matter. What's the use of a pistol when you've got to shut your eyes, press something and wait for a terrific bang?

While you were trying to perform, your assailant would have knocked you on the head, stolen your lipstick and powder puff and got away!' I asked her what had become of it and she simply said, 'Now, Inspector, how on earth should I know? I asked my husband to put it away in a safe place where it wouldn't go off unexpectedly and I never troubled any more about it.' Finally I got her down to something more definite. She thought it was put in a drawer of her bureau in the music room. Together we searched every likely place in vain. That pistol is missing and I'd like to bet a year's screw it's the one we want."

"She went and got the keys to the music room herself?" asked Vereker.

"Yes, but she never said anything about duplicate keys. A most exasperating kind of person to question. I asked her why the music room was kept locked and her only reason was that she thought ghosts ought to be kept in their place and not be allowed to wander all over the house."

"You know that she opened the music room door for Doctor Redgrave on the very night of the murder?" asked Vereker.

"Yes, she volunteered that information and said that after she had let the doctor out by the door into the garden she quickly locked both doors and hurriedly left the keys in Crawley's pantry."

"Redgrave was anxious to see the Manor ghost," remarked Vereker, lighting a cigarette.

"Yes," replied Heather quietly, "love's nearly as good as rum for instilling courage. What does a spook matter when you've got your arm round a young lady's waist?"

"Something rather shaky about that ghost-stalking, Heather," remarked Vereker. "It sounds so damned unconvincing!"

"Did you expect anything else from a pair who're sweethearting? It's just as incredible as the 'detained at the office' story and gives the show away as completely. Now you've already said you've an idea that the murderer entered and left by the music room or was in the house and left by it. You've already got your suspicious eye on Doctor Redgrave."

"Certainly, but before we go any farther let me tell you a very important fact."

"Out with it."

"The lock of the outer door of the music room has been oiled quite recently."

"Add that it was oiled with 'Three in One' oil, Mr. Vereker," laughed the inspector.

"True. Who oiled it?"

"God knows, and I couldn't find out."

"I think it's high time we ranged up and discussed our suspects," declared Vereker. "I'll take those in the house first. We'll start with the mistress, Mrs. Cornell. Your discovery that she once had an automatic pistol of small calibre is most important. Her frank admission and facetious way of dealing with your question may only be very audacious camouflage. From all accounts she's an exceptionally clever and cool woman. She may have had several motives for getting rid of her stepson. His fortune is tied up in the hands of trustees and by her husband's will reverts to her should the stepson predecease her without issue. With some types of murderer that alone would be sufficient motive. In her case there may be complications which might strengthen her resolution to such a desperate act."

"What other motive have you got in your mind?" asked Heather promptly.

"I've got a pet theory but it's purely intuitive and I'm not going to divulge it yet."

"The only other motive I know," said Heather, "is that the stepson knew that Doctor Redgrave, her lover, had got rid of John Cornell by foul means. I can't stretch my mind, elastic as it is, to the extent of considering that idea seriously. There is everything to show that John Cornell died a natural death."

"The coroner's jury said so and it is so," remarked Vereker ironically. "Never mind. We pass now to Doctor Redgrave."

"I think you can cut him out right away," declared Heather emphatically.

"No, Heather, my little theory won't let me do that. Besides, he was the last man in the music room prior to the shooting of young Cornell. The ghost business is a bit too thin to swallow. I'm going to keep him on my list of suspects for the present. Have you anything against Mrs. Mayo, Heather?"

"Not a suspicion."

"Neither have I, so we'll dismiss her without a stain on her character. And Miss Mayo?"

"I'm not so sure about that young lady. She belongs to the passionate, theatrical class that might rise to the shooting of her lover if she found sufficient cause. We've got to hunt for that sufficient cause."

"I'll supply a hypothetical one," remarked Vereker.

"Sounds damning. Has it anything to do with an intuition?" asked Heather.

"Be patient with me, Heather. The lady went to kiss her betrothed good night. She found that he had changed his clothes as if he were going out to keep an appointment. This runs contrary to her statement, but if she did the killing it's not likely she's going to incriminate herself by telling the truth. She finds that he has an assignation with some other woman and there's a quarrel and a pistol shot."

"You ought to be writing serials instead of your young friend Ricardo, Mr. Vereker. That's your true calling."

"One minute. Let us suppose that Frank Cornell had an appointment with a young lady. He had some kind of appointment with someone. That is fairly evident from the fact that he changed his clothes and put on a stout pair of shoes. He had the duplicate keys to the music room and let himself out that way. Miss Mayo follows very stealthily, discovers that she's not the only pebble on the Cornell beach, and as her lover returns meets him at the door of the music room and shoots."

"What did he do with the duplicate keys?" asked Heather almost impatiently.

"You ought to have asked, What did she do with the duplicate keys? If she wished to cover up her tracks, she'd get rid of them after seeing that the doors were locked. I have a strong suspicion that the shot was fired in the music room. A small-calibre pistol doesn't make a terrific report, yet if it had been fired on the landing or staircase it would almost certainly have been heard by someone on the first-storey corridor. Fired in the music room it wouldn't be heard at all. The walls of these old houses are thick enough to be thoroughly sound-proof. Against my idea is the absence of any bloodstains in the music room, but that anomaly doesn't disprove my theory."

"This sounds more plausible the further you go, Mr. Vereker, but it's unlikely young Cornell would have an assignation seeing he had recently become engaged to Miss Mayo. You know the danger of forming a theory too early in the day and then trying to make the facts fit it."

"That sounds like a judgment on modern science, Heather, but I see you're weakening. I'm going to try and get you on the run now. You have possibly heard that young Cornell and his cousin Stella Cornell were once lovers and I learned from the young lady herself to-day that they were secretly engaged at that time. The parents objected, young Cornell's feelings towards his cousin changed and he fell in love with Miss Mayo. Miss Cornell, on her part, was faithful to him to the last."

"This is getting quite important, Mr. Vereker. I congratulate you on your knack of getting behind the human scenes in a complicated case. Do you think Cornell had an appointment with Miss Stella?"

"I can't say definitely yet, but it's quite a likely supposition. The lady's statements are against such a supposition, but we don't put too much credence on anybody's statements, do we, Heather? Statements are ticklish stuff to deal with. What I did learn was that, during their courtship, to which their parents strongly objected, they used to meet secretly. The trysting place was the old oak seat by the lily pool in the formal garden."

"They'd hardly meet there on a wet night like the night of the murder, Mr. Vereker," suggested Heather with a curiously bright light in his eyes.

"By God!" exclaimed Vereker suddenly, as some idea assailed him, and then recovering himself remarked: "Heather, you're damned smart. You've already jumped to the conclusion that they used to meet in the music room on a wet night."

"It seemed a likely proposition," smiled Heather with quiet satisfaction.

"My theory begins to find itself on firmer ground," said Vereker as if speaking his thoughts to himself. "Miss Mayo is on the list of suspects. I think we'll put an asterisk against her name. But that confounded pistol..."

At these words Heather fumbled in one of his pockets and produced a tiny automatic pistol which he handed to the astonished Vereker.

"You don't mean to tell me..." commenced Vereker.

"No, no, it's not the pistol, but it's one exactly like it, I should say. You see, a small gun like that can be hidden very easily and if thrown away would take some finding."

Vereker carefully examined the weapon, tried its action and asked, "May I have the loan of this pistol for a day or two, Heather?"

"Certainly," replied Heather. "You might make some useful experiments with it. I can easily get another, Mr. Vereker."

"Thanks," said Vereker and slipped the miniature automatic into his waistcoat pocket.

"In our discussion we've dealt with Mrs. Cornell, the doctor, Mrs. Mayo and Miss Mayo. Let's look at Roland Carstairs. Have you picked up any information about him?"

"One rather important scrap," said Heather. "In conversation with the parlourmaid I think I made a great impression. She looked me up and down with that sort of eye that tells you you're being silently valued. If you watch a young woman looking at new hats in a milliner's window, you can tell immediately when she has spotted the one she wouldn't mind wearing. It was that kind of look and I naturally played up to it like a thoroughly wicked lady-killer. We had a cup of tea together later." Heather at this point of his statement curled his moustaches complacently and blinked his eyelids with complete satisfaction.

"What a Valentino you'd make, Heather! What was the scrap of information?"

"We got quite confidential on the subject of true love and were comparing it with that wicked thing which Miss Catchpole called 'a passing fancy.' Can't say I'm struck with the name Bella Catchpole; it's too near to 'catch police.' Well, as an example of true love she held up Mr. Carstairs' love for Miss Stella Cornell."

"I thought there was something like that in Carstairs' admiration of the young lady," remarked Vereker. "'One of the best women that ever breathed,' he described her. I suppose she doesn't return his affection."

"That's it. He has always loved her in spite of the fact that she loved his pal. This is a significant detail when you remember that his pal did the dirty on Carstairs' goddess, but I wouldn't call it a motive for murder in itself."

"You never know what love will drive men to, Heather. His pal's action might seem to the infatuated Carstairs a most heinous offence. I had a long conversation with him to-day. He was very frank, even eager, to discuss every phase of our case and be helpful. From my first impressions of the man I wouldn't put him down as a likely."

"I'm always suspicious of the witness eager to make a statement or give information. Frequently it's a case of exaggerated enthusiasm to assist and then the statement is generally hopelessly misleading. At other times it's the criminal's confidence in his own astuteness that drives him to the folly of trying to bamboozle the 'tec. He's a young man with a good notion of himself as far as I could sum him up."

"I think you're right there, but he's the type who has principles. He's not old enough to have become disillusioned about the validity of hard and fast rules. He's a steady fellow with a fairly reasonable outlook and I can't just feel cynical enough to think he was trying it on with me. We'll put him on the doubtful list with a slight bias in his favour. Now we've come to the servants. I've had a chat with Crawley, the butler, and George Tapp, the valet. I dismiss Crawley right away. He's a bit of a connoisseur of wines, and from my experience no one who's a judge, say, of claret would think of committing a murder unless someone offered him a bottle of champagne in preference to a bottle of 1878 claret. On the other hand, I'm not quite certain about Tapp. He's apparently a bit shifty and doesn't look a man straight in the eye."

"I've put Tapp off the map," said Heather. "I can see from his face that he's one of those blokes who have the inferiority complex very bad. Not much faith in himself and probably had such a rough time of it in his life that he hasn't much faith in other people. His wife ran away from him a couple of years ago and left him with two youngsters. His mother looks after the kids and Tapp sends her nearly all his money for their keep. I think he keeps five bob a week for himself out of which he saves half-a-crown during the steeplechasing season. During the flat he's a flat to the tune of that other half-dollar."

"Poor devil!" exclaimed Vereker and was lost in thoughtful pity over the unhappiness of some men's lives. He was remembering the fact that Tapp was a germ-carrier with a secret to hide from humanity, a pariah through no fault of his own and bound by the very fact to practise deceit in spite of any disposition not to do so. Still, there might be something questionable about his connection with Doctor Redgrave. Penury and his duty to his children might make him an associate in crime, especially if his nature had become embittered by his misfortune. Fate had played him a sorry trick and secretly his hand might be against the society which for its own self-preservation would have its hand against him if cognizant of his potential danger to the health of its members.

"I don't think we need trouble about the female servants," said Heather, breaking the silence that had fallen on them. "The young man was fond of a woman's charms and not too solidly proof against them, but he took care not to dirty his own doorstep. Even Miss Catchpole, who's the star turn for good looks, said he was a very nice young man and behaved 'most respectable' even though he used to rag the girls at times."

"We've come to those outside the house, Heather. The most important of these is, of course, Miss Stella Cornell. On the face of it she's the last person to commit murder, but a jilted woman's a dangerous explosive. If her love affair with young Cornell had exceeded the bounds which, for clarity, we'll say distinguish your relations with the fair sex, there's the very strong motive of revenge. A woman who has given her all to a man can be distraught to the point of mania if that man suddenly flings her aside like a 'sucked orange.' I think that's one of your expressive phrases, Heather."

"'Never throw a sucked orange on the pavement,' is another of my wisecracks, Mr. Vereker. It's dangerous to the next man coming along and you might tread on it yourself if you happen to come that way again yourself. The best thing to do with a sucked orange is to put it away in your pocket and make it think it's still full of juice till it's dry enough to leave somewhere with safety. Of course, it's only one of my wisecracks because I was never given to sucking oranges. As for Miss Stella, she's a strong favourite in my betting list. She's an injured woman or may think herself one. She knew the house and her man. She was the very person to make a secret appointment with him. She was intimate with Mrs. Cornell and probably knew that lady kept an automatic in the music room bureau, which, by the way, Mrs. Cornell never locked up for she's a most casual woman. Then you have the matter of the duplicate keys. Doubtless either young Cornell or she had got possession of that set after Mr. David Cornell handed them back. If they used the music room as a secret trysting place in wet weather, this seems a very safe supposition. She's a clever girl, I should say, with an excellent command of her feelings in some respects. She was certainly a bit nervous when I questioned her this morning, but I know the type well. When face to face with danger they lose every trace of nerves and become deadly cool and very difficult to upset. The very presence of danger seems to key them up and give every faculty an added sharpness. I was doubly cautious with her when I saw she had taken command of herself and by becoming friendly and confidential, tried to make her overconfident. I think she saw through this trick and countered it by being artfully naive and guardedly helpful. I tried to leave her with the impression that I thought she was above suspicion and ought to give us a hand in tracing her cousin's murderer. If I have lulled her into feeling fairly safe, it will give us a chance of watching her more closely and finally giving her a nasty surprise as soon as she makes a false move. Once upset she'd promptly fall to pieces."

"You horrible old humbug, Heather. I wouldn't have thought you capable of such guile only I know you too well. I have put a double star against the young lady myself, but still I'm open to rubbing them out. I haven't seen her father yet, but hope to do so to-morrow. He may be the very man we want."

"He's our man!" said Heather with surprising emphasis. "If this was a yarn by a story merchant, I'd arrest him right away as the most unlikely person. He can't see to shoot a haystack, which makes it doubly probable he fired the shot."

"Without joking, Heather, he's among the probables," said Vereker seriously. "If he loves his daughter he might lose all sense of proportion over such things as sucked oranges for instance. He knows his way to the music room even at night, for darkness is not an obstacle to the blind. They rely on other faculties such as hearing and touch to an amazing degree. He may never have handed back the keys to the music room or he may have quietly regained possession of them. He may have known all about the automatic pistol in the bureau and thought that his very disability was an excellent cloak against discovery of guilt. What do you say?"

"I lie low," replied Heather reflectively and glanced into his pewter mug. "Finished!" he remarked, "and seeing that it's getting late, I propose we call an end to the conference of The Big Two. The inquest is to-morrow and I'll call for an adjournment till we see things a bit more clearly. There's one little question on my mind which I must ask you. You needn't reply unless you like. What were the objects you were examining to-night under your microscope? Anything vital?"

"Two or three hairs, Heather, One I found on a lounge suit in Frank Cornell's wardrobe. It's a short human hair, almost black. I should say it came from the bobbed section of Miss Cornell's rather lovely mop, I visited her hairdresser to-day and in conversation found she'd had her hair cut last week. No inmate of the Manor has such perfectly black hair. It's a long shot, but I feel I'm not very wide of the mark. I found another of the same colour and texture, also a woman's hair, on the settee in the music room. Both of these hairs have sharp sections which, as you know, indicate that their owner recently had her hair cut. But the third hair's a bit of a surprise. As I've wandered into your domain just for the fun of orthodox detection, I'll tell you what it is. It certainly belongs to a ginger tabby cat. Now you've got something really distinctive to follow up!"

"Thanks for the information," said Heather ironically. "I'll go round the district and take a census of the cats and hunt down all the ginger tabbies in Marston. You've overlooked the fact that it might be the property of a tortoiseshell but that won't make any difference to me."

"I'd give up facts and take to the intuitive method, Heather, if I were you," said Vereker.

"The clue of the ginger tabby!" exclaimed Heather with a loud laugh and then remarked, "By the way, in the last chapter, so to speak, of our discussion, when we were jotting down the probables not living in the house, we didn't mention the possibility of a complete outsider."

"It went without saying. We have both thought of the contingency of someone living in London, say, who was a deadly enemy of the murdered man. A young fellow like Cornell, who goes about philandering with women, happens at times to put it across somebody else's woman and there's promptly a cause for war. The other man objects and to sooth his wounded pride and anger blots out his adversary. Besides, Cornell with his drinking and gambling propensities was almost certain to have run into a rather questionable crowd of people or, to put it better, a crowd of people with some very disreputable and reckless members. I've already written to young Ricardo asking him to inquire among his many legal friends if any of them knew a Frank Cornell who was reading for the bar. He has chambers somewhere in the Inner Temple, I believe. But you and your myrmidons, Heather, can carry out that end of the investigation more thoroughly and I'm relying on you, partner, to let me know if you get a suspect beyond the Marston circle of inquiry. It would be damned unfair to let me go on nosing round here and then spring an unpleasant surprise on me after many days by saying you'd had the man arrested— name, Smith, address, London, for choice."

"I'll play the game, Mr. Vereker, but I'm not bothering much about Smiths of London. Our hare is in Marston or I'm the biggest idiot ever. But I'm going to bed. Good night and God bless you."

Chapter Nine
More Food for Suspicion

People afflicted with the tragedy of blindness had always evoked in Vereker as long as he could remember a faint sense of the uncanny. This feeling he could not wholly dispel by reasoning, nor could his quick sympathy for those who suffer misfortune entirely eradicate it. That blindness had some powerful, morbid appeal for the imagination was evident from the very fact that it had been used as a basic theme in both literary and dramatic art. Secretly ashamed of this irrational attitude in himself, he had often tried to discover from what source it sprung. He had seen Maeterlinck's drama and read Wells's story in his youth and had at first been inclined to ascribe his sensations to an echo of the bygone impressions made on his mind by these two powerful imaginations. Later, he felt certain that they were due to some curious association in his mind of blindness with the mystery of death. The eyes of the blind were as the eyes of the dead. The faces of the sightless lacked the quick responsiveness to things seen. When reacting to things heard and felt, the living flash that lit the ordinary man's eye with excitement, fear, hatred, anger or desire was missing. On meeting David Cornell for the first time, he was again conscious in a marked degree of this sense of uncanniness. In spite of himself he could not keep his eyes off the man's face which in repose wore a strange resignation, some faint likeness to the marmoreal fixity of death, and as he watched he observed how his host's sense of touch and hearing rose to the difficult synthesis called perception by an added quality of sharpness.

Soon after his arrival at the bungalow, Miss Cornell had gone out and left him to talk music with her father. The topic was not long in coming to the surface of their conversation, and once roused the old man held forth vigorously. Vereker, ignorant of the subject, was pleased to play the part of a patient listener. David Cornell deplored the recent trend of musical art. He said it was the expression of an age without faith or belief in itself. Music was an emotional expression and our cold intellectualism and cynicism were antagonistic to greatness in the art, Vereker combated this theory by hinting that the mind of to-day was explorative and that modern musical art must necessarily be tentative, searching for a new outlook on which to base a faith. At length, after a disquisition on the beauty of the nineteenth-century romantics, the topic died out and David Cornell apologized for riding his hobby horse so long. To change the subject he suddenly asked: "What's your real profession, Mr. Vereker?"

"I'm supposed to be a landscape artist, but some time ago I took up criminal investigation as a mental relaxation and now it's playing a very prominent rôle in my life."

"It must be extremely interesting," said Cornell, "and do you think you'll manage to unravel the mystery of my unfortunate young nephew's death?"

"I came down to Marston with that intention. Success depends on so many things and hangs on such delicate threads that it'd be foolish to say just now how the business will turn out."

"Of course, of course, but I daresay you'll have formed some idea as to who committed the murder."

"No, I would hardly say that. You see, Mr. Cornell, in detective work the facts you gather range themselves together in your mind, then they seem to cluster in associated groups and finally turn your suspicion towards a person or several persons. You don't start with suspecting a person and then see if the facts agree. Preconceptions are amazingly easy to form and are often most dangerous to success. They frequently lead down the wrong road and are terribly hard to eradicate when once formed. Valuable time is wasted and your work rendered futile and exasperating."

"The facts you've already gathered must have given you some direction in the matter. You must surely suspect someone?"

"Oh, yes, I suspect two or three people in a tentative way," agreed Vereker, highly satisfied that the conversation had taken the turn he desired. He wanted Mr. David Cornell to talk. He was one of the Cornell family; he was the cause of the exhumation of his brother's body. He might unconsciously reveal some factor which up till now had evaded the investigator's pursuit. "Are you interested in detection, Mr. Cornell?" he asked.

"Yes, in a general way, but in this particular case certainly," replied Cornell at once. "I suppose you start on such a job by hunting for the weapon?"

"Well, yes, that's a very important factor, but so far we've been unsuccessful. The search is still proceeding."

"Have you searched the music room?" came the next question to Vereker's great surprise.

"Yes, but I hope you won't think me impertinent if I ask you what prompted your question?" replied Vereker observing the old man's face closely. A slight quiver of the upper lip, almost a hint of a smile was born on his passive features. The gentleness and nobility of his general expression gave place to a certain contemptuous hardness.

"No, I don't think you're impertinent. It's part of your job to ask questions. I mentioned the music room for the simple reason that Mrs. Cornell used to keep her automatic pistol in a drawer of the bureau near the door."

"Ah, yes, I see," said Vereker and decided that he must be cautious in dealing with Mr. David Cornell. Apart from his musical leanings, the broad forehead and shrewd, sensitive lines of the face hinted at an unusual breadth of intellect and quickness of intuition.

"It was a miniature automatic, what they call a vest-pocket automatic. I took a large .45 automatic out with me to France, satisfied that I had the latest thing in destruction. But for warfare they're not so useful as one would imagine. The mechanism is comparatively delicate and the action jams easily, especially when there's mud about. They're not nearly so good as a revolver for accurate shooting in my opinion. I gave up the .45 for the regular service revolver."

"You've never seen Mrs. Cornell's pistol?" asked Vereker casually.

"Hardly, but I've felt it," replied Cornell with a wan smile.

"Can you tell me if it was anything like this?" asked Vereker and drawing from his pocket the pistol he had borrowed from Heather, he handed it to Cornell. Cornell took the weapon in his hands and felt it carefully.

"Exactly similar, I should say," he remarked and holding the pistol by the barrel extended it to Vereker. The latter, satisfied that Cornell's finger-prints were now on the barrel, took the weapon by the grip and slipped it very carefully into his pocket once more.

"Not much of a weapon if you mean to kill," continued Cornell, "but, of course, useful to scare anyone in self-defence. Frank Cornell was an unlucky young man; he got the packet, so to speak, in the most deadly spot from such an uncertain weapon. Had he been hit anywhere else, he'd have been alive to-day. I should say the shot was fired at close range. What d'you think?"

"That's my opinion, but it would be unwise to be too definite," commented Vereker, an expression of surprise on his face.

"Of course. Were there any marks of powder?"

"I believe not. In any case with modern, smokeless powder they are not always present even when the shot has been fired at close range."

"That's very interesting, very interesting. I should say the shot was fired from the music room, wouldn't you?"

"Yes, I concluded it had from the fact that the report was not heard by anyone on the first floor corridor," replied Vereker, again surprised at David Cornell's power of drawing a likely inference.

"Quite so, but there's one thing that must puzzle you. How on earth did Frank Cornell stagger up the second half-flight of steps with a bullet in his brain? Seems impossible to me."

"Unlikely, but not impossible," commented Vereker now hanging on every word the man spoke.

"Might I make an amateurish suggestion, Mr. Vereker?"

"Do so by all means. I'm open to all kinds of suggestions bearing on the case."

"Well, I suggest the murderer dragged the body up the stairs after the shooting and left it there."

"And your reasons?" asked Vereker promptly.

"His reason was to try and hide the place of execution," replied Cornell blandly.

"You've settled the gender of the murderer, I see," said Vereker quickly.

The remark was received by Cornell with a sharp upward jerk of the head. "Well, yes, in a way. As a matter of fact I used the word, his, to cover male and female. But a woman seldom uses a revolver or pistol to kill, I'm told. They resort to gentler methods like poisoning. Isn't that so?"

"Generally speaking, yes, but everything depends on the circumstances. In this case the automatic pistol in Mrs. Cornell's drawer may have been the first means to hand and therefore a cardinal factor."

"You have an idea that it was Mrs. Cornell's weapon?" asked Cornell.

"I'm inclined to think it was but time will prove. We shall probably find the gun before long," replied Vereker with a smile.

"You must drag the lily pool if you haven't done so already."

"Inspector Heather is getting that job done to-day, I believe."

"Of course, it's an obvious measure. I hope I'm not boring you talking your 'shop,' Mr. Vereker."

"No, no, I'm never tired of talking detection. You must remember it's not exactly shop with me. I might soon tire if we began to discuss painting."

"Good, because I've thought a good deal about this crime. I have so much time to think that it's natural in a way I should brood on it. My idea of the shot being fired from the music room was based on a suspicion that the murderer entered the house by the music room."

"That implies possession of keys to unlock the doors," remarked Vereker at once.

"Naturally. There's a duplicate set missing. It's a set I once had in my possession. I'm certain I returned them to my brother John, but I wouldn't be positive. If I did, someone must have pinched them from Crawley's pantry."

"That someone must know the Manor customs. He must have known where the keys were kept," suggested Vereker.

"Your argument's sound, Mr. Vereker, but don't infer from my remark that I'm pointing the accusing finger at any inmate of the Manor. It was merely a factor which struck me as important."

"It's very important. We'd very much like to know how those keys disappeared, and more important still, who took them. May I ask why you possessed a duplicate set of keys to the music room, Mr. Cornell?"

"I used to sit and compose there at the grand piano. To be confidential with you, Mr. Vereker, I've never got on very well with my sister-in-law. I didn't think John was wise in marrying a woman so much younger than himself and I'm afraid I was indiscreet enough to say so openly. That indiscretion flung up a barrier between my sister-in-law and myself which our subsequent knowledge of one another failed to remove. I have no positive dislike for the lady, but I couldn't take her to my heart as I should have liked to. I absented myself from the music room after a year and trumped up some excuse about not caring for the atmosphere of the room. I traded rather blatantly on the ghost nonsense that had gathered round the apartment and John, who was a confirmed believer in spirits, swallowed my excuse. He bought me a piano as a result. I like the instrument; it has a finer tone than their old box of wires."

"I suppose your move in getting an exhumation of your brother's body didn't improve your relations with your sister-in-law?" asked Vereker pointedly.

"It fairly tore things!" exclaimed Cornell vehemently. "I couldn't help it. I won't go into details, but there seemed something fishy about John's sudden death. It preyed on my mind till I took action. Perhaps I oughtn't to have done so. The result simply knocked my suspicions on the head. In any case, I'm satisfied now and the less said about the subject the better."

"Perhaps you're right," continued Vereker boldly, "but I was inclined to think the affair had some obscure connection with Frank Cornell's murder."

"I don't follow you."

"Let us suppose that Frank Cornell by some means learned that his father's death was brought about by foul means. The murderer of your brother might, on learning this, take steps to remove your nephew."

"Yes, but that theory at once brings my old suspicions up again. The inquest settled the matter of my brother's death as far as I'm concerned, but you must, of course, work out the problem on your own lines. I think you'll eventually find your idea isn't worth considering. Seeing that your suspicions are so comprehensive, I daresay they include Miss Mayo, my daughter and myself?"

"A detective has to keep an open mind," replied Vereker with some embarrassment at the direct question.

"Certainly, no one is sacrosanct. I felt from the very first that suspicion would fall on Stella."

"It's a very delicate matter, Mr. Cornell, for you and me to discuss but the relations which existed between your daughter and the dead man were bound to attract inquiry."

"I suppose they were," said Cornell and a worried expression came over his impassive face. "My daughter loved Frank very deeply. I was dead against her choice and was rather intolerant about the whole matter. I forbade her to marry him. Girls of to-day don't seem to heed what their parents say and, of course, she could have ignored my wishes altogether if she had chosen.

The old patriarchal days are gone. Still, she wisely refrained from marrying him. I say, wisely, because I knew Frank's character. He was an altogether lovable man up to a point. Generous, amiable, easy-going, but he had no guts, to put it bluntly. An invertebrate, without definite ambitions, no steadfastness of character, and no serious outlook on life. He thought of nothing but pleasure. Drink and women were his ruling passions. His genial, inoffensive nature might have carried him through life without any serious mishap as a bachelor, but I couldn't see him in the rôle of my Stella's husband. Stella is of a finer texture than most women. In time he would have broken the girl's heart and her whole life would have become embittered and futile. I couldn't allow this to happen and I did all I could to frustrate it. This may sound a bit high-falutin to you, Mr. Vereker. I don't know. The cynical modern laughs at our old-fashioned faith in decent, purposeful lives. They say we lack a sense of humour and don't look at life from a progressive, scientific point of view. Sexual freedom, they aver, is merely a frank acceptance of Nature's law, and that to look upon work as the foundation of ordered living is merely mistaking the means for the end. Some even go as far as to say that the gospel of work is the invention of the hypocritical industrialist to feather his own nest. To return, however, to Stella. She is naturally bound to be suspected. She was the wronged woman, cast aside by her lover who had transferred his affections to Miss Mayo. In a spirit of revenge she shot the faithless fellow and trusted, if her crime were discovered, to some hope of mercy at the hands of her fellow creatures."

"I'm afraid she'd get little mercy at the hands of English law," said Vereker. "A murderer is a murderer and the unwritten law, as it is called, is merely a negation of all law."

"Just so and to add weight to the suspicions that the police and you yourself must entertain, Stella knew where the music room keys were kept and also where Mrs. Cornell's automatic pistol was hidden," continued Cornell bitterly.

"Those factors not only apply to her but to everyone in the house and even to yourself and Mrs. Cornell," said Vereker.

"Ah, yes, I'd quite forgotten myself," said David Cornell with strange gusto. "I shot Frank Cornell because he had broken my girl's heart. Quite a likely proposition when you come to examine it closely enough. I'm blind and would feel fairly safe from discovery behind my misfortune. Dear, dear, it's an amazing world!"

The old man ceased talking and letting his head sink on his breast seemed lost in profound thought and completely oblivious of the presence of his guest. Suddenly a light scratching noise was heard in the studio in which the two men were sitting. At once David Cornell rose to his feet and, crossing the room with remarkable assurance for a man who couldn't see, turned the door handle and flung open the door. It swung inwards on its hinges with an unpleasant creaking sound.

"Misty wants to see my visitor," he said as a grey Persian cat entered the room and stalked with uplifted tail to where Vereker was seated. Vereker stroked the animal which at once returned the friendly greeting by rubbing himself against his leg.

"That infernal door gets on my nerves," said Cornell irritably. Crossing to a writing-desk, he pulled open a drawer and extracted a small can of oil. The action at once arrested Vereker's attention and he immediately rose to his feet.

"Let me do it for you, Mr. Cornell," he said.

"Thanks very much," replied the old man extending the oil can to his guest. "You'll find that it's the bottom hinge that's got the soprano voice."

Vereker took the can, oiled both the hinges, swung the door noiselessly to and fro, and returning to his chair handed the small can back to his host.

"Splendid stuff that 'Three in One,'" he remarked with suppressed excitement. "It really does the work thoroughly. But I must be getting back, Mr. Cornell. It's nearly lunchtime and I've a lot of work ahead of me."

"Very well, don't let me detain you. Drop in whenever you feel like it. You're a good listener and I'm fond of talking. Besides, I'd like to know how you're getting on with your detective job. It's more interesting than reading about the game in books or rather having them read to me."

"I don't know so much about that," replied Vereker. "I think it was a gangster called Jack Diamond who said detective yarns were 'bunk,' but I'm afraid he found out at last that actual crime was the sublimest bunk of all. I'll take you at your word and look in when I've got a moment to spare. Good morning."

On leaving David Cornell's bungalow, Vereker made his way across the paddock towards the belt of woodland which cut off the grounds of Marston Manor from the surrounding lands. His intention was to pass through the Manor grounds, see what success had attended Heather's dragging and searching operations, and then pass out by the lodge gate nearer Marston village. As he slowly crossed the paddock he was lost in his own thoughts and those thoughts were centred on David Cornell. Swift as he usually was in weighing up the general character of a man as left on him by first impressions, he found on this occasion that no such picture would form clearly in his mind. He ascribed his inability to form a rough and ready judgment in the first place to Cornell's blindness. In his conversation with him he had felt all the time the presence of a curious barrier. It was as if he had been talking to someone standing on the other side of an opaque screen. Secondly, he had formed the opinion that David Cornell did not present a mere portrait of himself with his words. He had talked openly, even volubly, but the ideas and opinions expressed might be merely intellectual counters flung about in the game of conversation and not rising straight from the heart. It was a common trick among sophisticated people. Even when the words were charged with emotion, it was merely the simulated emotion of an actor playing a part. That part was almost invariably the character the player wished his hearer to ascribe to him. Vereker had entered the bungalow harbouring only the tentative suspicion against Cornell which facts forbade him as a detective to disregard. He had been prepared to leave it completely convinced that the blind man had no vestige of connection with the murder of Frank Cornell. Now he was not so sure. There was something about Cornell's inferences regarding the manner in which the crime had been committed, the spot from which the shot had been fired, the theory of the removal of the body from the half-landing to the first storey corridor, which was very unusual, to say the least of it. For a man without trained observation his theoretical deductions were startling enough to rouse suspicion. He had jocularly designated the motive that could have driven him to such an act as if to minimize its cogency as a motive. All this might be the astute attempt of a cunning brain to mislead the investigator. The one great safeguard against suspicion Cornell possessed was his inability to see. The man who fired the shot was either an expert marksman or had reached the most deadly spot by mere chance. Was there any method or ruse by which Cornell could have made sure of hitting the desired mark, were he the man who had used the automatic pistol? He was well acquainted with the type of weapon. He had also known where to lay his hand on one. Vereker asked himself these questions and began to formulate all sorts of theories which would render such a feat possible. Suddenly as he was about to leave the paddock and enter the boundary wood of the Manor grounds, he stopped dead.

"Good Lord!" he exclaimed. "Why didn't I think of that before? I really must pull myself together; I'm getting rusty!"

For fully five minutes he stood almost motionless. His eyes seemed to be examining the beautiful markings on the bole of a silver birch in front of him, the forefinger and thumb of his right hand caressed his chin with a slow, rhythmic motion, his lips were tightly compressed. Inwardly he was bubbling with excitement over some bright intuition, his thoughts playing round it swiftly with the most searching criticism. Having evidently decided the matter to his satisfaction, he quickly passed through a gap in the thorn hedge bordering the wood and walked rapidly along the beaten path that traversed it and led out to the gate in the Manor garden wall. He had not gone far when he heard voices ahead of him. He stood and listened. The speakers were evidently a man and a woman and they were approaching at a slow pace. All at once they came into view in the distance and Vereker saw that they were Roland Carstairs and Stella Cornell. They were so engrossed in the subject of their discussion that they failed to notice him. Not wishing to meet them at this moment, Vereker swiftly stepped off the path and secreted himself behind a dense clump of hazel undergrowth nearby. He would let them pass and then proceed on his way. As they approached their voices grew more distinct and the tones disclosed that the speakers were labouring under strong emotion. Vereker, not altogether an unwilling eavesdropper, listened intently and when the pair passed within a few yards of where he stood he heard Stella Cornell say:

"It's no use, Roly. I wish you wouldn't plead with me."

"Stella, I implore you to change your mind. I'll stand by you and take all the blame if you'll only consent to marry me. Can't you see it's the only effective way out of the situation?"

"It's a heroic suggestion on your part, Roly, but I cannot consent. I've made up my mind. It wouldn't be fair to drag you into the mess. I'll face the music alone."

"Think it over before you act, Stella. I'm showing you the one way out and you are foolish to refuse to take it."

"I've done all the thinking I'm going to do."

"Am I to take that as final?"

"Absolutely final!"

Here the pair got out of definite earshot but the conversation continued and it appeared as if Carstairs' words became almost angry in tone, for Miss Cornell sought refuge in sobbing which was distinctly audible. Vereker, satisfied that they had almost passed out of the wood, regained the path and made his way rapidly to Marston Manor.

He entered the formal garden by the door in the north wall and saw to his surprise Heather seated alone on the oak seat by the lily pool. He was quietly smoking his pipe and appeared the picture of contentment.

"Well, Inspector," said Vereker as he came up and took a seat beside his friend. "Any important discoveries?"

"None," replied Heather.

"You've dragged this pool for the pistol?"

"Yes, we've scraped every inch of the bottom for pistol and missing keys. No luck. Simply ruined the lilies and scared the goldfish off the gold standard. It's only a couple of feet deep and my men took off their boots and socks and paddled in it. Goss said it was a cushy job and very refreshing for the feet. I promised to buy him a tin bucket and a wooden spade if he found the pistol. Where have you been hiding?"

"I've had a long chat with Mr. David Cornell over at the bungalow."

"What do you make of him? Rather a rum sort of customer in my opinion. I interrogated him about his daughter's relations with young Cornell. He fairly let fly on the subject of his nephew. Thinks he was a young wastrel. The old boy seems to have his wits about him and made some very shrewd remarks on the whole case. He's blind, but he sees more than most men once he gets the hang of the facts."

"I agree, but I don't quite know what to make of him at the moment. I went into his bungalow thinking he wasn't worth worrying about in this business, but I left with quite a different notion, Heather."

"Ah!" said Heather with a curious note of surprise in his voice. "You were always good at reading between a man's words. I had a similar experience with him."

"There's something about David Cornell's knowledge of this case, Heather, that intrigues me," said Vereker. "He seems to know just a shade too much about the whole business."

"It puzzled me, too," replied the inspector, "but his is the type of mind that troubles to draw conclusions from facts. You see, Mr. Vereker, he gets the case minutely described to him, questions the speaker for more details, arranges the facts and begins to think. In a way he resembles yourself. He makes intuitive deductions and, being blind and having nothing much to do, has plenty of time to think things over very carefully. Besides, he's a musician and I'm sure after all my experience that in a way an artist has a peculiar knack of jumping at the truth where men like myself have to climb up to it slowly step by step."

"First time I've heard you admit it," said Vereker smiling.

"I'm in the mood, a peculiarly fair mood at the moment. Of course the artist frequently jumps into a nasty mess of error which the practical detective always avoids, but we'll not argue the point. What struck you as unusual about Cornell's ideas?"

"He came to the conclusion that the shot was fired from the music room. Now unless he had a very careful account of the bloodstains, he could hardly arrive at such an opinion. He would have to be certain that there were no bloodstains in the hall or on the lower half-flight of stairs. We know there are no stains on the lower half-flight, but we're not sure there was none in the hall because the maid washed the linoleum before the arrival of the police. He doubtless got his account of the affair from his daughter Stella, and I don't think it likely that that young lady would give her father such a detailed, almost professional, description as would be necessary for him to work out such a theory."

"He also has an idea that the body was dragged up to the first-storey corridor," remarked Heather.

"He would strike on that explanation because, like me, he probably thought a man shot in the brain couldn't run up the steps himself. But his reason for coming to such a conclusion was that the murderer wanted to conceal the way he entered the house and left it. As you know, Heather, there must be some point in such a concealment, and the only point I can see is that the murderer wanted to hide the fact that he had possession of the duplicate keys of the music room. Mr. Cornell once had possession of them. Those keys are a very dangerous pointer to a detective. They narrow the question by giving some idea as to the person who could easily get hold of them or had possession of them."

"Now, Mr. Vereker, you're getting into your old form. I like to hear you talk like that. Anything else?" asked Heather puffing vigorously at his pipe.

"Another point. In talking about the missing weapon he promptly asked me if we had searched the music room."

"Oh!" exclaimed Heather with some surprise.

"I pulled him up rather too abruptly, I'm afraid. I'm not as clever as you at leading witnesses up the garden. I asked him his reason for putting the question. His reply, Heather, was an amazing one to me. He replied that he had asked it because Mrs. Cornell used to keep an automatic pistol in a drawer of the bureau near the music room door."

"By Jove, Mr. Vereker, this is the real stuff!" exclaimed Heather. "You naturally wondered why he should drag in Mrs. Cornell's miniature automatic. He couldn't possibly have known that the weapon that had fired the shot was an automatic. He had heard nothing about the nature of the bullet. Only Doctor Redgrave and ourselves know anything about the bullet and Redgrave was particularly cautioned not to mention anything about it. Not that he would in any case. He's a professional man and knows his job better than to talk about such things even in confidence."

"Exactly, Heather. How could he possibly have known that the murderer had used a miniature automatic? I think Cornell at once saw he had made a dangerous mistake. He went on to talk about a .45 pistol he'd taken out to France and so forth to fling up conversational dust in which to hide his slip. I let him ramble and asked him if he'd ever seen the weapon. He had felt it, was his reply and I promptly produced the one you lent me and asked him if Mrs. Cornell's resembled it. After carefully feeling it, he said it was exactly similar. I've handled your gun very gingerly since because he has left some nice finger-prints on the barrel. You might get these photographed and developed. They may come in useful," said Vereker and extracting the pistol carefully from his pocket, handed it back to the inspector.

"Everything's useful at times," commented Heather and placed the weapon in its original cardboard box which he produced from some obscure part of his anatomy.

"I tried to bowl him a body-liner on the pistol business a little later, but he was too wary. Referring to the weapon we want he naively said, 'You've an idea it was Mrs. Cornell's pistol?' I'm afraid it wasn't too bright an effort to cover up his former mistake, but it showed me clearly that he knew he'd made a mistake and was eager to retrieve it. Then after further polite conversation he boldly broached the subject of suspects in the case and jokingly said that our list probably contained his daughter and himself."

"Shrewd chap," remarked Heather. "If you're fishing for information there's something very disarming about a blunt question. It has a knack of toppling over a man's finer judgment."

"I must admit it was embarrassing, but I'm rather good at slipping round the direct thrust. He saw I was going to be diplomatic and then gratuitously supplied reasons why his daughter should be one of our chief suspects. It was a novel experience for me, Heather. It was the first time I'd encountered this bold type of gambit. He may have thought it amazingly clever, but its only effect was to rouse my suspicions all the more. He was trading on the assumption that no man would supply damaging suggestions to the police for suspecting his daughter unless he knew his daughter was absolutely above suspicion. I didn't rise to it and he learned nothing about how his daughter stood in our eyes. He tried the same move by giving me a motive why he should be the man who shot Frank Cornell. This was trying a supreme bluff if he had anything to do with his nephew's murder. I was all on my toes to catch every shade of expression on his face, every intonation of his voice..."

"Did you learn anything?" asked Heather with some impatience.

"There was something in his whole attitude which struck me as false and artificial. An absolutely innocent man might do it as a joke, but it's not a subject that any innocent man would joke about. A guilty man would have to be a supreme actor to be natural enough to carry it off successfully. Of course Cornell was only toying with an amateur like myself, but the stratagem was weak. As you know, Heather, jocularity is a very common resort of the criminal. His conceit in his astuteness leads him to try this bluff and it's a feeble one to try on any experienced police officer. The younger the man is in crime, the greater his readiness to undervalue his official opponent's intelligence."

"Thanks, Mr. Vereker," interrupted Heather complacently. "Not often we get such a nice pat on the back. You've certainly got your teeth in Mr. Cornell's trousers and he's a poor, harmless, blind man. Not quite fair but as I've got him down in my bad books, I'll not blame you on this occasion. Did he give himself away on any other point?"

"Be patient, Heather. After all this talk which, to put it briefly, seemed to me only a move on Mr. David Cornell's part to see how his daughter and he stood with regard to us in the business, something made a scratching noise at the door. Cornell rose and opened the door, which creaked loudly on its hinges, and in walked a fine grey Persian cat."

"I thought you were going to say that the ginger tabby made its bow," interrupted Heather.

"You're too eager, Inspector, and jump too hastily to conclusions. The grey cat doesn't concern us, but here's a striking detail. After Cornell had opened the door he complained about the grating noise it made on its hinges. Crossing the room to a desk, he took from a drawer an oil can and was going to oil the door hinges when I offered my services. The offer was accepted and I found to my delight that the can was a 'Three in One' oil can."

"That's excellent, Mr. Vereker. We both know that the lock of the outer door of the music room was recently oiled with 'Three in One' oil. It gives point to a very curious remark he made to me. When we were talking about the music room he said the lock and hinges of that door creaked very badly and if he had been the murderer he'd have oiled them thoroughly before trying to enter the house that way, because from the bedrooms over the music room it was easy to hear the music room door opened if the occupants of those bedrooms slept with their windows open."

"Amazing! It looks as if the man knew every clue we were likely to pick up and was cleverly trying to bluff us off tracing them down to him!" exclaimed Vereker thoroughly perturbed at this piece of information.

"To tell the truth, Mr. Vereker, I'm getting very uncomfortable about Mr. David Cornell. He worries me in a way I've seldom been worried before and I don't know exactly how I'm going to deal with him."

"I'm not surprised, Heather. I've reached the point of asking myself how he could possibly have shot a man with such deadly aim in a dark room."

"Ah, that's the rub!" exclaimed Heather. "But it's getting near lunchtime and I propose we return to Marston and refresh. I've a lot to tell you and I daresay you've got a packet of news for me. We'll discuss things over our grub. We're going to have a roast capon for lunch and an apple pie with real Marston cream, I can't be bothered with business with that staring me in the mind's eye."

I had another strange experience this morning which I haven't told you about yet, Heather," said Vereker to the inspector as they sat at lunch.

"I daresay," said Heather. "There'll be all sorts of little things you're keeping hidden up your sleeve, but to show you I bear no malice I'm going to help you to the liver wing of this lovely bird. When I've finished carving, I'll sit down quietly and listen to your yarn, but not one moment before. I like to make a neat job of carving a capon, so I'll trouble you not to bother me. By the way, they haven't brought in any beer. Now go and get it yourself and save Mrs. Borham the trouble of coming in and interrupting us when we get busy with our discussion."

Vereker disappeared and when he returned he found that Heather had completed his task and was sitting waiting for him.

"Now we're O.K.," said the inspector. "Step on the gas and let her rip. What was your strange experience?"

"After I left the bungalow this morning," said Vereker, "I cut across the paddock and was making my way through the wood when I heard voices. Shortly afterwards two figures came into sight in the distance. They were Carstairs and Miss Cornell. They were talking very earnestly to one another and didn't spot me. I was anxious not to meet them at the moment because I wanted to get to Marston Manor and catch you before you left, so I just stepped off the path and hid behind a thick clump of hazels while they passed. I naturally kept my ears open to hear what they were saying."

"Dear, dear, Mr. Vereker! This is too bad. Just a common eavesdropper and I thought you were a perfect gentleman. This detection business is demoralizing you, there's no doubt about it. Doesn't matter about me, I never was what you call a gent, but you! What were they saying? I'm eager to hear."

"I only heard a fragment of the conversation and it wasn't at all conclusive, but as far as I could gather Carstairs was asking the lady to marry him."

"Stout fellow! I thought there was something sticky between them and it bears out Miss Catchpole's story about him being the faithful but disappointed lover. They were together this morning in the garden some time before you saw them in the wood. They were evidently making their way to the bungalow. I had my eye on Romeo and he's badly smitten. He was talking like a politician who'd got warmed up to telling his constituents what he was going to do for his native land and he looked like a hungry cat watching a bowl of goldfish. What did the young lady say to the marriage proposal?"

"Turned it down definitely and finally but his exact words were, 'I'll stand by you and take all the blame if you'll consent to marry me. Can't you see it's the only effective way out of the situation?' and in her reply she used the words, 'It wouldn't be fair to drag you into the mess. I'll face the music alone.' What dread secret lies behind this conversation, Heather?"

"Sounds rather suspicious," remarked Heather. "Looking at it in the worst light, it would seem that the young lady had something to do with the death of her former lover and that Carstairs was in the know."

"It may be something entirely different and innocent, Heather, but it gives one food for thought. I heard no more of the conversation, but from the subsequent tone of Carstairs' voice, I think he was getting shirty. In fact he reduced Miss Cornell to loud sobbing."

"Men are unkind beasts," remarked Heather. "If they can't get what they want by going on their knees and praying for it, they begin the bullying game. Of course he could force her hand considerably if he knew that she was in any way guilty of the crime."

"I can't think that of the man," said Vereker reflectively, "but in these affairs one never knows and it's no use having a favourable bias towards anyone."

"Not even towards Miss Cornell and she doesn't strike me as a particularly likely person to shoot a man. But I also have some news which I can't hold back from you, and you must keep your eyes open all the more after hearing it. It won't be very agreeable news for you because it introduces an unknown party into our hunt."

"Good Lord, Heather, I hope you're not going to spring Smith of London on me at this stage!"

"That remains to be seen, as the burglar said when he chalked something nasty on the nark's front door. I was asked by Tapp, the valet, if he could have a word with me this morning. He said he had a statement to make which had been worrying him for some days. He thought he'd better see me and get it off his chest. I agreed with him."

"I was never quite sure of Tapp," commented Vereker, "though you seem to have acquitted him long ago."

"Well, it has nothing to do with him personally but he concealed an important bit of information when I first questioned him about the case. It seems that Tapp on the night of the murder had a secret appointment with the daughter of old Braber the gardener. He met her in the garden about eleven o'clock and they were together till long after midnight."

"He's a married man with two children, isn't he?" asked Vereker.

"Yes and it was this fact which he had to break gently to the gardener's daughter. It seems that for some time he has been on very friendly terms with the girl and she with him. She's such a dear that he hadn't the heart to tell her right away that he was another woman's husband, but like many things it had to come to pass and he screwed up his courage to spill the beans. He told her fair and square that he was married but that his wife had left him for another. Also, which was more important, he had two youngsters to support. The economic snag is the worst in such cases."

"Poor devil, I suppose there was an awful row!" interrupted Vereker.

"The young lady fainted, he said, and it took him a long while to bring her round. That's why the interview lasted so long, he was careful to explain. When she recovered he expected a display of fireworks, but to his surprise the girl said she was very sorry for him. She hoped he and his wife would make it up and live happily ever after. Tapp said that would never be and as soon as he could afford a poor man's divorce he'd get one. 'That makes all the difference,' remarked the young lady and said she'd think the matter over before breaking off their innocent friendship. Well, she thought very rapidly and told him she didn't see why they shouldn't continue as before. Tapp reminded her of the two youngsters again, so as to make his position quite clear, and it then transpired that the girl simply adored children. Tapp said he felt in the seventh heaven of delight at this news and promptly proposed. He was accepted and the girl put the icing on the cake by saying, 'You see, George, the kiddies will be a great comfort to us should Providence not grant us any of our own.'"

"But what has all this rigmarole to do with our case, Heather?" asked Vereker.

"Well, on that night of the tryst, after the gardener's daughter had kissed George good-bye provisionally, George was making his way stealthily back to the house when he heard footsteps hurrying along the garden path and coming in his direction. He got the wind up and diving into the summer-house shut the door. The midnight prowler quickly passed the summer-house and ran towards the formal garden. Tapp opened the door to see if he could see anything, but it was not light enough for clear observation. Though visibility wasn't good he saw it was a man. The fellow was in the deuce of a hurry but Tapp is certain he wasn't wearing a hat. At first Tapp decided to follow up in case the house had been burgled, but then thought of his own predicament if questioned as to his business in the garden at that time of night. He played for safety and let the matter drop. Now that he doesn't mind it coming out that he was trysting with the gardener's daughter, he decided to give me a possible line on the murderer of Frank Cornell."

"This is too bad, Heather! What are you going to do about it?"

"We'll have to go more thoroughly into Mr. Frank Cornell's history, or that portion of it which belongs to London. He may have some enemy in town and we'll have to get a search going among his friends and acquaintances. I think you said you were going to ask your accomplice in crime detection, young Mr. Ricardo, to make inquiries. You can start him off as soon as possible, if you haven't already done so, and I'll get my men to work. Together we may find out something."

"These wide fields of inquiry rather put me off my stroke," remarked Vereker with a show of depression. "But I wired Ricardo this afternoon and let him loose. It's just the kind of thing he loves; a roving commission with a big cheque to cover his expenses."

"He has been useful before," remarked Heather. "He put the finishing touch to the Pleasure Cruise Mystery, if you remember. I've got to see Doctor Redgrave this afternoon, so I won't waste any more of your time."

Heather rose and left the room and a few minutes later Vereker saw him walking briskly along the main road outside the "Dog and Partridge." He sat and finished his cigarette and then thrusting his felt hat on his head sauntered out from the inn towards the village green. At one of the pumps on the green was a man filling a bucket. Accosting him, Vereker asked him if he knew where Lister, the village carrier, lived. The old man, after taking in with some difficulty what Vereker wanted, turned round and looked steadily across the green. Then slowly stretching out his hand pointed to a thatched cottage standing next to the village post office.

"That be Jack Lister's cottage," he said solemnly and without further word began to pump water into a second pail which he had hung on the pump's spout.

Vereker thanked him and crossing the green went up to the cottage door and knocked. A middle-aged woman answered his summons and looked at him inquiringly without speaking.

"I believe Mr. Lister lives here," said Vereker.

"Yes, sir, but he's out on his carrier's round to-day," replied the woman. "What would you be wanting? I could give he your message when he come home. I be his wife."

"Thanks, Mrs. Lister, but I don't particularly want to see your husband. I came to ask you when it would be convenient to see your daughter. She's in service with Mr. David Cornell and I'd like to have a chat with her on her half-day off if that could be arranged."

"She's at home this afternoon, sir, and in the house just now. Will you please come in?"

Vereker entered, was shown into a little sitting-room and asked to take a seat while Mrs. Lister called her daughter. A few minutes later Mary Lister entered the room and closing the door behind her stood nervously hesitant, waiting for Vereker to declare his business.

"Miss Lister," said Vereker rising, "I've come to have a confidential talk with you if I may."

"Is it about the murder at the Manor?" asked the young woman directly.

"Well, no, not altogether," said Vereker tentatively.

"For if it is, I know nothing about it, sir," continued Mary with an air of finality. "Are you one of the detectives?"

"I'm a newspaper correspondent," ventured Vereker reassuringly for he could see that Miss Lister was alarmed at the idea of being questioned by a detective.

"Oh," said Mary with returning composure. "You gave me such a fright. I thought you belonged to Scotland Yard. In any case I don't think I can help you much because I know nothing of what goes on at the Manor."

"I wasn't going to ask you anything about the Manor," replied Vereker. "You see, I've got to write up this case for the papers and I must write about something. It's a difficult job to fill up the column of a newspaper and I've got to say something about the friends and relatives of the dead man. Any piece of news about them is welcome. You understand?"

"I see and will my name be in the papers if I can tell you anything?" asked Mary.

"Not unless you want it to be. If you'd rather I didn't mention your name, I won't."

"I don't want to be in the papers at all..." commenced the young woman.

"Then you certainly shan't, Miss Lister. Please sit down and let me ask you some questions."

"I won't promise to answer everything you ask," said Mary and took a seat, sitting rather uncomfortably erect on the corner of a chair.

"Don't be afraid. I'm not going to ask you anything unpleasant or anything you can't answer without the least hesitation. You're in service with Mr. David Cornell, the blind brother of the late Mr. John Cornell?"

"Yes, sir, I've been with him two years in January next."

"You ought to be very comfortable there, I should say. Mr. Cornell is a charming man and his daughter, Miss Stella, must be very easy to get on with."

"I'm comfortable enough, sir, and they're easy people to work for. My wages are none too good. Two pounds a month is all I get beyond my keep. Do you come from London, sir?"

"Yes, but why?"

"They say a good general with plain cooking can get as much as a pound a week in London."

"Yes, I daresay you could get that quite easily. Good servants are scarce and there's always a demand for a good general who can cook. But London's a dear place to live in and it's not like this lovely countryside."

"The country don't appeal to me. I've lived here all my life and it's a dull old hole. If you want to go to a cinema you've got a one and sixpenny bus fare into Bury and there are only two days a week you can do that."

"Still you might not get into such a nice family as the one you're with. There are only two in the house and your work must be fairly light."

"Oh, yes, the work's easy and Miss Stella always does a big share of it though I wish she wouldn't."

"You like Miss Stella?" asked Vereker.

"She's all right, sir. A bit particular, that's all."

"You don't come home to sleep, Miss Lister?"

"No, sir. I'm up at six o'clock. Breakfast's at eight in the bungalow and it's more convenient for me to sleep there."

"Do your employers keep late hours?" asked Vereker.

"Oh, yes, they stay up to all hours burning good oil. Miss Stella usually goes to bed at eleven and Mr. Cornell about midnight."

"And yourself?"

"They have a meal about seven o'clock at night and after I've cleared away and washed up I can do as I please. Sometimes I sit up till ten if I've got a good book to read, but I'm generally in bed and asleep by nine."

"What time did you go to bed on the night of Mr. Frank Cornell's murder?" asked Vereker.

"Now what has that to do with it?" asked Mary with sudden truculence.

"I was going to ask you if you'd heard anything unusual that night between midnight and, say, one o'clock. Any car passing by the bungalow on the main road, for instance."

"No, I heard no car, though I was lying awake with the toothache."

"You have my sympathy. I sometimes get it myself. You should go and get the tooth pulled."

"Not me. I don't want false teeth just yet," replied Mary, and laughing, showed a perfect set of natural ones.

"Did you get up and take anything for it?"

"I took an aspirin and it relieved the pain."

"And you positively heard nothing unusual during that time?"

"I heard either Miss Stella or Mr. Cornell moving about, but that's nothing unusual."

"What time would that be?"

"I looked at the clock and it was just after one."

"It would probably be Mr. Cornell," suggested Vereker.

"I was almost certain it was at first, but I know Miss Stella's footsteps and then thought it was her. I listened particular to satisfy myself but couldn't be certain."

"Had she gone to bed before that?" asked Vereker.

"Oh, yes, I heard her come upstairs about eleven o'clock. I spoke to her about it in the morning, but she said I'd made a mistake because she was sound asleep at that time. Then I said it must have been Mr. Cornell, but she said Mr. Cornell was also in bed and that I must have been dreaming."

"Do you think you made a mistake, Miss Lister?"

"It's quite possible, sir. I was in such pain I wasn't heeding overmuch, but later on when I was talking to Mr. Cornell, he said he'd got up to let Misty, the cat, in. Then I remembered I'd heard the back door opened and closed and never thought about the thing any more."

"You're certain that somebody was about at that hour, anyway," commented Vereker.

"As certain as one can be, sir."

"Of course Miss Stella was terribly upset next morning when she heard the news of her cousin's death?"

"Not so upset as her father. Miss Stella went about her work as usual though she was as white as a sheet, but Mr. Cornell looked as if he was half-dead."

"He took it to heart more, I suppose."

"No, I don't think that. Miss Stella was Mr. Frank's sweetheart until this Miss Mayo vamped him. But she's terribly strong-willed and wasn't going to show she was upset."

"They were very fond of one another, so I hear, but their parents wouldn't let them walk out," remarked Vereker.

"They used to walk out in spite of their parents, if you ask me, and so would I if it was me who was in love," said Mary defiantly.

"They met secretly in the Manor garden, I believe."

"Yes, and as you know all about it I may as well tell you they used to sit together in the haunted room when it was wet."

"That took some pluck," said Vereker encouragingly. "Would you risk sitting in a haunted room with your young man, Miss Lister?"

"Of course I would, because the room was never haunted," replied Mary firmly.

"What about the young lady who wears her wedding dress and plays the piano?" asked Vereker.

At these words Miss Lister burst into merry laughter. "So you, too, have heard that story?" she asked with a superior air.

"Yes and I believe it. I know a lot about haunted houses."

"You wouldn't believe in that one if you knew as much as I do," remarked Miss Lister, hinting darkly.

"It depends on what you know, but I've heard of ghosts walking about in wedding dresses. They were usually murdered on the eve of their weddings."

"It wasn't a wedding dress at all," said Mary contemptuously. "It was a muslin frock."

"Then you've seen the ghost?" asked Vereker eagerly.

"Well, yes and no, but are you going to put all this in the papers?"

"I'll only put in what you want me to put, and as I shall be paid for the ghost story, I'll share what I get with you. I may get a couple of guineas for a good ghost story."

"It's not much of a ghost story," said Mary despondently, "because the ghost was Miss Stella. She had gone to meet Mr.

Frank in the music room and had just sat down at the piano when Mrs. Cornell came in. Miss Stella began to play the piano and Mrs. Cornell screamed and ran out of the room."

"Didn't she see it was Miss Cornell?" asked Vereker, amused at this tame laying of the Manor spectre.

"No; it was dark. Miss Stella told her all about it some days afterwards and as they are great friends they had a good laugh and kept it all to themselves. Miss Stella told me on the quiet, so you mustn't put that in the papers."

"Never mind, I'll sell the story all right and I'll give you your guinea now," said Vereker, "but tell me, Miss Lister, how did Miss Stella get into the music room?"

"By the door from the garden, of course. How d' you think?"

"Yes, but how did she get hold of the keys? The doors are always kept locked."

"But we've always had a set of keys to the music room in the bungalow. They used to lie on Mr. Cornell's desk, but they haven't been there for some days."

"They were there when you last dusted the desk, I suppose?"

"Mr. Cornell never let me dust his desk, but I saw them there only last week when I put a bowl of flowers on his desk."

"You're quite certain about that, Miss Lister?"

"Perfectly certain, sir. There are two keys tied together with a piece of string and there's a tab on the string with 'music room' printed as large as life on it. But may I ask why you're anxious about those keys?"

"If I'd known Mr. Cornell had them, I'd have borrowed them from him, but I was led to understand that they'd been lost. Now I know there's no ghost in a wedding dress haunting the music room, I shan't trouble any more about them. I'm rather sorry in a way because if I'd seen the ghost I'd have got a lot more for my story from a newspaper."

"Can't you tell them you've seen one?" asked Mary helpfully with an eye to a larger share of profits.

"Impossible, Newspapers never print anything but the truth and if I told a whacker they might find out and get me into trouble. In any case I'll get a couple of guineas and I'll give you your share now."

Vereker produced his note-case and handed Mary a pound note.

"Beg pardon, sir, but you said guineas," she commented as she picked up the note.

"Of course, of course, I was forgetting," laughed Vereker handing her the odd shilling. "And, Miss Lister, don't tell anyone about our story. We must keep that a dead secret."

"Is it a Sunday paper, sir?"

"No, but why do you ask?"

"If they wanted my photo, I might let them have one."

"They never publish photos, Miss Lister, so it wouldn't be of any use to me. I've got to hunt round for more stories, so I think I'll make a move."

"If you want to know anything else, sir, I'm always at home on Wednesday afternoon and you'd better come here if you want to see me."

"Thanks. I won't forget, Miss Lister," said Vereker and after another careful injunction as to secrecy took his departure.

The front door of the cottage had just closed behind him and he was about to cross the village green when a motor-cycle, coming along the road bordering the green, sounded its horn and slowing down pulled up just behind him.

"Good afternoon," said a female voice as the rider, whom in the distance he had taken to be a bareheaded youth in jumper and grey flannels, got off the cycle and approached him, pushing her heavy machine slowly beside her.

"Good afternoon," returned Vereker, raising his hat, "I simply didn't recognise you, Miss Cornell."

"I suppose these togs rather misled you," remarked Miss Cornell indicating her grey flannel trousers. "I wear them for gardening and they're much handier for a motor-bike than skirts. I was busy in the garden after lunch and then I suddenly remembered I wanted to see Mary Lister, our maid, so I jumped on my machine and came down as I was. It's her half-day off. Did I see you come out of the Listers' cottage or was it the post office?"

"It was the Listers' cottage," replied Vereker casually, but with his eyes on Miss Cornell's face.

"Oh!" she remarked and a curious flash of uncertainty invaded her eye. "I simply wondered. I couldn't see very well as I was coming up parallel with the frontage of the buildings on this side of the green."

"I heard that Lister was a carrier, in fact the only carrier in the village," said Vereker, hoping that his suggestion would be taken and save him the necessity for a misleading explanation.

"Yes, he's our Carter Paterson and a most obliging man," replied Miss Cornell in a satisfied tone.

"Unfortunately he's out on his round," continued Vereker, pleased that his ruse had succeeded, "but I'll call again this evening. My business is not very pressing."

"Are you returning to London, Mr. Vereker?" she asked, looking up at him quickly.

"No; I shall wait until the adjourned inquest is over. As far as I can see it'll be the usual open verdict. We've made little headway in the investigation and the case will probably be added to the long list of unsolved mysteries."

"Ah!" said Miss Cornell and after a few moments' silence continued, "I'm glad you called at the bungalow this morning. You've made a great impression on father and he's looking forward eagerly to your next visit. But I must catch Mary Lister before she goes out."

"Do you think I'd find Mr. Carstairs at the Manor if I called this afternoon? I was on the point of making my way up there now," asked Vereker.

"Almost certain. I saw him this morning and he said he was going to be in all afternoon as Mrs. Cornell has gone to see her solicitors about some probate business."

Thanking her, Vereker turned and walked leisurely across the green on to the main road running through the village and leading past Marston Manor. As he walked slowly along in the warm autumn sunshine, his thoughts were busy about the young woman he had just left. As he remembered her slim girlish figure in jumper and grey flannels, her pale olive-coloured skin, luminous dark eyes and her beautifully-shaped head with its shining black hair, he had to admit to himself that she was a very prepossessing creature. The hint of self-assured modernity suggested by her boyish garb was belied by her grave, thoughtful face and quiet, almost shy, manner. Susceptible to beauty in all its forms and especially in its most potent form, he found it extremely difficult to keep an open mind about her connection with the terrible tragedy which formed the subject of his investigation. He warned himself that he must be utterly dispassionate in his attitude and harden his heart against the warm appeal of feminine beauty which was so apt to bias his judgment. It was the cardinal weakness of the artist against which he had to be alertly on guard. From all the facts in his possession she was as likely a person to have fired the shot as anyone else. Her motive, too, was one of the strongest: the anger of a discarded woman who, faithful to her lover during the most romantic years of her life, suddenly discovers that she has been irrevocably supplanted by another. If she had shot her lover there was something in the injustice of her treatment which would partially condone her act even in minds firmly chained to the inviolability and sanctity of the law. At the bar of English justice, probably the most impartial and logical in the world in its decisions, she might be condemned and yet evade the legal death penalty by the appeal of her cruel position to the emotional sympathy of a people on the whole staunchly sentimental. Vereker put this aspect to himself and resolved not to allow any sentiment whatever to deflect him from the hard canons of the profession to which he had so often given his time and devoted services. He recapitulated all the factors which pointed to Stella Cornell as the likely culprit. The powerful motive; her possible access to the music room keys even if the duplicate set was not already in her possession; her knowledge of the existence of an automatic pistol in the drawer of a bureau in the music room; her ability to secure a secret appointment with her cousin at such an hour possibly with the idea of making a last appeal to his better nature; her thorough acquaintance with the house and grounds which would render her entry and departure safe from observation and as free from any chance encounter as it was possible to anticipate. That she and her cousin had made the music room a secret trysting place during inclement weather, even Inspector Heather had shrewdly hinted at, and Mary Lister, the Cornells' maid, had just confirmed. Against these arguments and apart from the fact that a firearm has seldom been used by woman in acts of revenge or even in self-defence, there was the young woman's amazing self-assurance and complete composure after the crime. In discussing the subject with a detective she had been supremely cool. She had been absolutely frank in the admission of her love for the deceased and of her chagrin at her deposition from the status of a secretly betrothed by his open engagement to another. She had denied all knowledge of the duplicate keys to the music room with the downright air of one speaking the truth. He clearly remembered her facial expression when he had asked her if she knew what had become of them and the direct gaze of her eyes when she had replied to him, "Not the slightest. Crawley ought to know where they are." If she had lied, Stella Cornell must be an actress of the first order, thought Vereker, and in that case he must be infinitely wary in dealing with her. He instinctively felt that underneath her assumed trustfulness of him—in other words the natural attitude of an innocent person—she was secretly convinced that he suspected her. A momentary unsteadiness in the eye, born and gone in a flash, an almost imperceptible twitch of the short upper lip, had been clear indications to his super-sensitive awareness. Her discovery that he had called at the Listers' home and her

uncertainty as to the purpose of that call had, in their meeting of
only ten minutes ago, brought that nervous questioning glance
into her eye. Perhaps a guilty conscience had suggested to her that
his visit to the Listers' cottage might be to interrogate the maid,
and that same guilty conscience had temporarily blinded her to
the fact that he might have wanted to see Lister on the latter's
ordinary business of a carrier. He had most clearly detected the
swift note of relief in her voice when the latter possibility had
been deftly suggested to her and readily accepted. Silently but
surely in Vereker's mind was forming a grave suspicion that Stella
Cornell, if not the guilty principal, had some connection with or
knowledge of the crime and its perpetrator which she was anxious
to conceal from the world. He was loth to entertain this suspicion
against such a beautiful and seemingly good young woman, and
in her presence he was almost inclined to reproach himself for a
cynicism that bordered on the sordid. Wrapped in these thoughts,
he had nearly reached the Manor gates when the rapid explosions
of a motor-cycle's engine some distance behind him made him
take to the safety of the footpath. In doing so he glanced back
and at once recognized the approaching rider as Miss Cornell.
Something in the hatless head with its raven hair fluttering in the
wind, something in the light grey flannel trousers which, in spite
of any argument in their favour, seemed an incongruous article
of attire for a woman, stirred a vague and fleeting association in
Vereker's mind. He tried to grasp it clearly, but for some moments
it was elusive and formless. Then, by some mental trick, the idea
of being hatless rose to prominence in his effort at recollection
and at once brought up a memory picture hanging by that frail
thread of association. It flashed upon him at last with a lively
feeling of satisfaction that the elusive association which Miss
Cornell's hatless head had stirred in his mind was concerned with
the belated statement which George Tapp had made to Inspector
Heather. In that statement Tapp had declared that he was in the
Manor garden with the gardener's daughter about midnight. She

had just left him and he was stealing back to the house when he was startled by the sound of footsteps hurrying in his direction. Tapp, eager not to be seen, promptly sought refuge in a summer-house and let the midnight prowler pass. Though visibility was not good, he saw that the prowler was a man; that he was not wearing a hat, and that he made his way in the direction of the formal garden. With this active recall, Vereker at once asked himself if the person not very clearly seen by Tapp could have been Stella Cornell in her present attire. It was quite possible, and to return to the bungalow she would certainly make for the formal garden and let herself out by the green door in the north wall. With this question there also crossed his mind Mary Lister's account of hearing noises of movement in the bungalow at one o'clock on the same night. Mary Lister, however, had been uncertain whether those footsteps had been Miss Stella's or her father's. At this point in his speculation the motor-cycle overtook him and, slowing down, came to a halt by the footpath.

"Are you going to call at the Manor to see Mr. Carstairs, Mr. Vereker?" asked Miss Cornell as she let her machine tilt over so that she could support it standing on one foot.

"That was my intention," replied Vereker, and looked with disconcerting directness into Miss Cornell's eyes to see if he could discover whether she had learned from Mary Lister the reason for his call at her father's cottage.

Miss Cornell returned the look with disarming frankness which ostensibly satisfied Vereker and continued: "I asked you because I want you to do me a great favour. Would you kindly give him a note for me?"

"With the greatest of pleasure," replied Vereker, noticing the flush of colour that had mounted to the young woman's cheeks.

"Thanks so much. It will save me running up and besides I don't particularly want to see Roly to-night."

"Shall I tell him that?" asked Vereker maliciously.

"For heaven's sake don't do that!" exclaimed Miss Cornell seriously and seeing Vereker's smile, laughed, her whole face lighting up with mischievous merriment. "We've had a slight tiff and I'm not in the mood for forgiveness just yet," she added.

"Mr. Carstairs is apparently very fond of you," ventured Vereker boldly.

"He must be if you've noticed it already," parried Miss Cornell. "I'm afraid he wears his heart on his sleeve. But to return to my request, I'll run home, write my note, and meet you in the drive as you are going up to the house. Please don't walk too fast as I may keep you waiting a few minutes."

"Don't take any risks, Miss Cornell. I'll give you plenty of time. I'm not in any hurry at all."

"Thanks ever so much, Mr. Vereker," she said and next moment with a roar from its exhaust the motor-cycle flashed up the road, swerved swiftly to the left to clear a speeding car, and was lost to sight round a curve.

"She certainly has cool nerves," thought Vereker and promptly associated the fact with his suspicions regarding her. He continued his way leisurely, stopping every now and then to admire the serene pastoral landscape drowsing in the autumn sunshine. Finally he turned up the drive by the gate near the bungalow and was sauntering lazily in the chequered shade cast by the avenue of chestnuts bordering the well-kept gravel, when Miss Cornell's girlish figure suddenly appeared through a mass of rhododendrons and waited for him to approach. She held an envelope in her right hand, and when Vereker came up with her he noticed she had changed into a smart tweed suit and wore a neat felt hat which shaded her large dark eyes and lent them a bewitching softness and lambency. A closer glance revealed that she had been weeping and was doing her utmost to hide her distressed feelings.

"I suppose you think I've got a colossal cheek making a postman of you, Mr. Vereker," she said, handing him the letter.

"Don't mention it, Miss Cornell. I hope, however, I'm not going to be the bearer of bad news," replied Vereker, boldly eager for any scrap of information.

"No," she replied thoughtfully. "What appears bad news at first often turns out to be the reverse. As you've already guessed, Roly is in love with me and I'm sorry to say I don't return his affection. I like him immensely, but that's not sufficient. I couldn't marry him without love. Sometimes, I suppose, a mere liking may turn into something stronger. I don't know and time alone will tell. I've asked him for time in this letter. I think that's only fair to him and to myself. What do you think?"

"It's fair enough, Miss Cornell, but I'm afraid a mere liking seldom turns into love. Time, however, may alter your opinion about love being the *sine qua non* for marriage."

"Perhaps. I'm inclined to agree with you about the matter of love. It's often called love at first sight, but I think all love is really at first sight and the first expression is merely the development of the state. The germ is born at once and gathers force according to the constitution of the afflicted person."

"Very clearly put, Miss Cornell," said Vereker and was lost for some moments in romantic reminiscences of his own. He looked up quickly and caught a pair of large dark eyes gazing at him with almost an appeal for friendship in their sombre depths. At once he felt he must summon all his reason to counteract this allurement, and his glance wandered from the neat, brown felt hat down the trim, shapely figure to a pair of brown walking shoes almost hidden in the lush grass. There it settled on a dandelion with its globe of downy seed; it was a comforting distraction in a moment of emotional embarrassment.

"How are you getting on with your investigation, Mr. Vereker?" came the question in a casual conversational tone. "Any nearer a solution?"

"Still in the dark, Miss Cornell, but things are beginning to take shape. Little facts are discovered, they suddenly, almost unconsciously, group themselves into a persuasive pattern and begin miraculously to glow. The light gradually grows stronger and then there's a flash of illumination. The secret lies bare and the time has come to strike."

"It sounds horribly cruel and fiendishly clever. Suppose, for instance, that when the secret lies bare as you call it, you find that a murder is justifiable, what do you do?"

"No murder is justifiable, Miss Cornell. Homicide may be at times, but a planned and executed taking of a human life is not justifiable."

"You mean at law, I suppose, but in your experience you must have come across a case where a human being is wronged and has no redress at law. The wronged person takes the law into his own hands and kills, what then?"

"I've had no such experience, but suppose one came my way I'm not allowed to constitute myself a supreme judge. The final judgment lies with twelve good men and women and that's as far as we can go in human affairs. Of course, there's a final Supreme Judge and I'm afraid His ways are inscrutable."

"Yes, they apparently are," said Miss Cornell with the suspicion of a sigh, "but to return to the subject of my letter. I want you to hand it to Roly when you take leave of him. He's terribly impetuous and if you hand it to him on your arrival he'll promptly dash down to the bungalow on the spur of the moment. I have to return to the bungalow before I go out and I don't want him to catch me in. I want to give him time for reflection and I shall be out for some time. When he has had leisure to think things over calmly, he'll decide that it will be better not to see me. Will you do that for me?"

"Certainly, Miss Cornell," said Vereker and could almost have added that he would do anything for so charming a woman.

"Thanks and I'll say good-bye for the present," said Miss Cornell extending her hand. "I daresay we'll meet again. I don't know whether I shall be called as a witness at the inquest, but I presume I shall. I don't look forward to it."

"I hope you'll be spared the ordeal," said Vereker and took her proffered hand.

For a few seconds she let her hand remain in his. She stood strangely hesitant with downcast eyes and heaving breast and then said, "I wish, Mr. Vereker..." but her face suddenly changed with a swiftly-born resolution and she left the sentence provokingly unfinished.

"So do I," said Vereker quietly, but with a toss of her head and a matter-of-fact good-bye, she turned on her heel and made her way rapidly through the rhododendrons.

"On the very brink of revelation and then darkness. Not even a glimpse from some soul's Pisgah!" soliloquized Vereker. "Alas, it's the common experience of the detective. Ah, well, Anthony, you always were a damned fool with a pretty woman and perhaps it's all for the best that she rang off at the critical moment. There are some things in life that even experience fails to teach and the wisest fail to learn."

Chapter Eleven
Mr. Carstairs Speaks Out

When Vereker arrived at the Manor he was shown into the drawing-room and more than five minutes elapsed before Mr. Roland Carstairs entered.

"Sorry to keep you waiting, Vereker, but I was in the midst of packing up my kit. I'm leaving Marston after tea," said Carstairs apologetically and sank into a chair as if mentally and physically exhausted. Vereker at once noticed the drawn, haggard features and the tired light in the man's rather fine grey eyes. He looked as if he had passed through some overwhelming emotional ordeal and had reached the limits of human endurance.

"You look rather done up, if I may say so," said Vereker sympathetically.

"I feel it, too," continued Carstairs and for some moments sat in silence as if uncertain whether to unburden himself further. Then, as if unable to restrain himself, he remarked, "They say the way of the transgressor is hard, but I'm inclined to think that the way of the man who tries to do the right thing in difficult circumstances is infinitely harder. Do you believe in being born under an evil or unlucky star, Vereker?"

"I've often wondered whether there's anything in the saying," replied Vereker. "A great number of people are firmly convinced that the stars have an occult influence on our lives and fortunes. I've never gone into the subject myself, but personally I've no faith in astrology. Still there's no denying the fact that there are some people whom misfortune seems to dog in spite of all their efforts, and there are those who sail gaily along on the perennial crest of good luck. The hidden cause behind events is the mystery and may have nothing to do with the stars."

"Possibly not, but it's as good a way of explaining a mystery as any other," said Carstairs despondently. "I was born under a damned unlucky star. I'm sure of that."

"What's your trouble? Is there anything I can do to help you?" asked Vereker.

"Very kind of you to suggest it, but I'm afraid you can do nothing," replied Carstairs, touched by Vereker's ready sympathy.

"Perhaps an affair of the heart?" hinted Vereker hopefully.

"Not only of the heart, Vereker. I'm unlucky all round. Anyhow, I'm leaving this place this afternoon and shan't be sorry either. If I could find any solace in drink I might go and get drunk. That's how I feel!"

"Wine's a great companion when you're happy, but a sorry one when you're fed up," remarked Vereker. "Why have you decided to leave in such a hurry?"

"The chief cause of my leaving hurriedly is Doctor Redgrave. We had a bit of a row this morning and if we hadn't been in Jo's presence we'd have come to blows."

"What was the trouble? It'd do you good to get it off your chest," said Vereker encouragingly. "Sort of psychic deflation. Better than keeping it to yourself and brooding over it."

"Yes, I think so, too, and I can trust you to let it go no farther," said Carstairs lighting his pipe. "You'll probably have guessed, Vereker, that I don't feel too well disposed towards Redgrave. There's that germ-carrier business which I've told you about. It seemed fishy to me, look at it in any light you like. Since my tiff with Redgrave this morning, I've taken the trouble to tell Inspector Heather all about it and I hope he digs into it pretty thoroughly. To add to my suspicions in the matter, Redgrave has taken Tapp into his service. I don't know exactly what has been said by Tapp to Redgrave, but they've evidently put their heads together and discussed it pretty thoroughly. In their discussion my indirect share in the affair was certainly brought to Redgrave's knowledge and that put the fat in the fire. He has got his knife in me now and no mistake."

"To interrupt you, Carstairs, what's your private opinion of the man, Tapp?"

"He's apparently an underhanded sneak, to put it bluntly. In the first place he has hidden his secret affliction from everybody. This was almost to be expected, though in a way it's unpardonable. I was inclined to be sorry for him at first. To make matters worse, he has been carrying on a flirtation with the gardener's daughter. I happen to know he's a married man and quite by accident I spotted him one night from my bedroom window. He had his arms round the girl and was ostensibly making violent love to her. That's none of my business and I've said nothing about it, but now I think the young woman ought to be told the fellow's history. However, I'm not going to be the informer. I'm beginning to learn that interference in other people's affairs only gets one into unnecessary trouble. The part that concerns me is that he knows I'm acquainted with his history, and I daresay he has told Redgrave that I started the ball rolling in the exhumation of old John Cornell, though I was not directly responsible."

"Was that the cause of your stormy interview with Redgrave?" asked Vereker.

"It wound up in that. The passage of arms started with an innocent enough trifle. Redgrave is one of those superior persons who treat you with a kind of supercilious tolerance as if you were one of Nature's funny mistakes. At least that is how he has always treated me. I admit I'm none too clever, but I object to it being rubbed into me like an embrocation. He invariably adopts the same attitude to Stella Cornell. I resent that kind of attitude very strongly. This morning the conversation started with some remark about a sense of humour and when I made some comment, Redgrave said I ought to write a serious monograph on the subject. He remarked that it would be great reading, almost as funny as Bergson's work on laughter which was one of the most humorous things he had read for many years. I replied rather warmly by saying that some people had a very strange idea of humour and asked him if he could give me a good example of the ludicrous. He confessed that it was a difficult task, but he agreed with Schopenhauer that a tangent to a circle was one of the funniest things he knew. The very reply was an impertinent assumption of superiority. I told him he was being damned offensive and not in the least funny. Then the matter took a grave turn and we became abusive. He lost his temper and said I was a meddlesome idiot and that it was my mischievous interference in other people's affairs which had brought unnecessary pain on Mrs. Cornell and had put him in a very serious position locally. I had, he continued, come within an ace of ruining his practice and career."

"Did he give any satisfactory explanation of the introduction of Tapp into the Cornell household?" asked Vereker.

"No. He declared he had a perfectly satisfactory explanation of his share in that affair, but he wouldn't condescend to discuss it with a dangerous lunatic."

"What did Mrs. Cornell say to all this?"

"Of course she sided with her lover. I must say she took a kindlier view of my action and in a way tried to argue that as a friend of Frank's I had only thought I was doing my duty, but Redgrave asked her not to try and excuse my behaviour which was downright caddish. At this I lost my wool and said I was now going further in the matter by making a full statement to the detective-inspector in charge of the case of Frank Cornell's death. This brought him up to boiling point and he threatened to break every bone in my body if I did so. I told him he'd better start right away, because it was the only way to prevent me carrying out my decision. We were on the point of settling matters with fists and it was only Jo's presence and intervention that stopped a fight."

"It's not a bad way of settling a dispute," was the only comment Vereker could offer to the now thoroughly roused Carstairs.

"I was quite willing to put the matter to the test," continued Carstairs. "I was dying to punch his film features out of shape, I can assure you. It may come to that yet if we meet again alone. But while we're discussing the case, I may as well tell you, Vereker, of another little item which you ought to know. There was some talk a day or two back about missing keys to the music room. They were found this morning."

"Oh, and where were they found?" asked Vereker with sharply-roused interest.

"Doctor Redgrave found them, or rather said he remembered that John Cornell had locked them up in a small drawer in his study some weeks before his sudden death."

"How did Doctor Redgrave know that? Did he say?"

"He frankly avowed he knew all along where the keys were because he was with John Cornell when he locked them away. He said he hadn't heard that there was any question about missing keys or he would have mentioned the fact before. Of course, I am biased against the man, but to me it sounds the lamest story I've heard for a long while."

"I wonder why he left the house by the music room door on the night of the tragedy?" asked Vereker, almost in soliloquy.

"You may go on wondering. I daresay he has got some ready-made yarn to cover his action, which was an unusual one to say no more. However, it's up to you people to find out all about his movements on that night. To me they appear damned suspicious and it's remarkable how the missing keys should have been found by our worthy leech. While you're about it, I think you ought to make a very rigorous inquiry into the secret history of Redgrave's discovery of Tapp as a valet for old John Cornell. He may be able to give you a satisfactory explanation; it's more than he was willing to give me. If I were in the inspector's shoes, I'd have a good search in his house for any evidence of germ culture. I believe it's a simple process on the whole and malignant germs can easily be injected."

"You mustn't lose your sense of proportion, Carstairs," remarked Vereker quietly. "In anger one is apt to say and do irrational things."

"Perhaps you're right. Once roused, I'm inclined to go the whole hog and it's a dangerous propensity. I beg Redgrave's pardon for the insinuation of germ culture and injection."

"I think you ought to patch up the peace with him," suggested Vereker. "After all, you didn't accuse him of introducing Tapp into the Cornell household with any nefarious purpose and he ought to look at the matter in the same light. It was Frank Cornell who caused all the trouble by talking foolishly to Stella Cornell."

"No, I'm not going to run to Redgrave with a white flag. He was the first to lose his wool. I've said good-bye to Mrs. Cornell and I'm rather sorry I shan't see her again. But these things happen and can't be helped. In any case, I shall be glad to forget all about Marston and the Cornell family."

"Even Miss Stella Cornell?" asked Vereker boldly.

"Well, no. In her case the boot is on the other foot. She'll be glad to forget me. I've proposed to her umpteen times altogether and been refused. It's not much use my returning to the charge. I've almost decided to quit."

"You mustn't lose heart. She may yet capitulate," suggested Vereker sympathetically.

"I'm afraid not. You don't know the lady's temper, Vereker. Once she has decided on a line of action, there's no hope of deflecting her. I've never come across a person of more resolute will. She's the stuff martyrs and fanatics are made of. In some ways, too, she's obstinate and will adhere to a course which she knows is wrong rather than give in."

"Has she a violent temper?" asked Vereker.

"She has a temper all right, but it's not what I'd call violent. It's an icy cold one which is infinitely worse, because a violent temper is transient and the other type persists and eats away sanity. She only declares it by a frigid light in the eye and the intense pallor of her face. In her favour, I must say it's never roused by trifles, but if she scents injustice or a cruel wrong, she's implacable and would go to any length to redress it. She inherits it from her father who has the same temper in a greater degree. He's a tiger when roused."

"Your outlook's not too bright, Carstairs, but one never knows what's on the lap of the gods. By the way, is Miss Cornell in any secret trouble or afraid of any secret danger at present?" asked Vereker.

The question put in a quiet, conversational tone had a most unexpected effect. Carstairs suddenly sprang to his feet, his face white, his hands clenched.

"Who, who told you she was in any secret trouble or fear of danger?" he asked eagerly.

"Calm yourself, Carstairs," interrupted Vereker in a cold, peremptory tone. "No one has told me anything about Miss Cornell. I spoke to her this morning on the Marston road and I thought she looked rather ill and worried. From her distrait manner, I drew my own conclusions and wondered what her trouble might be. As you are an intimate friend of hers I thought you might know. There was nothing more than that in my question."

"Thank God! I thought you had discovered something that was hidden from me," said Carstairs with evident relief, and after a brief period of silence he asked with sudden earnestness, "Tell me, Vereker, you surely don't suspect Stella of any hand in Frank Cornell's death?"

"We suspect everyone till we find they're above suspicion. We even consider that you yourself may have had a finger in this unsavoury pie."

"Of course, of course, I suppose you must work on some method like that. As far as I'm concerned you can wash out all your suspicions. Whoever shot Frank Cornell, I had no hand in the rotten business."

"I believe you, Carstairs," said Vereker sincerely. "At present I can see no motive that would drive you to such an act."

"No motive in the world could drive me to such an act in any case. If a person commits murder, I'm sure it must lie in the hidden character of the person and not in any extraneous thing such as a motive, though a motive is the match that causes the final explosion."

"Decidedly. Now, if it's a fair question, do you think Miss Cornell could be driven by some hidden motive to shoot her lover?"

"Good Lord, no!" exclaimed Carstairs emphatically and after a few moments' reflection added, "but perhaps I'm not the person to answer such a question. If you love a woman you can think no evil of her and, whatever her character may be, you look at it from quite a different angle to the ordinary observer."

"Very true, Carstairs, and I agree it wasn't quite fair of me to put the question to you."

"But surely you don't think Stella did it?" asked Carstairs with a look of surprise and horror on his face.

"Now, Carstairs, you're jumping to rash conclusions. I never think anyone has committed a murder till my observations clearly show me that he did. I don't know enough about this case yet to think definitely about it. If I put Miss Cornell in my list of suspects, I'm looking at the matter from a purely professional point of view—quite a different angle from yours as you've just admitted."

"Ah, well, that amounts to nothing, anyway. I know Stella has had a damned rough time at the hands of Frank, and his engagement to Valerie Mayo must have been a terrible shock to her pride and self-esteem, but I don't think she'd kill him on that account. Is there anything else I can tell you, because I must finish my packing? It's now four o'clock and I must catch the five train for town. I suppose I'll have to put in an appearance at the adjourned inquest and I'd better leave my London address with you and the inspector." Carstairs produced his card case and handed Vereker his card. "That's my address, Queensborough Gardens," he added. "When you're back in town, I'd be glad if you'd look me up any evening. We've met under rather rotten circumstances, but I shouldn't like to think I'd never see you again. Ring me up if you decide to blow round my way."

"Thanks, Carstairs. I'll certainly drop in and see you if you're sure it wouldn't bore you to entertain me. I'm not a very bright person socially."

"I'm not a good entertainer but I'll be delighted to see you. I'd like to hear all your theories and conclusions in this case when it's over."

"We'll take that as fixed," said Vereker rising and then exclaimed, "Oh, by the way, I've a little note for you from Miss Cornell. I saw her in Marston village this morning and she asked me if I'd deliver it to you."

Vereker produced the letter and handed it to Carstairs who promptly opened and read it. As his eye ran over the contents, his face paled and a frown gathered on his brow. Vereker stood waiting in the hope that he might hear something from the impetuous lover, but he was disappointed.

"Thanks," was the only word he could utter and he did this with obvious distress. Then with a sigh of bitter resignation he thrust the letter in his pocket and held out his hand.

"*Au revoir*," he muttered, and his whole face was expressive of suppressed agony.

"So long," replied Vereker and added, "I won't forget your invitation."

When Vereker arrived at the "Dog and Partridge" he found a letter from Manuel Ricardo awaiting him. Tearing it open he read:

My Dear Algernon,

Many thanks for your commission and the money to carry it out in my usual masterly fashion. After a very good lunch at Jacques, I set forth and called on my old friend Laurie Harwood to see if he had heard of the young man Cornell whose mysterious murder you are now investigating. Harwood, as you know, hangs out in the Inner Temple and has a very wide circle of friends, all engaged in the romantic business of making a living at the law. But let me say at this point in my letter that your request came as a gaoler might come to set a prisoner free. I was busy on my thriller and was very sorry I'd embarked on such a project. I had settled on a genuine antique plot. A body with its nose cut off is found in the ventilator of one of the latest luxury liners. I think this is rather a dinky place to find a corpse, but it's the only new point I dared introduce. I have made the captain the head of a Mysterious Gang who are in the pay of every Foreign Power to get rid of their dangerous politicians. Wroth Vandeleur is on the Trail. It intrigues even me why Wroth should poke his inquisitive nose into that funnel-shaped ventilator, but let that pass. He is eventually captured by one of the Gang and they are about to torture him to death for interfering with their profitable though laudable pastime. A Lovely Girl appears at the very moment they have smeared Wroth with honey and are going to put him stark naked in the path of an army of warrior ants on their trek in an African forest. (Delighted shudders from reader.) The warrior ants were beginning their enjoyable work of devouring the strong, and still silent, Wroth, when the Lovely Girl suddenly operates on the Gang who are gloating oilily over the jolly show. She has in her possession an invention of Wroth's. It's a mysterious lilac ray gadget that blinds and paralyses everyone coming in the line of its invisible beam and so forth. It's what the critics call "real honest-to-goodness stuff," and I had started the bell-ringers on the wedding peals when your letter arrived. Feeling rather prostrate after a series of motor chases, hold-ups, policemen shot gaily to pieces with machine-guns, aeroplane crashes, and a submarine sunk in the Polar seas by a mysterious battleship leaving Wroth clinging thirstily to an iceberg, I think I was due a quiet lunch at Jacques. I've been very comfortable in your flat. Your man, Albert, is a gem and has been most attentive.

Yours ever,

MANUEL.

P.S.—Harwood had never heard of Cornell, so we arranged a nice little dinner at his favourite eating house. We went to a first-class show "The Corybantic Canon." You must see it on your return if its brilliant plot and witty dialogue haven't damned it before then. I have parted with Brenda. She has a soul like a Swiss watch and can only boast a cigarette card education. M.R.

Thrusting the note with a gesture of impatience into his pocket, Vereker repaired to the little private room of the inn for tea. There he found Inspector Heather who, having finished his meal, sat smoking in an easy char. His face was thoughtful, almost lugubrious, but on Vereker's appearance it lit up with a good-natured smile.

"I've a bone to pick with you, Mr. Vereker," he said as he knocked the ashes out of his briar and began to refill the bowl.

"Say nay, say nay, Heather. You were looking rather warlike when I came in. What's all the bother?"

"I had a long statement from Mr. Roland Carstairs this morning. It concerns the man George Tapp."

"I have just left Carstairs and he warned me he had told you. To put the matter in a nutshell, he thinks Redgrave introduced Tapp, who is a germ-carrier, into the Cornell household with malice aforethought. He also has a suspicion, though he doesn't frankly say so, that Frank Cornell's murder may be a sequel to the first nasty bit of business."

"You knew about this germ-carrier idea and hugged the secret to yourself without letting your faithful friend into the know. I'm feeling very hurt, Mr. Vereker."

"Carstairs told me the story in the strictest confidence and I felt sure he'd tell you before long. Do you really think there's anything in it, Heather?"

"I've been weighing the matter up in my own mind. At present the whole thing seems too farfetched to me. I see no connection whatever, but it gives us a line on which to keep our eyes skinned. There's one objection to putting much stress on Carstairs' story; he clearly dislikes Doctor Redgrave. He makes no bones about it. They had a wordy set-to this morning."

"Yes, he told me so, but I think his dislike of Redgrave has arisen chiefly out of this germ-carrier affair. It was at bottom the cause of their row because, in the first instance, it was indirectly the spring that set David Cornell into getting his brother's body exhumed."

"Frankly, what's your opinion of Carstairs?" asked Heather.

"On the whole he impresses me favourably, Heather, but he's rather an uncommon type and I don't know altogether what to make of him. At times he appears cautious and guarded and at others blurts out what a reserved man would never mention. I should say he was rather an idealist in some ways and you don't meet many of them nowadays. He's a strong lover and would doubtless make a relentless enemy."

"Struck me as a bit eccentric. A man who clearly knows that a girl doesn't return his affection and yet moons after her year in year out instead of finding another just as good isn't quite normal. He might at least forget her and be happy with his fret-saw work, racing pigeons, or any other old hobby."

"I must say his constancy to the girl he loves gets me on a soft spot, Heather. It's romance in the grand manner and wins me over every time. I can't say why, but the expert psychologist could doubtless tell us all about this romantic complex."

"Would you behave that way yourself?" asked Heather sharply.

"No, I don't think I would, but I can't help admiring a man who can be utterly true to one woman for so many years in spite of the hopelessness of his passion."

"Yes, I can admire him in a book because you can blow the candle out, stuff the book under your pillow and fall asleep with the comfortable feeling that it's all a yarn. When you meet the bloke in real life he's rather terrifying. You feel so damned sorry for him that he annoys you. And then a man who can be so single-minded in love can be fanatical in other lines of behaviour. I don't feel too comfortable about young Mr. Carstairs. If he loves Miss Cornell so strongly he'd be a dangerous man to anyone who harmed her, even to his friend Frank Cornell."

"I agree, Heather. There's a lot in what you say, but I can't work up a feeling of handcuffs about him so far. Did he tell you that the duplicate keys to the music room had been found at last?"

"Yes, in a drawer in John Cornell's study. He also hinted that it was strange that Doctor Redgrave should have known they were there all the time."

"It struck me as significant if not peculiar. We must keep in mind that Redgrave and Mrs. Cornell were ghost hunting in the music room on the night of the murder and that Redgrave left by the music room door."

"But why should Redgrave take the trouble to mention that he knew where the keys were at this hour and that he had known all along? If he had had any guilty connection with the loss of those keys, he'd have said nothing about them. He'd have let us find them ourselves. His explanation seemed to me wholly above-board and just the explanation an innocent man would give."

"That's possibly exactly what he wants us to think. His methods may be the cunning methods of a very astute brain. If Redgrave is a criminal he's certainly not in the category of stupid ones. I feel more comfortable about Carstairs than I do about the doctor. I should like to meet Redgrave and form my own opinion of him after observing him in the flesh. What you hear of a man from others is really half-dead stuff in comparison with what you find out by seeing him. Every shade of expression in the eye, the naturalness or artificiality of his gestures, the deadly information unconsciously disclosed by nerves that refuse to be utterly controlled, the very inflection of the voice and bodily pose when making a statement are so vitally informative to the man who has eyes to see."

"True, Mr. Vereker, but there's one thing about the discovery of those keys that strikes me as important. If Redgrave knew they were there all the time, it almost proves that they were not in the possession of David Cornell or his daughter on the fatal night."

"You've come round to a piece of information I gathered this afternoon and was going to tell you. After lunch I called at the Listers' cottage. Mary Lister, the daughter, is a maid at the bungalow. She saw those music room keys on Cornell's desk only last week. I have been very suspicious of Miss Cornell all along and this piece of news came to me as really important. She herself told me definitely and without any hesitation that she didn't know what had happened to those keys and that Crawley, the butler, ought to know what had become of them."

"There's just a possibility that there's a third set," suggested Heather, "and as I suspect both David Cornell and his daughter, I'm inclined to think that they or one of them had a private third set made. Such a set would be extremely handy for Miss Cornell when she wanted to meet her lover secretly in the music room. She could also speak with downright truthfulness when she said she didn't know where the duplicate set had vanished to."

"That's a bright suggestion, Heather. I see you don't wish to relinquish your suspicions about David Cornell. Neither do I, if you wish to know my feelings in the matter. There's another important point I gathered this afternoon which points to Miss Cornell. She rides a motor-cycle and is fond of gardening. When engaged in either of those pursuits she wears flannel trousers, a jumper and goes without a hat. She could easily have been taken for a man by George Tapp when he peered out from the summer-house on the night of the murder and saw a hatless man making his way through the garden towards the formal garden."

"Yes, Tapp could easily have fallen into such an error. On the other hand, I know Mr. David Cornell never wears a hat, and the man whom Tapp saw might just as easily have been Cornell."

"Sound stuff, Heather. Father and daughter are now running neck and neck in my black list. A final piece of information I gathered from the obliging Mary Lister. On the night of the crime, one or other of the Cornells was moving about the bungalow at one o'clock. Mary heard footsteps and also the back door opened and closed. She was suffering from toothache and didn't pay particular attention to the matter because it was not unusual for one or both of them to be up at one o'clock in the morning."

"Did Miss Lister tell you that Frank Cornell once worked up a crush on her?" asked Heather quietly. "She was also a bit sweet on him."

"No, she didn't. That's important, Heather; it shows why she took so much trouble to learn of Frank and Stella's trysting arrangements. She would be jealous and rather inquisitive about their movements. Did the affair go farther than mere flirtation?"

"I can't say. The gentleman was an eager lad and I should say Miss Lister would be none too bashful if it meant the possible capture of a rich young man or a fair solatium if marriage was out of the question."

"This brings in another factor," remarked Vereker thoughtfully. "The ramifications of this case become more bewildering every day. If young Cornell had a guilty liaison with the girl Lister, there's just a possibility she'd resent being cast aside on the eve of the lover's marriage. She's a forceful young woman, I should say, from the brief interview I had with her, and might at a pinch use a pistol. Against this theory is the fact that she knew nothing about the pistol hidden in the bureau in the music room."

"I think we can safely dismiss her from our search, Mr. Vereker. What we want is one really good clue to drive us along the correct path."

"There's my clue of the ginger tabby," said Vereker.

"Oh, damn the ginger tabby!" exclaimed Heather bluntly.

"I don't know so much about that, Heather. You surely remember the French murderer who was brought to justice by the evidence of a plumed seed found on his coat? It belonged to a comparatively rare plant in the district, and the detective investigating the case found one of the plants only a couple of feet from the dead body. In the struggle one of the seeds had attached itself to the murderer's coat."

"Yes, yes, I remember, but in our case this hair was found on the settee in the music room. Anyone might have carried it there, even the wind. It's so inconclusive at the present moment but, of course, we won't utterly neglect it." Heather lapsed into ruminative silence and then suddenly asked, "I wonder if you'd do a little job for me to-night, Mr. Vereker?"

"Certainly, Heather. That's what I'm here for. What's the job?"

"Before you returned I had a message from Mrs. Cornell and she said she'd like to have a talk with me after dinner, say, about eight o'clock. Now, I'm terribly busy with other lines of inquiry and I've an idea the good lady's going to waste my time. As I've said before, she's an exasperating sort of person to question. I wish you'd take my place and hear what she has got to say. You've not met her as yet and the opportunity presents itself now. Besides, I've great faith in your powers of dealing with a woman of her class and temperament. I might send Goss, but it would be something like using a Big Bertha to shoot a swallow. Will you turn up at the Manor and say I've sent you as my proxy?"

"By Jove, Heather, this is just the kind of job I like. I'm your man."

"I thought you'd jump to it, Mr. Vereker, but before we go any farther, there'll be no necessity for you to go to the music room with the lady to hunt for the Manor ghost. You can safely leave that sort of thing to Doctor Redgrave."

"Ah, you've not heard the true story of the Manor ghost, Heather. Mary Lister definitely laid the spook this afternoon. She told me that the bride in the wedding dress who played the piano on the occasion that Mrs. Cornell saw the ghost, was none other than Miss Stella Cornell. She was waiting in the music room for Frank Cornell to turn up when Mrs. Cornell entered and saw her. Some days after, Miss Cornell told Lister the truth about the business and they thought it was a good enough joke to keep as a secret between themselves. Even Mrs. Cornell knows the secret."

"I'm glad we've not got to deal with the supernatural," remarked Heather wearily. "The case is complicated enough without any interference from the other world." With these words

Heather rose and knocked out his pipe in the empty fireplace. "I'll see you to-night before you turn in, Mr. Vereker," he added as he crossed the room and, opening the door, slowly disappeared.

Chapter Twelve
Mrs. Cornell's Story

At about half-past seven Vereker left the "Dog and Partridge" and turned into the main road which led to Marston Manor. As he was passing out of the village he overtook a young woman walking at a smart pace in the same direction. She turned and glanced somewhat nervously at him, and at once Vereker recognized that she was Mary Lister.

"Good evening, Miss Lister," he said. "I suppose you're on your way to the bungalow?"

"Yes, sir," she replied. "Are you going there?"

"No; I was making my way up to the Manor. If you don't object, I'll keep you company. I'll go as far as the bungalow gate with you and then turn up the farther Manor drive which is near."

"Thanks very much, sir. I'll be glad of your company because I'm a bit nervous on this road by myself in the evening, especially since Mr. Frank's murder."

"Naturally. I'm glad I've met you because since I saw you this afternoon I found there were several questions I wanted to ask you and forgot. Did you know Mr. Frank Cornell at all well?"

"How do you mean, sir?" asked Miss Lister guardedly.

"Well, to speak to, for instance?"

"Oh, yes, sir, when I first went into service at the bungalow he used to turn up there almost every day. Then his father objected to his courting Miss Stella and he only came rarely. He was always ready to talk to anyone, and if Mr. Cornell and Miss Stella were out, he'd come into the kitchen and talk to me as if I was his equal. I did like that about him. He didn't put on any side and was always full of fun."

"He had rather a soft spot for a pretty girl," remarked Vereker pointedly.

"So everyone says, but you'd hardly call me a pretty girl, would you, sir?"

"If you're asking my personal opinion, Miss Lister, I should certainly say you had your fair share of good looks."

"Lor' bless us! You're the first man I've ever heard say so," replied Miss Lister with a nervous little laugh. "Still, I think Mr. Frank was a bit partial to me."

"I'm not surprised, but if I'm a judge of character, you kept him at arm's length."

"I don't know so much about that. I must say I thought he was a very nice gentleman, and if circumstances had been different I think I could have liked him very much."

"Did he ever pay you any marked attention?" asked Vereker bluntly.

"Now you're asking something," replied Mary. "On one or two occasions I happened to be alone in the bungalow. He was inclined to be a bit fresh, but I showed him straight I was having none of that. He actually kissed me once, but when I got wild with him and told him I'd tell Miss Stella, he was sorry and begged me not say anything about it."

"Of course you told her," suggested Vereker mischievously.

"Not me, sir. I wasn't going to create no trouble just because the young gent thought he'd got a soft mark and found he hadn't. There was nothing in it because I clearly showed him I wasn't going to stand for any nonsense. After that he behaved himself as he ought and I liked him all the better then. After a time I could almost have wished I hadn't been so stiff with him. He used to tease me all about my young men and say he was sorry for them, but, of course, I had no young men. I think he got quite fond of me as time went by and never called me Lister as he used to. He nicknamed me 'Quite Contrary' because my name's Mary."

"Rather a nice nickname," commented Vereker and added, "What a pity he didn't become engaged to Miss Stella!"

"Mr. David Cornell wouldn't hear of it all because Mr. Frank liked his drop of beer and was always ready for a bit of mischief. There's no harm in beer in moderation and although Mr. Frank got into one or two scrapes there was no real wickedness in him. Miss Stella would have made him a good wife; anyway, better nor Miss Mayo. She's just a vamp if you ask me."

"I've not met Miss Mayo, so I can't say, but there's one thing I particularly wanted to ask you, Miss Lister. Do you remember what dress Miss Stella was wearing on the night that Mr. Frank was killed?"

"Yes, sir, I remember quite clearly. She had been out on her motor-cycle all afternoon and was wearing a jumper and her flannel trousers. She didn't change into a dress that evening at all and was wearing her flannels when I went to bed."

"She wasn't wearing the muslin frock she wore when Mrs. Cornell mistook her for a ghost?" asked Vereker.

"No, sir, I'm quite certain of that."

For some moments the conversation lapsed and the two walked along as if lost in their own thoughts. The silence was at length broken by Vereker who asked: "Do you know anyone in the village who has a ginger tabby cat, Miss Lister?"

"What a funny question to ask!" remarked Miss Lister with a note of surprise in her voice. The question had been so alien to their former conversation that for a moment she wondered whether her companion was joking.

"Well, ginger tabby cats are rather rare and I'm fond of them. I was wondering if I could buy one to take back to London with me. I've got mice in my flat and I want a good cat to clear them out. Has anyone in the village got a ginger tabby?"

"I've got one myself, but he's not for sale. I call him Sandy and he came from my aunt's at Long Melford. I think he's the only ginger tabby in Marston."

"I'm sorry you won't part with him. Have you had him long?"

"I got him the day before Mr. Frank was shot. I brought him up to the bungalow that morning to show Miss Stella. She fell in love with Sandy at once and wanted to keep him because Misty, her cat, is getting old and won't bother about catching mice now."

"Mr. Cornell seems very fond of Misty," suggested Vereker irrelevantly for his thoughts were elsewhere.

"He hates cats and won't let them come near him," replied Miss Lister emphatically. "He only puts up with Misty because Miss Stella is fond of her."

"That so," remarked Vereker and at this point the conversation widened out on the subject of cats of every kind, colour and temperament until the lights of the bungalow brought it to an end. Bidding Miss Lister good night, Vereker turned and, walking at a rapid pace, made his way to Marston Manor. His brief interview with the maid had given him food for thought and he was soon lost in speculation as to the importance of the clue of the ginger tabby in his investigation. Was it irrelevant as Heather had almost suggested, or would it assist him in the solution of the problem on which they were engaged, a problem which at the moment still appeared an impenetrable mystery? Moreover, he felt he must not take Heather's jocularity about ginger tabbies as the inspector's real opinion. No one knew better than Heather the importance of the most trifling clue. Often from his marvellous memory he would quote cases in which vital conclusions had been drawn from some seemingly unimportant detail. Vereker particularly remembered the case in which a microscopic particle of thread attached to a chisel at the junction of blade and handle had been identified as belonging to the pocket of a waistcoat worn by the criminal on the day of the crime. No, he would persist in attaching some importance to his singular discovery of that ginger-coloured hair. As he pondered on the subject, he concluded that if the hair had been brought into the music room by an accidental attachment to human clothes, it pointed at once to three people as possible agents. The music room had been vacuum-cleaned on the morning preceding the murder and fresh covers had been fitted to the chairs and settees. It could therefore be argued that the hair had been introduced by someone entering the room and using the settee subsequent to the cleaning operations. Marston was a small Suffolk village, and Miss Lister had declared that her cat was the only ginger tabby in the village. Ergo, somebody who had handled Miss Lister's cat or come in contact with him must have entered the music room subsequent to the cleaning. This, in a way, narrowed the problem to three people: Miss Lister, Miss Cornell and Mr. David Cornell. Though the last-named had not fondled the animal, it was quite possible that his clothes had accidentally picked up and retained one of its hairs. Dr. Redgrave and Mrs. Cornell had certainly been in the room on the fatal night, but at the moment there seemed no connection between them and ginger tabby cats. On the other hand, there might be several mysterious and accidental ways in which the hair had come to rest on the settee, and it was this lack of conclusiveness that had doubtless deterred Heather from attaching too much importance to the clue. Vereker was still weighing his discovery in a searching critical analysis when he arrived at the main entrance to Marston Manor. On explaining his business he was at once shown up to Mrs. Cornell's private sitting-room. From Heather's brief allusion to her good looks, Vereker was prepared to see a comely woman who, with the aid of art, might appear considerably more attractive than nature had made her. He was certainly not expecting the serene vision that met his eyes on entering Mrs. Cornell's sitting-room. Auburn haired, with large, limpid brown eyes and a dazzlingly beautiful complexion, she reclined with graceful ease on a settee. On Vereker's entry she excused herself for not rising and extended a delicate and exquisitely-shaped hand. In a few sentences, spoken with a soft, lazy intonation, she put him at his ease.

"Bring a chair quite close to me, Mr. Vereker," she said. "I want to speak confidentially to you. Please help yourself to cigarettes.

You'll find a box on the table near the door. Also whisky and soda, or if you prefer something else to drink, I'll ring."

"Thanks, I'll smoke if you don't mind, but I'd rather not have anything to drink just now. I think you understand, Mrs. Cornell, that I've come instead of Inspector Heather."

"So Crawley told me. I believe the great man's very busy and couldn't come himself." With these words Mrs. Cornell raised herself to a more comfortable posture for conversation and continued, "I wanted to discuss this dreadful business of Frank Cornell's death. You've decided it's a case of murder, I believe?"

"We've been obliged to conclude that his death wasn't accidental or suicide, Mrs. Cornell."

"Just so. Personally I know nothing about these things and I'm not in a position to contradict you. What I want to do is to make my own position quite clear once and for all. As you may guess, it has been a very painful affair for me. I'm not much moved by what other people think of me, and I've tried hard to keep a non-committal attitude throughout the whole business, but there are times when one can't remain detached. This affair has shown me that I cannot. It's no use my trying to hide the fact, but I feel I'm the centre of a great deal of nasty suspicion."

"You're not alone in that, Mrs. Cornell," ventured Vereker diplomatically.

"I daresay not, but I don't feel any happier for being one of a company of suspects. As you probably know, Mr. Vereker, I was only twenty-six years old when I married John Cornell. I'm not going into a long explanation why I married a man so much older than myself. That's purely my own business, but I can tell you quite truthfully that his wealth had nothing to do with my choice of John Cornell as a husband. You may not believe me and only a few of my intimate friends did. It's natural for the world to judge people by its own material standards and I can hardly blame it for thinking I was a cunning little gold-digger. I suppose you know the provisions of my husband's will?"

"Only from hearsay," replied Vereker.

"Under my marriage settlement I have an income of five thousand a year. I didn't benefit under the terms of John's will to any great extent and most of his property, real and personal, went to his son, Frank. As you will see, my marriage settlement provided for me amply and I'm not an extravagant woman. I've never spent anything like my annual income. But John inserted a clause that if Frank predeceased me without issue, the whole of the property and investments reverted to me."

"I understood that to be the case," remarked Vereker.

"Very good. His death means that my income is now about ten thousand a year. I'm sure I'm not exaggerating when I say that in a case of murder the capture of five thousand a year would be considered a sufficient motive."

"Quite an appreciable motive," agreed Vereker dispassionately.

"Anyhow, I feel it's quite a good reason for suspecting me of having committed the crime," continued Mrs. Cornell, idly admiring a large, single-stone ruby ring which gleamed from the forefinger of her left hand. "But the matter, as far as I'm concerned, didn't begin with Frank's death; it had its origin in my husband's death. Long before the latter occurrence I'd become very friendly with Doctor Stanley Redgrave whom I hope you'll meet later this evening. For some months previous to John's death I was very much in love with Doctor Redgrave. I suppose from a rigid social point of view this was reprehensible."

"I'm afraid people would say it wasn't quite the correct thing," said Vereker in a tone devoid of all expression.

"Exactly. I ought to have severed the friendship before it grew into love, and shown myself a perfect example of reason and correct conduct. Well, I damned well didn't!" said Mrs. Cornell with airy impatience and then with sudden emphasis, "But I didn't do what the world thought I'd do as an ordinary human being—as a common example of itself. I'd made my vows on my marriage with John and I kept them strictly. His sudden death released

me from that stringency of behaviour, but it brought quite an
unexpected load of mischief in its train. I suddenly discovered that
people began to think that John's death was not due to natural
causes and that I possibly had some hand in it. I'm not going to
try and defend my conduct as far as falling in love with Stanley
Redgrave is concerned. It simply happened. I can only make the
excuse that I was helpless. My instincts were stronger than any
precepts I'd swallowed in my youth as to what one ought to do,
but you can imagine my distress on learning that I was being
suspected of murder to satisfy a guilty passion. It was terrible—it
was damnable!"

Overcome by her emotion, Mrs. Cornell buried her face, now
scarlet with anger and shame, in her hands. For some minutes
there was silence, a silence more embarrassing to Vereker than he
had ever before experienced. At length, recovering her composure,
Mrs. Cornell uttered a sigh of weariness and continued:

"I presume we shape our conduct or ought to shape our
conduct to win the esteem of our fellow-beings. The sexual side
of that conduct is the most intractable of all and the most open
to suspicion and attack. That side of my life I've tried to live
blamelessly. If I had erred and given John cause to divorce me, it
wouldn't have been considered a very terrible thing in these days.
I would simply have been classed as one of the many hundred
people who in a year are parties to undefended cases and are
forgotten if not altogether forgiven by the world at large. Life's
no longer provincial. But I had too lively a regard for that kind of
conduct which, generally speaking, makes for orderly and happy
living, to entertain the idea of divorce. I'm orthodox and have a
touchy social sense. Therefore I was illogically suspected of going
the length of murder to preserve the esteem of my fellow-beings!"

"Strange to say that has often been done, Mrs. Cornell. It's
logical enough: the murderer stakes everything on the chance that
the major offence won't be discovered. He wants his cake but isn't

prepared to steal it. He'd like it to appear that the cake had fallen into his lap by a dispensation of Providence."

"That's the outlook of a lunatic and I hardly expected anyone to think I was mad. However, I was evidently classed as such and had to suffer the consequences. My brother-in-law, David Cornell, made representations to the Home Office and as a result my husband's body was exhumed. The result of the official analyst's report was only partially satisfactory to me, for there's always a suspicion that in poisoning, say by vegetable alkaloids, the poison cannot always be detected. Since the affair I've regained my peace of mind to a certain extent. On looking at things from a matter-of-fact point of view, I've had to admit to myself that David Cornell probably acted from motives which he thought justifiable. I've forgiven him and though we've never been very good friends we're not what you'd call hostile to one another."

"Your position was certainly most unpleasant, but who do you think was at the root of the trouble, Mrs. Cornell?"

"It all started with Roly Carstairs discussing with Frank Cornell the presence of George Tapp in our household. Now Roly's a very conscientious, well-meaning fellow and he had no idea he was going to set match to such a train of gunpowder. He knew that Tapp was a germ-carrier and he knew that Stanley Redgrave had recommended him to my husband as a valet. The discussion ended there as far as Roly was concerned, but Frank was not always sober enough to be responsible for what he said. He foolishly hinted on one occasion to Stella Cornell that his father's death was not altogether above suspicion. He made no definite statement about the man, Tapp, or the subject of germ-carriers, and Stella, in turn, stupidly repeated the conversation to her father. David Cornell, who is at times terribly impetuous, at once suspected that his brother had been poisoned and wrote to the Home Office."

"You were always on good terms with your stepson?" asked Vereker.

"Always. I liked Frank very much up to a point. Times without number I've straightened out his financial affairs in order to save him from his father's anger, but it was useless. The only real quarrel we ever had was over Mary Lister. It came to my knowledge that he was in the habit of paying her quite unnecessary attentions when he happened to find her alone in the bungalow. Perfectly sober, he wouldn't dream of such a thing, but under the influence of drink there's no saying what any man will do. The girl was naturally flattered by his advances and I foresaw that she might encourage him to the point of misconduct. I had a straight talk to him about it and he told me to mind my own business. I wouldn't have minded that, but he hinted that his relations with Mary Lister would compare favourably with those existing between Stanley Redgrave and me. I repeated this to Stanley and the two men had it out together on a later occasion. Still, all these differences had been forgotten and we were all on quite friendly terms prior to his mysterious death."

"Mr. Carstairs left for London this afternoon, I believe?" asked Vereker tentatively.

"Oh, yes. He and Stanley had words this morning and fortunately I was present to prevent the matter going farther. Roly's a sensitive man in many ways and simply can't stand having his leg pulled. I must admit Stanley's rather provocative on occasions and it really was his fault that they quarrelled. I tried to persuade Roly to forget the matter, but in vain. He said he would return to London by the five train and in the end I was obliged to let him go."

"The discussion turned to the subject of Tapp being a germ-carrier, I believe," remarked Vereker.

"I see Roly has told you all about it. I won't express any opinion on the matter at all. Stanley has a perfectly straightforward explanation of that nasty business and he'll doubtless tell you all about it when you see him."

"If it's a fair question, Mrs. Cornell, may I ask if you've any theory about your stepson's death?" asked Vereker.

"In the first place, I declare I had no hand in the matter, though I daresay I've come under official suspicion. From the police point of view, I had a powerful motive and it looks very much as if the murder was committed with my little automatic pistol. It's to clear up this last point finally that I wished to see Inspector Heather, but as you've come as his proxy, I may as well clear it up with you."

Mrs. Cornell rose to a sitting posture and stretching out her hand to a shelf by the settee on which she reclined picked up a small nickel-plated automatic which she handed to Vereker.

"That's the weapon John gave me some years ago during a scare in the district. It used to be in a drawer of a bureau in the music room, but in going through John's private chest of drawers in his bedroom, Stanley found it beside the duplicate keys of the music room for which he was searching. I suppose you'll hand it to the inspector."

"Thanks," replied Vereker with suppressed amazement as he took the pistol and placed it carefully in his pocket. "Is it loaded?" he asked.

"For the life of me I couldn't tell you, so please be careful. I know nothing of the mechanism of such a thing and can't touch one without a feeling of revulsion."

"You've no idea where your husband bought this pistol?" asked Vereker, now doubly alert to every shade of expression on Mrs. Cornell's face.

"I'm not quite sure, but I think it was bought in Ipswich. I believe David Cornell was with him when he bought it," replied Mrs. Cornell with matter-of-fact calm. "I've an idea it was prior to the time when police permits were necessary, but I can't be definite on the point. In any case I've told the inspector and he said he'd make some inquiries in Ipswich as a matter of form."

"Then this can't be the weapon that was used to shoot Mr. Frank Cornell," ventured Vereker in a casual tone.

"Utterly impossible. It was locked up in my late husband's chest of drawers and the keys of those drawers have been in my possession since my husband's death."

"No one had access to the keys, of course?" asked Vereker.

"Only Stanley and I knew where they were," replied Mrs. Cornell frankly. "After my husband's death he helped me to go through most of my husband's papers and belongings and we locked the keys in my safe in my bedroom where I keep the few jewels I possess."

At this point a knock sounded on the door and a few moments later a tall young woman in fashionable evening dress entered the room.

"I hope I'm not interrupting you, Jo," she exclaimed as she closed the door behind her.

"Not at all, Valerie," replied Mrs. Cornell, and after introducing Vereker to the newcomer, asked, "Is there anything wrong? You look as if you'd seen our spook."

"Your telephone rang and I answered the call," said Miss Mayo breathlessly. "Your brother-in-law, Mr. David Cornell, was at the other end of the wire. He says that Stella left the bungalow early this afternoon and hasn't returned."

"Did she go out on that dreadful motorcycle?" asked Mrs. Cornell with sudden alarm.

"No. The cycle's in the shed. She left a note simply saying that she had gone and begged her father not to make any inquiries after her; that she was utterly worn out and wanted a rest and was going to stay with some friends until she was quite well again. She had left written instructions with Mary Lister to carry on in her absence."

"Poor Stella!" exclaimed Mrs. Cornell with a swift resumption of calm. "She's in a highly-nervous state and if she has gone away to seek quiet, it's about the best thing she could do. She has had a dreadful time of it lately with one thing and another. It'll do her good to get a complete change. Apart from other things, I'm afraid her father worries her considerably. He's not an easy man to live with."

"I hope there's nothing more serious in it," said Miss Mayo. "You don't think she'd have any suicidal intentions, Jo?"

"Good gracious, no, nothing of that sort. Stella's too level-headed, Valerie. I shouldn't worry any more about it, dear. Did you finish your crossword puzzle?"

"I'm wriggling out a solution with Stanley's help. He arrived about half an hour ago and I told him you were having a private interview with Mr. Vereker. He said he wouldn't interrupt you. He's in the drawing-room."

"Tell him I'll join you shortly," remarked Mrs. Cornell and Miss Mayo left the room. For some minutes after her departure Mrs. Cornell sat absorbed in her own thoughts. Then she rose, took a cigarette from a silver box on the table, and lit it.

"I think that's all I've got to tell you, Mr. Vereker," she said as she stood with one hand resting on her hip. "I've tried to make matters clear as far as I'm concerned in this business. Is there any question you'd like to ask me, anything you're in doubt about? Don't be afraid to be blunt to the point of rudeness."

"Might I ask, Mrs. Cornell, if you and Doctor Redgrave managed to get a glimpse of the Manor ghost on the night of the tragedy?" asked Vereker with as much seriousness as he could summon.

"I see what you're driving at, Mr. Vereker," replied Mrs. Cornell with an arch smile. "You want to know exactly why we went into the music room. In the first place, Stanley wanted to speak very confidentially to me. Though we are lovers, I can assure you it had nothing to do with the subject of love. We chose the music room because it was private, but the main reason was that Stanley wanted to leave the house by the path through the gardens. He had to see Miss Cornell professionally that night and he took the shortest cut to the bungalow to save time. Have I made the point clear?"

"Perfectly clear, Mrs. Cornell. Was Miss Cornell ill, may I ask?"

"I'm afraid I can't answer that question. I know why Stella wanted to see Doctor Redgrave, but I cannot divulge a doctor's professional secrets. I oughtn't to know myself but a lover is a privileged person. You must ask him yourself. Whether he'll answer your question, I can't say. He'll have to use his own discretion. Anything else?"

"Only one more question, Mrs. Cornell, and please don't think I've taken leave of my senses in asking it. Have you seen a ginger tabby cat lately?"

"No, I certainly haven't!" replied Mrs. Cornell with a laugh. "Your question reminds me of a doggerel that was very popular in America some years ago. It ran:

'I've never seen a purple cow
And do not wish to see one,
But I'd rather see a purple cow
Than be one!'

I see my own black cat every day if that's any use to you, but why do you ask?"

"That's a professional secret, Mrs. Cornell, and I'm afraid I can't divulge it," replied Vereker smiling. "Is there anything else you'd like to tell the inspector?"

"Oh, yes. I didn't want to alarm Miss Mayo about Miss Cornell's sudden disappearance, but I certainly think Mr. Heather ought to be told at once of the fact. The girl's in a very dangerous frame of mind, and though I don't think she would do anything rash, it would be advisable to find out where she has gone and what she's up to. If you can trace her whereabouts, perhaps you'd let me know and I'll go immediately and see her myself. She's very fond of me and I've a great deal of influence with her. My help and advice might be just what she needs at this time. The sooner you can do this the better, Mr. Vereker."

"I'll return at once to the 'Dog and Partridge' and see the inspector," replied Vereker. "Thanks very much. I wish you'd call tomorrow morning and see me. I'd like to know what you've done about Miss Cornell and how you're getting on with your investigations. There may be other things which I'd like to discuss with you which I can't think of just now. Call any time you like after nine o'clock. But before you go, come downstairs and let me introduce you to Doctor Redgrave. I'm sure he'd like to make your acquaintance."

As they were about to leave Mrs. Cornell's private sitting-room, she stood for a few moments as if trying to recollect something she had forgotten. Then turning to Vereker and looking him frankly in the face she said: "There's one question I've been dying to ask you all the time, Mr. Vereker, and haven't had the pluck. Your manner's so diplomatic that I'm almost scared to ask it now. Who do you think murdered Frank Cornell?"

"I really can't say, Mrs. Cornell. Naturally a detective has suspicions, but he never suspects definitely till facts permit. I'm busy gathering all the facts of the case together. I'm a complete stranger to the dead man's relatives and friends, and I've to find out everything about him and them. This is a difficult and tedious business. Now you knew Mr. Frank Cornell as well as anyone, I should say. You ought to have some inkling as to the person who was likely to kill him, either in a fit of anger or with premeditation. Whom do you suspect?"

"I've thought about it till my head ached, but I haven't the vaguest notion. At times I've thought Stella was the guilty person on account of motive, but I know Stella so well that I simply dismissed the thought as impossible. I've suspected Roly Carstairs, but I really can't say why. There may be some hidden motive which might drive him to such an act. He has loved Stella for many years and would marry her now if she'd consent. Then

there's Mary Lister. She's a resolute little woman with some of
the directness of an animal. I don't know how far she may have
let Frank go in his philandering with her. Jealousy might drive
her to revenge. Then, of course, Frank had innumerable friends,
especially women friends in London. Some of them, I've heard, are
of rather questionable character. I don't know; the whole thing's
a mystery to me and I'm glad I'm not a detective trying to solve
it. In any case, I hope you'll find out before long. This suspense is
painful to all concerned. Now let's go to the drawing-room."

Chapter Thirteen
The Doctor's Story

In the drawing-room Mrs. Mayo was seated at a card table intent
on a game of patience. Dr. Redgrave and Miss Valerie Mayo, close
together, were discussing with laughter "No. 21 down" in the *Daily
Telegraph* crossword puzzle for the day.

"What on earth can it mean?" asked Miss Mayo tapping
her very scarlet lips with the butt end of her pencil. 'Medico's
encouragement to the sea.' Really, Doctor Redgrave, this is your
chance for being brilliant and you're only facetious. I'm waiting for
you to scintillate... 'Medico's encouragement to the sea'..."

"I'm trying hard to twinkle but it's no use. I've never given any
encouragement to the sea anyhow..."

The cheerful comfort of the house and its inmates struck
Vereker at the moment as a glaring contrast to the shocking
tragedy that had so recently been enacted within its walls. The
sordid details of that tragedy lurked grimly and persistently
at the back of his own mind and his presence among this little
company of cheerful people seemed to him incongruous—an
intrusion. Introductions followed and the subject of Miss Stella
Cornell's sudden disappearance from Marston was immediately
discussed. During the conversation Vereker was silent and seized
the opportunity for carefully observing the talkers, especially

Miss Mayo and Dr. Redgrave. The former impressed him as an ordinary specimen of young womanhood, in spite of her good looks, her perfect figure and a certain forced brightness of manner and conversation. Her opinions and the words in which she expressed them were the stock opinions and phraseology of the set in which she moved. She had a grace of carriage and manner acquired in the study of acting which were hardly yet perfect enough to appear natural. The brilliance of her fair hair and blue eyes were marred by a hint of weary cynicism and her mouth, of which she seemed perennially conscious, suggested a love of ease and a proneness to self-indulgence. She was an actress and seemed incapable of forgetting the fact, a type which Vereker found particularly irritating. Dr. Redgrave, on the other hand, was a man who would be impressive in any company. Six feet in height with broad, sloping shoulders and possessing a body which suggested the strength and quickness of a boxer, he looked every inch an athlete. His face, in contrast, was that of a thinker. Large grey eyes, long lashed and slumbrous, gazed with a curious innocent concentration from a shapely head which he carried with an air of quiet dignity. His manner was easy and unstudied and had the quick unconventionality of a man sure of himself and competent in everything he did. His open-hearted frankness at once disarmed suspicion and inspired confidence in Vereker who had an unshakable faith in first impressions.

After a lengthy discussion of the incident of Miss Stella's sudden disappearance, on which Miss Mayo was inclined to be tragic, Mrs. Mayo desultory, and Mrs. Cornell clear-headed, Dr. Redgrave glanced at the clock and addressing his hostess, remarked:

"Look here, Jo, it's getting late and I think the best thing in the circumstances is for me to call at the bungalow and see Cornell himself. He's sure to be terribly upset and I'll try and put him at ease. He'll want someone to talk to and he can get it off his chest on me though I'm not a great favourite with the gentleman. It'll possibly be a suitable occasion for improving our relations with one another, for I'm one of his sincere admirers though he possibly doesn't know it. What d'you think?"

"A good suggestion, Stanley. Tell him we've already got Inspector Heather on the girl's tracks, and as soon as we've found out where she is, I'll immediately go and see her. In the morning we'll either call or ring him up and let him have all the news. The inspector can 'phone up the police of the whole county and that's all that can possibly be done to-night."

"Good, and perhaps Mr. Vereker would like to accompany me," suggested the doctor.

"No, Mr. Vereker is going back at once to the inn to see the inspector," replied Mrs. Cornell, "but you could accompany him to the lodge and talk things over before you call at the bungalow. Will that meet the occasion?"

"Admirably," said the doctor and after bidding the ladies good night the two men left the Manor together.

They had only gone a few yards down the drive when the doctor broached the subject that was uppermost in his mind.

"I suppose, Mr. Vereker," he began, "you know all the ins and outs of this wretched business from the exhumation of John Cornell's body to the murder of his son, Frank?"

"I think I can say I've gathered in conversation and otherwise the general hang of the affair, doctor."

"Then I won't waste your time recapitulating. Carstairs has told you—I couple you with Inspector Heather—all about the unfortunate Tapp and my share in the business of bringing him to Marston. You haven't heard my version of the affair and I'm going to tell you briefly the part I played in it. I introduced Tapp into the Cornell household. He's what is called a germ-carrier. Now the whole question of germ-carriers, important though it is from the point of hygiene, can be over-stressed by the layman. Every doctor knows that about two per cent. of the whole population of the country are germ-carriers. I'm not going into any lengthy discussion of the problem with you because it's quite irrelevant to the present case. Tapp was a milk roundsman in Kingston some years ago when I was in practice there. An epidemic of cerebro-spinal fever was traced to him by certain experts who inquired into the origin of the epidemic. As to the validity of their findings I've nothing to say. What concerns me is that although I remember all the facts of the outbreak of the epidemic, none of my patients caught the disease and I never met the man Tapp in my life before he was brought to my notice by my housekeeper, Mrs. Jordan, who is his widowed sister. She heard that John Cornell was in search of a competent valet and asked me if I would use my influence to get her brother, who was a married man with a family dependent on him, the job. She told me his name was George Tapp but, as the epidemic at Kingston occurred some years ago, the name conveyed nothing to me. She naturally concealed his unfortunate history from me and in all innocence I recommended him to John Cornell. As it happens, John Cornell died of pneumonia—that was my professional opinion—and if it hadn't been for Carstairs' very indiscreet chatter to Frank Cornell about Tapp's history, the matter would have ended there."

"You're quite sure John Cornell didn't die of cerebro-spinal fever, Doctor?" asked Vereker.

"Perfectly certain—as certain as any human being can be. It's a difficult subject for a doctor to discuss with a layman, but pneumococcal meningitis may very closely resemble cerebro-spinal fever. I was fairly well acquainted with the latter and tested my patient for Kernig's sign which is one of the few reliable tests. I also made a lumbar puncture."

"What is Kernig's sign, Doctor?" asked Vereker feeling completely out of his depth at this juncture.

"To put it as plainly as I can, when a patient is propped up in bed in a sitting posture he is unable to straighten his legs. But these medical details are unnecessary. The presence of George Tapp, however, was unfortunate. My friendship with Mrs. Cornell which had ripened into love was the factor which made the whole affair doubly unfortunate. Whether Carstairs actually thought I'd devised a damned cunning method of getting rid of John Cornell so that I could marry his widow, I don't quite know. The suspicion probably entered his mind and he confided his knowledge of Tapp's history to Frank Cornell. Now Frank, lovable fellow though he was, could at times be an infernal idiot. He promptly suspected me of the crime of removing his father for my own ends, or rather, in a drunken mood, hinted at something of the sort to Miss Stella Cornell. You know the rest of the story."

"You and Carstairs didn't hit it off very well together, I believe?" asked Vereker.

"No; but that was not my fault. In the first place, when he discovered that Tapp, a germ-carrier, had been recommended by me to John Cornell as his valet, in fairness to me he ought to have come to me and had an open discussion about the matter. If my explanation had been at all unsatisfactory, he'd have been completely justified in carrying the matter farther. Instead of that he indiscreetly talks about it to an irresponsible fellow like Frank Cornell. Put yourself in my place and consider how you'd have felt in the circumstances. Even if there wasn't a fragment of basis for his suspicions, and there wasn't, the very discussion of it endangered my whole life and career. I was nearly driven mad with rage and anxiety. I tried hard to be fair but I found it devilish hard to be civil to Carstairs afterwards. Doubtless he's a good enough fellow but he's opinionated, lacks humour, and though a man of his type is capable of even heroic actions, he's equally capable of the blindest folly in acting on rigorous and unquestioned principles. Instead of losing my temper with him over the affair, I pretended to ignore it. I avoided discussing it with him; to have done so at this juncture would, I felt, have been professionally undignified and I hoped that an attitude of jocularity might meet the occasion. I was wrong. He resented my facetiousness and lost his temper altogether. We quarrelled openly and he left Marston this afternoon. It's the best thing he could have done: otherwise, I'd have been obliged to punch his head good and hearty."

After this outburst the doctor walked along in silence for some moments.

"There's another matter I'd like to thrash out with you now, Mr. Vereker," he continued at length. "There was some nonsense about missing keys to the music room and a missing automatic pistol of Mrs. Cornell's. I presume the importance attached to the keys arose from the fact that Frank Cornell was shot on the landing adjoining that room or in the room itself. If the point had been raised in my presence, I could at once have informed the inspector where the duplicate keys were. I knew that John Cornell had locked them up in a drawer in his bedroom. When I heard that they were in request, I promptly told Mrs. Cornell where they were. She asked me to get them. On going through the contents of the drawer, I also found the missing automatic pistol."

"We have an idea that the pistol which Mrs. Cornell kept in the music room might be the weapon the murderer used."

"Quite a legitimate supposition but it won't hold water now. In any case the type of weapon's a fairly common one though I don't think a man would use one."

"Which suggests that the murderer was a woman," remarked Vereker.

"It suggests nothing of the sort," quickly rejoined the doctor. "Such a pistol may have been the first weapon to hand in this case. A large-calibre automatic isn't a comfortable thing to carry and cannot be easily concealed on one's person or hidden after it has been used."

"Quite so," agreed Vereker, pleased with the doctor's shrewd reasoning.

"To revert to the music room. On the night of the tragedy I left the Manor by the music room door leading into the garden," continued the doctor calmly. "I was perhaps the last person to use the door prior to the murderer, if by chance he entered the house that way. This might throw suspicion on me. The question naturally presents itself, why should I leave the Manor by the music room door at that time of night? The front door was obviously my nearest way home and the conventional method of departure for a guest. I left the house by the music room door because I had to pay a professional call at the bungalow. Miss Stella Cornell wished to see me on an important matter concerning her health."

"I suppose it's quite out of bounds for me to ask the nature of her complaint?" asked Vereker frankly.

"In the ordinary course of things I should simply refuse to answer you, but I think present circumstances warrant my waiving strict professional etiquette. Miss Stella's sudden disappearance to-night made up my mind for me in the matter. Her action will certainly be construed by the police as very suspicious and they'll take steps to find out where she is and why she vanished. They'll most certainly discover her and I'm only anticipating events by telling you the reason for her departure. She asked me to call on her that night for a very grave reason. She believed she was pregnant and I merely confirmed her in her opinion. I presume, though I don't know, that Frank Cornell was the father of the child. That makes the incident of her leaving the bungalow perfectly intelligible. She has gone away to give birth to her child."

"Does her father know of her condition?" asked Vereker.

"That I can't say."

"Do you think she's a woman who might commit suicide in such a crisis, doctor?"

"My personal opinion is that she wouldn't, but in pregnancy, as you know, women are sometimes quite abnormal and one can't be dogmatic on such a point."

"I ask because Mrs. Cornell wants me to put the inspector on to making inquiries. She evidently fears that Miss Cornell may do something rash. Otherwise it might be the kindest thing to let the girl get over her trouble without harassing her."

"A sympathetic way of looking at the matter, but I think Mrs. Cornell knows what she's about. She and Miss Cornell are very intimate friends and you must use your own discretion after telling Inspector Heather of the real reason for her disappearance," replied the doctor.

"Very good," agreed Vereker and having reached the Manor lodge gate bade Dr. Redgrave good night.

He then made his way slowly to the "Dog and Partridge." His mind was reviewing with feverish activity all the happenings of a thoroughly eventful afternoon; his talk with Mary Lister which had confirmed Heather's information about her relations with the dead man and revealed the whereabouts of the only ginger tabby in Marston; his interview with Mrs. Cornell and her amazing production of the missing automatic pistol; the sudden disappearance of Miss Cornell and its ostensible cause as revealed by Dr. Redgrave. Carefully as he weighed up these factors in their relation to his investigation, they absolutely refused to surrender any definite light on his problem. At one moment the clue of the ginger tabby seemed fraught with the gravest importance, and on further analysis seemed to fade away into inconclusive insignificance. During his interview with Mrs. Cornell and subsequently with Doctor Redgrave, he had been very favourably impressed by their unequivocal directness and apparent truthfulness. Both had spoken about the tragedy and their own positions in relation to it as people quite above suspicion; they had given satisfactory explanations of those actions of theirs which might appear to an investigator as open to question and requiring elucidation. Again on reconsideration, they might be in a subtle conspiracy to prevent the discovery of their guilty participation in a crime. They both had sufficient motive for the removal of the unfortunate Frank Cornell, and they were both people of more than ordinary intelligence, capable of using a disarming frankness to mislead an investigator. Lastly, the disappearance of Stella Cornell which had momentarily seemed to inculpate her and declare her a fugitive from justice had been occasioned by a tragedy sufficiently serious to drive her from the narrow and censorious world of Marston-le-Willows. In a state of bewilderment and mild exasperation he arrived at the "Dog and Partridge" and at once sought out Inspector Heather. The latter was sitting smoking after his supper with an expression of complete satisfaction on his rotund, good-natured face. Looking up on Vereker's entry, he blew a cloud of smoke with quiet deliberation into the air and asked: "Well, Mr. Vereker, did you see the Madonna of the Manor?"

"I've seen everybody and heard everything, Heather; Mary Lister, Mrs. Cornell, Miss Mayo, Doctor Redgrave..."

"Sounds like Widdicombe Fair with Uncle Tom Cobley and all. Nice lady, Mrs. Cornell, don't you think?"

"Charming," replied Vereker flatly and thrusting his hand into his pocket he produced her miniature automatic pistol and flung it on the table. "That's her gun, if it interests you."

"Dear me, this is quite exciting," said the inspector as he picked up the pistol and extracted the magazine from the grip to see if it was loaded. Pulling back the ejector mechanism, he inserted a small piece of paper torn from the margin of *The East Anglian Times* into the breech and peered down the barrel. "Quite clean, but that doesn't tell us who first brewed beer. Who found the gun?"

"Doctor Redgrave. It was in the same drawer in which the duplicate keys to the music room were found."

"This doctor man's becoming more helpful to us every day. I don't know what we'd do without him."

"As far as I can see it's not the weapon we want," remarked Vereker.

"We'll try it out, but I don't think the bullet we've got will give us much information. Whoever fired the shot took care to pick up the ejected cartridge-case which might have told us more.

Anyhow, I'm fairly satisfied it's not the weapon we want. Any other surprising news items?"

"Miss Stella Cornell has done a bunk. Her father rang up the Manor while I was busy interviewing Mrs. Cornell. Miss Mayo took the message and told Mrs. Cornell in my presence."

"Yes, I've heard about that. Mr. Cornell sent his maid down to me and asked me to circularize the Suffolk police to see if they can trace her and bring her home. I've done that by 'phone, but I don't put much stress on her disappearance. I don't think the young lady is likely to go far, though, of course, one can't be certain if she had any hand in the murder of her lover."

"In my interview with Doctor Redgrave—we walked down the drive together—he told me that the young lady is in what is politely termed 'an interesting condition' and that she'd doubtless gone away somewhere where she's not known to get over her trouble in peace."

"That's important," replied Heather with the first excitement he had displayed during the conversation. "Do you know, I half-suspected something of the sort but couldn't be certain. I'd found out that the doctor had called at the bungalow about half-past ten on the night of the murder and I bluntly asked him why. He merely said it was a professional call and naturally I couldn't expect him to tell me the nature of it. I jumped to conclusions, however, and now things are really becoming clear. The dawn's breaking, Mr. Vereker."

"Do you think Miss Cornell killed her lover in a fit of anger or revenge?" asked Vereker eagerly.

"No, I don't, though that's quite possible."

"But how did she get hold of the pistol? Could she possibly have had access to Mrs. Cornell's?" For a moment Vereker sat bolt upright as his thoughts busily took a new trend and then, turning to the inspector, asked, "By Jove, Heather, could she have done it? Is there a conspiracy among all the people in the house that night to shield her?"

"That's a new suggestion," said Heather as if weighing up the possibility, "but I don't fancy the idea. In our interviews and examination we'd surely have found some discrepancy that would have given the show away. We'll bear it in mind nevertheless. I'm on another line and want to know where the pistol that shot Frank Cornell is."

"I wouldn't object to knowing that either," remarked Vereker somewhat disappointedly.

"Mrs. Cornell told me that her husband bought her pistol in Ipswich and I've had very searching inquiries made in that town," continued Heather. "I've found the gunsmith who sold the pistol to John Cornell, and at the same time I've discovered something far more important."

"What's that?" asked Vereker with renewed interest.

"That Mr. David Cornell accompanied him and also bought an exactly similar weapon at the same shop."

"Did he buy it for his daughter?" asked Vereker, surprised at this information.

"Presumably."

"Then Miss Cornell once more becomes a principal suspect," commented Vereker.

"I wouldn't say that. The existence of that second pistol throws suspicion on all three members of the bungalow; Mary Lister, Miss Cornell and Mr. David Cornell. I have tested Mary Lister by handing her the little automatic I lent you and on which we've got David Cornell's finger-prints. She clearly knows nothing about firearms and their use. Miss Cornell utterly refused to touch the gun. She had a woman's horror of pistols of any kind. You yourself discovered that David Cornell knows all about automatics. I've not told him I've found out that he bought a pistol in Ipswich some time ago, but I'll have a quiet talk to the old gent and bring the occurrence to his memory. I see possibilities in the interview."

"Things appear to be definitely on the move now, Heather, but I'm still all at sea. I was at first favourably impressed by

Mrs. Cornell and Doctor Redgrave, but if you discount mental impressions in sleuthing you must still keep these two people under suspicion. They may be very subtly hiding the fact that one or other of them committed the crime. The pistol Mrs. Cornell produced may be the weapon that was used. If so, it has, of course, been cleaned since. Its coming to light with such apparent innocence is a devilish clever bit of bluff if either Mrs. Cornell or the doctor is the culprit."

"There's such a thing as going too deeply into things, Mr. Vereker. Again and again in criminal investigation I've found that the simple explanation is the correct one. Unless a crime is premeditated and carried out by a super-clever criminal, the more obvious explanation is the one to back. The cold-blooded murderer is rarer than the impulsive one and the former is generally a bit cracked. Up to a point he works with amazing cunning and then commits the silliest blunder which eventually brings him to the gallows."

"Well, following your advice about the inmates of the bungalow, Miss Cornell is the star suspect. All three had access to the weapon. Your pistol tests with the two females may easily be wrong. A guilty person would naturally profess ignorance of the use of firearms. The cardinal factor that points to Miss Cornell is the clue of the ginger tabby. There's only one ginger tabby in Marston and it belongs to Mary Lister. On the afternoon preceding the murder she brought the cat up to the bungalow to let Miss Cornell see it. Miss Cornell fondled the animal. Mr. David Cornell hates cats and we can take it for granted that he didn't touch the tabby. Now, I discovered the hair of a ginger tabby cat on the settee in the music room. Who carried that hair? Either of the three people under discussion may have done so, but the odds are on Miss Cornell."

"Yes, but an odds-on favourite often fails to win the race. In my little gambling on the turf—I have a couple of bob occasionally on a 'sure thing'—I've found that the odds-on favourite is generally among the also ran. But it's getting late and I'm going to bye-bye. Good night, Mr. Vereker. I feel we're on the eve of great events as they say in the classics. I hope you won't dream of ginger tabby cats. It's a clue all right, but it wobbles all over the place instead of throwing a steady beam in any direction."

With these words the inspector rose and quietly left the room. For some time Vereker sat smoking and trying to evaluate Heather's information of David Cornell's purchase of another automatic pistol in Ipswich. It was now clear to him that Heather's suspicions were centred on the blind man, David Cornell. Though the inspector had said nothing about it, Vereker felt certain that before long Heather would make a surprise search of the bungalow in quest of that weapon. There was an air of satisfaction and confidence about the detective's manner with which Vereker was well acquainted. He knew by his remark about being on the eve of great events that the morrow would probably bring forth some startling developments in the Marston Manor mystery. At length he rose from his chair, went quietly up to his room, and before many minutes had elapsed was sound asleep.

Shortly after nine o'clock next morning Vereker called at Marston Manor as Mrs. Cornell had desired him to. Inspector Heather, in his customary way, had risen much earlier and set out immediately after breakfast on his own business. He had left no message for Vereker but the latter had a shrewd suspicion that he would visit David Cornell's bungalow and make a surprise search of the place. When Heather was feeling sure of his facts he lost no time in putting his thoughts into action. On arriving at the Manor, Vereker was at once shown into the drawing-room. There he found Miss Mayo nonchalantly puffing at a cigarette and glancing through the pages of a morning paper. A sheaf of correspondence through which she had waded lay in an untidy heap on the settee beside her.

"Good morning, Mr. Vereker," she said on the latter's entry into the room. "You're a bright and early bird this morning. I can scarcely call Mrs. Cornell a worm, but I suppose she's what you're after at this unholy hour."

"She asked me to turn up any time after nine, so here I am. I hope I'm not putting her to any inconvenience."

"Mrs. Cornell never lets anything inconvenience her, so you're all right. She's busy at the moment but the maid will tell her you're here and I daresay she'll be down shortly if you care to wait. I hope you will because in the interval I'd like to have a chat with you."

"I've nothing of any importance to tell her, but I think I'd better see her and let her know that the inspector has already instituted inquiries as to Miss Cornell's whereabouts."

"Please take a seat, Mr. Vereker, and let me talk. I've a bit of a confession to make and I want to get it off my mind. You know, of course, that I was Mr. Frank Cornell's fiancée?"

"Yes, I think it was fairly common knowledge in Marston."

"Marston always knows everything, even before it's published, but that's neither here nor there."

"To interrupt you, Miss Mayo, may I ask if Mrs. Cornell is being interviewed by the inspector?"

"Oh, no. She's closeted with her brother-in-law, Mr. David Cornell. He turned up here before breakfast and said he wanted to see her. Mrs. Cornell asked him to join us at breakfast, but he said he'd already had a meal. To pass the time he went into the music room and amused himself strumming on the piano. He calls it improvising, I believe, but it's mainly a regurgitation of other people's work. First a phrase from Beethoven followed by a bumpy hesitation on a couple of chords and then a snatch of Mozart or Dvorak, or any other mothy old composer. I told him one day that he should write his improvisations down and call them 'Unconscious Memory,' but he didn't like it and sat on me heavily. I daresay I deserved it; my tongue runs away with me at times. To revert to a most important person, myself, I hope you don't think I had any hand in this affair of Frank Cornell's death."

"You would hardly have sufficient motive, I should say," ventured Vereker in the hope of eliciting some information.

"No, just the reverse. By his death I've lost a very great deal indeed. I was passionately in love with him," continued Miss Mayo daintily applying a lace handkerchief to her eyes to remove the traces of swift emotion. "There might be jealousy, of course, but you can disregard that for Frank was simply crazy about me. The important thing with regard to myself was this. Apparently I was the last person to see and speak to him. The inspector so impressed me about the seriousness of my position that he nearly scared me out of my wits."

"But you've never possessed an automatic pistol?" asked Vereker immediately.

"Not of my own and this is where my confession comes in. Out of sheer funk I've hidden very weighty information from Mr. Heather. When I became engaged to Frank Cornell, I discovered I'd supplanted Miss Cornell in his affections. He'd often spoken to me of his cousin but he had never told me prior to our engagement that they had been lovers. This didn't upset me much because, after all, it's open to every one of us to change in matters of the heart. I was, of course, very sorry for Miss Stella, but I wasn't going to give up Frank on that account. I loved him body and soul and was determined to be his wife. Eventually he had to break the news to Miss Cornell and when he did so, I believe she flew into an uncontrollable passion and said she'd destroy me. I quote the word 'destroy' because it fairly put the wind up me. I must confess I'm a shocking coward, and when Frank told me the result of his interview, I almost decided to hand him over to my rival. A more courageous outlook followed and I said nothing further about the matter. Events took their course and apparently Miss Cornell became resigned to her fate. Then one day Frank confided in me that he had made a very strange discovery. He had been staying at the Manor, and one morning when on his way to the bungalow he heard several sharp explosions which echoed through the belt of woodland that lies just beyond the north wall of the garden. He wondered what was happening and entering the wood, quietly made his way in the direction from which the sounds had come. As he was proceeding very cautiously there was another sharp report close at hand and through the screen of undergrowth in the wood he saw Miss Cornell practising with a small automatic pistol. She was taking pot shots at an envelope she had pinned to one of the trees. He didn't make his presence known, and after a few more shots Miss Cornell removed her mark from the tree and returned to the bungalow. Frank seemed very much perturbed by this discovery. It was so unusual a thing for Miss Cornell to do, he said. At length he told me about it and remembering the lady's threat to destroy me, I quaked for days after. Although I was in London, I went about in fear and dread and never alone at night. When at last I was asked to come down to the Manor, you can imagine my feelings. It took Frank a long while to persuade me to accept his stepmother's invitation. I'll never forget the occasion when I first met Stella. Mrs. Cornell introduced us and Miss Cornell shot out her hand with a funny jerky manner she has. I simply leapt into the air and almost fainted when I came down again. I pretended on the spur of the moment that I had a spasm of lumbago. It was a bright inspiration and carried me over my embarrassment. But I'm digressing. After accepting Mrs. Cornell's invitation, I began to brood over possible consequences and in a few days looked positively fly-blown. I happened to meet an old friend of mine called Dick Cavenham. He's the actor; perhaps you've heard of him. Dick has always been more or less in love with me, but I couldn't possibly marry him. He hasn't a bean. Besides, he's getting very bald, sniffs objectionably, and won't wear socks suspenders. Still, he's a frightful dear. We lunched together and as I was aching for sympathy I told him my secret trouble. He was too sweet for words and ordered another bottle of fizz to cheer me up. He took a very grave view of the situation indeed and said by going to Marston I was simply walking into

the lion's den without as much as a hatpin as a weapon. I didn't
fancy a lion's den as a holiday resort, so I asked him what should
I do. He hinted that I ought to play for safety and give up Frank
to the cowgirl with the pop-gun. I told him that was out of the
question. I'd prefer to be chewed up by any number of lions rather
than give up the man I loved. This sounds rather melodramatic
for me but champagne always makes me feel as if I had a star part
at the Lyceum. The only other suggestion he could make was that
I also should carry a pistol. This didn't strike me as coruscant but
as neither of us could think of anything better, except my wearing
bullet-proof corsets, I fell in with the plan. Dick went back to his
flat and got me a property pistol he possessed. I asked him if it was
a dummy, but he assured me it was the real bumping-off article. I
took it and have carried it in my bag ever since."

Miss Mayo here picked up a bag from the settee and extracting
a small automatic pistol of Belgian manufacture handed it to
Vereker. Vereker examined the weapon carefully, noted that it was
a .22 calibre and was fully loaded.

"I think Inspector Heather will want to take charge of this
weapon for a few days, Miss Mayo," suggested Vereker.

"The dear man can have it for keeps if he wants to. Carrying it
about has raised a bunion on my smart new bag and to part with
it feels like giving away a cobra. I've been in mortal terror that
someone would ask me what was making my bag look as if it had
a lump of toffee stuck in its cheek. I couldn't very well whisper
hoarsely, 'A loaded pistol.' It's so un-English. It's different in the
States. There, it's almost as civilized to carry a gun as it is to have
false teeth or chew gum. To return to my subject, there's another
very important bit of news I have for you. When Mr. David Cornell
arrived this morning I was busy in my room tearing up all the
letters I had written Frank. Mrs. Cornell had given them back to
me the day before and I was running through them when there
was a knock and she and her brother-in-law came into my room.
After we had talked a while Mrs. Cornell and I went down to

breakfast and Mr. Cornell to the music room. Breakfast over, I thought I'd finish my job of destroying my correspondence and I was feeling broken-hearted over it, because those letters recalled so many happy moments and times I'd had with Frank, when among the last few letters in the bundle I came across a note which was not in my handwriting and which Frank had evidently thrust among them in a hurry. I glanced at the note to see what it was about and found that it was from Mr. David Cornell to Frank. It is dated on Friday afternoon and, as you know, Frank was shot on Friday night or early Saturday morning. The contents gave me a terrible shock for the note is just a brief affair saying that Mr. Cornell would meet Frank in the music room at midnight instead of Stella who was too unwell to keep the secret tryst she had made with him. He would give the usual signal with an electric torch. It begs him not to fail to attend because the writer has something of vital importance to communicate on behalf of his daughter."

"I hope you haven't destroyed the note, Miss Mayo?" exclaimed Vereker with excitement.

"No. I very nearly did so, but on thinking of the gravity of the contents, I kept it. You see, it means that Mr. David Cornell saw Frank after I did before he was murdered, and this completely alters my unhappy position in the business."

"Have you told anyone about this note? Mrs. Cornell, for instance?" asked Vereker.

"No; I only came across it a few minutes before you called. Mrs. Cornell and her brother-in-law were together in her private room and they've been there ever since. I came down here to the drawing-room immediately after I found it. I'd heard that you were expected, so I thought the best thing I could do was to tell you. It would be a serious matter for me if I concealed such important information from the authorities and I suppose you'll inform Inspector Heather."

"I think you decided wisely, Miss Mayo. To have destroyed the note or tried to suppress its contents in any way would have been criminal," replied Vereker with suppressed excitement and asked, "Can you let me see it?"

"Here it is, and you'd better take charge of it," said Miss Mayo producing the letter from her jumper pocket and handing it to Vereker, "but I think it only fair that you or I should tell Mrs. Cornell all about it, don't you?"

"No; for the time being I must ask you to keep the matter very strictly to yourself. To tell Mrs. Cornell wouldn't help matters in any way. She has enough to think about just now without our adding further to her worries. You'll see the necessity for discretion when you reflect that the note may have no bearing whatever on the tragedy of Mr. Frank Cornell's death. At first glance it puts Mr. Cornell in a very serious position. We'll have to see him about the matter and ask him if he had the interview with his nephew which he asks for in the note. The appointment may have been cancelled subsequently and doubtless Mr. Cornell will be able to give us a perfectly satisfactory explanation of the whole affair. The less the matter is discussed at the present juncture, the better for all concerned. I think you'll see I'm right in taking such a line, Miss Mayo."

"Of course, you know best and I'll leave the matter entirely in your hands. I only hope I won't be brought too prominently into the affair."

"No one need know how the note came into our possession for that matter," replied Vereker, eager to assuage Miss Mayo's rather lively apprehensions as to the correctness of her own conduct. "In the meantime, keep your own counsel and I think you'll find that matters will adjust themselves all right."

Vereker had hardly spoken these words when a maid knocked, entered, and said that Mrs. Cornell was now free and would like to see Mr. Vereker. Following her out of the room, Vereker dismissed her at the foot of the stairs leading to the first floor, telling her that he knew his way to Mrs. Cornell's private sitting-room. He then quickly ascended the thickly-carpeted stair to the half-landing on to which the music room opened and to his surprise noticed that the door was ajar. As he passed he instinctively glanced into the room and saw that it was occupied. Against the light of the far window was silhouetted the figure of a man bending over the settee on which Vereker had found his treasured clue of the cat's hair. Instantly Vereker recognized the figure as that of David Cornell and, struck by the man's unusual attitude, halted, and was on the point of greeting him. The impulse died as soon as it was born and he stood as if uncertain what to do. Evidently Cornell, intent on his own business, had failed to hear his approach. After carefully running his hand over the cretonne cover of the settee as if to smooth it out, the blind man stood erect and walked over to the door leading from the music room into the garden. Tentatively extending his hand, he touched the door, sought and found the door handle, and quietly let himself out on to the flight of steps which descended to the wide gravel path. At once Vereker, instead of going up to Mrs. Cornell's study, entered the music room and decided to follow Cornell. He allowed his man to get some distance ahead and then stepping on to the grass verge, so that his approach could not be heard, went slowly in pursuit. Though Cornell did not carry the usual stick as a guide, he walked with considerable pace and assurance. Use had evidently taught him every inch of his way and without faltering he proceeded into the formal garden and came to a halt beside the lily pool. There, he thrust his hand into the pocket of his jacket, produced something and flung it with great judgment into the pool. Vereker's eye followed the trajectory of that mysterious object, heard the splash of its entry into the water, and saw the circular ripples extend till they broke and vanished into the floating raft of lily leaves around. Quickly stepping on to the gravel path, he walked briskly towards Cornell who almost instantly heard his approach and turned round.

"Good morning," said the blind man and waited to discover who the oncomer might be.

"Good morning, Mr. Cornell," replied Vereker.

"Ah, I think I recognize the voice. Aren't you the *Daily Report* correspondent?"

"Quite correct," said Vereker, "I thought it was you in the distance, but I wasn't quite certain. I merely wanted to ask you if I might call at the bungalow some time to-day."

"Do so by all means. I'm afraid I shall be busy all afternoon and I dine at seven o'clock. Would you care to drop in about eight or is that too late for you?"

"That'll suit me admirably, thank you," said Vereker. "I'm in a great hurry at the moment. I have an appointment with Mrs. Cornell and I'm already rather late. *Au revoir.*"

With these words Vereker turned and made his way back to the house at a double. Entering the music room, he crossed at once to the settee and ran his hands all over its surface. Then he thrust them into the interstice between the cushioned seat and the back. Almost at once his right hand came in contact with something hard and irregular which he carefully extracted between his finger and thumb. It was a nickel-plated automatic pistol of .22 calibre. Taking a small cardboard box (an article he always carried as part of his investigator's equipment) from his pocket, he dropped the pistol into it. Returning the box to his pocket, he swiftly left the room and ascended the stairs to Mrs. Cornell's private sitting-room.

"Good morning, Mr. Vereker," said Mrs. Cornell with a pleasant smile. "I sent the maid for you ten minutes ago."

"I must apologize, Mrs. Cornell," interrupted Vereker, "but on my way upstairs I saw Mr. David Cornell leave the house by the music room. I wished to speak to him on rather an important matter, so I overtook him and made an appointment for this evening."

"Is that all? I thought you were unable to tear yourself away from Miss Mayo. She's rather lovely and I think you're impressionable."

"If that were the case, Mrs. Cornell, I would have dashed upstairs ten minutes ago," replied Vereker boldly.

"You're an impudent flatterer as well as a smart detective," replied Mrs. Cornell genially. "Have you any news of Miss Cornell for me?"

The inspector has put the search machinery into motion, but so far we haven't heard any news of her.

"Did Doctor Redgrave unburden himself to you last night?" asked Mrs. Cornell.

"Very frankly. He has been extremely obliging and helpful."

"That's his nature; he can't help himself. Did you learn anything about the professional secret that was mentioned yesterday in our talk?"

"Yes, he decided that it was his duty to tell us an important fact about Miss Cornell which in other circumstances he wouldn't have divulged on any account. It explains the girl's disappearance and helps to clear away suspicion that she has vanished from criminal motives."

"So I thought, too, but it afterwards struck me that it added weight to the question of motive for revenge. Still, I'm glad you feel satisfied on the point. You'll let me know at once when you get in touch with her. I'm beginning to feel very anxious as to what she might do."

"I'll ring you up from the village post office as soon as we get any news, Mrs. Cornell, and if there's nothing else I can do at the moment, I'll get back at once to Marston."

"There's nothing else, thanks, Mr. Vereker. Don't let me detain you a moment longer. I'm frightfully busy, too, and half the morning's gone already."

"There's one little item I've forgotten to mention, Mrs. Cornell. Would you mind if I removed the old-fashioned lock on the door leading into the music room from the half-landing? I'll take it away with me and replace it in a day or so."

"Take the whole door with you, Mr. Vereker," replied Mrs. Cornell with a laugh. "But what on earth do you want that lock for? We've got duplicate keys if that's what you're after."

"It's another professional secret and the inspector would be furious if I divulged it now," replied Vereker smiling.

"Please don't upset the inspector on any account," said Mrs. Cornell rising. "I'm getting quite intrigued with your detective methods. What with ginger tabbies and old-fashioned locks it sounds like something of Mr. Lewis Carroll's. I hope you'll tell me all about these mysterious things when you've found the culprit and finished with the case."

"If you're really serious, Mrs. Cornell, I should very much like to," replied Vereker.

"Now that's very nice of you. You said the words so sincerely, Mr. Vereker. Just drop me a line or ring me up and we'll fix up things. Only later on you must come and stay with Stanley and me. I shall be leaving the Manor after a certain happy event, but I'll post you our new address without fail."

Thanking Mrs. Cornell for her invitation, Vereker let himself out of the study and at once descended to the music room. Producing a screwdriver from his pocket, he set to work and very carefully detached the old-fashioned lock from the door. This lock he at once wrapped up with meticulous care in several sheets of paper and, carrying it as if it were a delicate piece of porcelain, left the Manor at his fastest walking pace. He arrived at the "Dog and Partridge" breathless with haste and excitement and inquired of the landlord if Inspector Heather had returned. Learning that Heather was in his room, Vereker at once dashed upstairs and entered without even the ceremony of knocking. Heather, who was carefully brushing his hair before going down to lunch, turned round in his slow manner and looked at Vereker.

"What's up, Mr. Vereker. You look like a pack of hounds in full cry. Anything really important?" he asked and, laying down his hairbrushes on the dressing-table, picked up a screwdriver from beside them and quickly put it in his pocket.

"Now, Heather, what's that mysterious object you've surreptitiously slipped into your pocket?" asked Vereker with a smile lighting up his eager face.

"Only my old screwdriver," replied Heather, producing the tool once more and returning it to his pocket. "I never go anywhere without it. It's as good a pal as my old pipe and doesn't smell."

"You won't need it in this case, Heather," replied Vereker looking mysteriously at the inspector who, observing his friend's unusual expression and the parcel held carefully in his left hand, exclaimed eagerly: "You don't mean to tell me you've got the lock to the music room door, Mr. Vereker? I was going up after lunch to get it myself."

"You've guessed right first time, Heather. This parcel contains that lock. From your guess I realize that great minds think alike. We're both on the trail at last!"

"This is really first-rate, Mr. Vereker, absolutely first-rate," said the inspector with gusto. "I hope you've been most careful in detaching it."

"You couldn't have been more careful yourself. After all, Heather, I detached the lock for the same reason as prompted you to the job. Time is essential and to avoid wasting it I risked anticipating you. It's wrapped in several sheets of paper and I've carried it as gingerly as if it were an auk's egg."

"Good, Mr. Vereker. I congratulate you. Shake on it!" said Heather.

The inspector extended his brawny fist and wrung Vereker's hand with painful heartiness. "But lunch is ready," he added, "and I'm really thirsty for once in my life. Let's go downstairs and discuss things thoroughly. First let me put that lock carefully away and then I'll be able to do justice to the grub. It's boiled beef and carrots, of which I'm passionately fond."

Chapter Fourteen
The End of the Trail in Sight

Now, Mr. Vereker," said Heather after they had finished lunch and had lit cigars over coffee and liqueurs, which had been ordered to emphasize the importance of the occasion, "You seem to have had a hectic morning. Let's hear all about it."

"In the first place, Heather, I saw Miss Mayo when I called at the Manor. Mrs. Cornell was having a pow-wow with Mr. David Cornell in her private sitting-room, so while I was waiting for an interview, the young lady entertained me in the drawing-room. After declaring she had no hand in the crime, Miss Mayo confessed she possessed a small automatic pistol and asked me to hand it over to you as a keepsake. Here it is," said Vereker and passed the weapon to the inspector.

"Very kind of her. I'll be able to start a gunsmith's shop when I've finished with this case," remarked Heather without emotion and, after a casual glance at the pistol, thrust it in his pocket. "Why did she carry it?" he asked.

"She was afraid of Miss Stella Cornell, who once in a fit of jealous temper threatened to destroy her. She discovered subsequently through Frank Cornell that Miss Cornell had been practising with an automatic in the wood beyond the Manor grounds and decided when she came on a visit to Marston to be ready for retaliation should her rival attempt to carry out her threat. To cut a long story short, she found that Miss Cornell's threat was just the idle threat that anyone might make in a fit of anger. The pistol is fully loaded, so be careful with it. Then she coughed up a really vital bit of information. Accidentally tucked away among the letters she had written to Frank Cornell during their courtship, she found this note from David Cornell to his nephew. It had evidently been put there by the dead man in mistake."

Vereker produced the note and handed it to the inspector who read it very carefully.

"This is the goods, Mr. Vereker," he said; "it bears out my suspicions to the letter. When I first suspected and then became almost certain what Miss Cornell's real trouble was, I naturally put her on the black list. After speaking to the girl and then to her father and hearing what the latter thought of Frank Cornell, I wrote him down as a more likely culprit. When roused he's a man of violent temper and very resolute. The great difficulty in his case was to discover how he, being blind, could have used a pistol with such deadly effect. This I overcame in the same manner as you have overcome it, but we'll discuss that point later. Anything else of importance from Miss Mayo?"

"No; our interview ended by the maid entering and saying Mrs. Cornell had finished her talk with her brother-in-law and was free to see me. I dismissed the maid and went upstairs alone. As I passed the music room door I was surprised to see it half-open. I glanced in as I was about to pass and there I saw our friend David Cornell leaning somewhat mysteriously over the settee. I couldn't imagine what he was doing and stood for a moment watching him. He left the settee, crossed the room, and passed down into the garden. Being a bit inquisitive, I followed him. Also I'd decided to ask for an appointment so that either you or I might discuss the contents of that note with him. I followed him as far as the lily pool, keeping on the grass verge so that he couldn't hear me. To my astonishment he stopped at the pool, took something from his pocket, and flung it into the water."

"Did you see what it was?" asked Heather with puckered brow.

"No, but we can wade in this afternoon and fish it out," replied Vereker.

"I wonder if it was his automatic pistol," said Heather.

"I'm certain it wasn't that," replied Vereker.

"Possibly a third set of keys to the music room. I hunted up all the locksmiths in the neighbourhood and eventually found that Cornell had ordered a third set in Bury and that Miss Cornell had called and paid for them. As a matter of fact, the young lady wanted a set for her own special use after the duplicate set had been returned to Mr. John Cornell. She managed to get a loan of No. 1 set for the purpose of getting No. 3. Mr. Frank borrowed them for her as far as I could ascertain."

"So nobody in the Manor itself knew of the existence of a third set except the dead man?"

"Exactly, but go on with your yarn, Mr. Vereker."

"After Cornell had passed the lily pool, I stepped on to the gravel path and followed him. He heard me at once and waited till I overtook him. I fixed up an appointment for eight o'clock this evening and hurried back to the house. Passing through the music room, it suddenly flashed across my mind to examine the settee. I wondered what Cornell had been doing at that spot. I pushed my hand into the niche between the seat and the back and found this, Heather. I'm sure you'll be interested in it," said Vereker, producing a cardboard box and giving it to the inspector.

"Great Scott, we've got the damned thing at last!" exclaimed Heather with real emotion when he opened the box and saw the automatic pistol which Vereker had withdrawn from its hiding place in the settee. "An experiment or two will probably tell us that this is the weapon that fired the bullet I've got in my possession."

"But before we go any farther, Heather, there's one point that worries me. Why on earth should David Cornell want to hide his pistol in the settee and fling the keys in the pool? Why not fling both into the pool together? There seems something fishy about this to me."

"Both the music room and the pool have been most thoroughly searched and are therefore the safest places in the world to hide dangerous articles in," commented Heather. "The odds were a million to one against our searching them again. We had done the job thoroughly and the local police had done it fairly comprehensively before us. As for hiding the pistol in the music room and the keys in the pool, the explanation is obvious. Cornell didn't want to lose the pistol altogether. He could recover it easily enough after the trouble had blown over. The keys he evidently wanted to get rid of for good and all."

"A neat piece of reasoning, Heather. I didn't think of it and hand you the biscuit. To return to the bullet that was extracted from the dead man's skull, I presume you'll fire another shot from Cornell's pistol and have the two bullets examined under a comparison microscope?"

"That'll be one of the tests, Mr. Vereker, but there'll be several others. Fortunately the weapon hasn't been cleaned and if there are minute particles of metal in the barrel, they'll agree in chemical composition with that of the bullet. But now we come to that conspicuous groove on the bullet. You've an idea what caused that groove?"

"Yes, Heather, it was not caused by coming in contact with, say, the orbital bone of the dead man; the bullet, as we know, didn't touch the bone surrounding his eye. I thought a lot about that, and when I hit on a theory showing how a blind man might hit his mark with such deadly effect, the point was at once as clear as day. It finally flashed on me that one way a blind man could shoot and hit his mark in the eye was through a keyhole. At first the idea seemed a bit far-fetched, but on closer examination it began to fit all the facts of the case with remarkable appropriateness. The old-fashioned lock of the music room door has a large keyhole. I thrust my pencil through it on my first visit to the Manor and found that the pencil passed quite comfortably through the circular portion of the aperture. As you remarked earlier in our investigation, an ordinary lead pencil is a quarter of an inch in diameter and therefore a .22-calibre bullet could pass through the circular hole of the aperture if the pistol barrel was in good alignment. In our case the barrel wasn't held in quite dead alignment, and the metal of the lock tore a small groove out of the bullet during the latter's passage."

"Astonishingly good, Mr. Vereker. We agree in our findings all along the line. The reason I was anxious about your being careful in detaching the lock was that I didn't want to lose the particles or metal torn from the bullet in its journey through the keyhole. There will also be particles of unconsumed cordite in the lock if a shot was fired through it. Once we're definitely satisfied that a shot was fired through the keyhole of the music room door, we'll both be convinced, I think, that Mr. David Cornell fired the shot. I'll run up to London this afternoon with that lock and put it in the hands of our expert microscopist and he'll settle the point once and for all. If things are as we expect them to be, it'll be high time to think of handcuffs."

"If David Cornell fired the shot, Heather, I wonder exactly how he managed to induce Frank Cornell on the other side of the door to put his eye to the keyhole?" asked Vereker reflectively.

"That point has occupied my mind, too," replied Heather. "There must have been some secret arrangement between Miss Stella Cornell and her lover to show she had arrived at the trysting place. They would obviously avoid creating noise from fear of waking a light sleeper on the corridor above or rousing the attention of anyone who might be awake. Still, it would be almost instinctive for Frank Cornell to peep through the keyhole to see if he could see, say, a human silhouette against the window opposite the door. Miss Cornell would doubtless put her father up to any secret arrangement. The blind man's very acute hearing would tell him quite definitely that Frank Cornell on the other side of the door had stooped to look through. In any case, it's a minor point and might be achieved in a dozen ways. We'll possibly hit on the method employed later on."

"What made you first suspect David Cornell, Inspector?" asked Vereker.

"I felt I was on the scent after my first interview with him, and when you related the points of your conversation with him that had struck you as strange, I began to have a livelier suspicion. Though he had apparently not visited the Manor after the murder, he had an almost uncanny knowledge of every detail of its execution, say, as you or I would figure it out after close observation. He made a disastrous slip when he mentioned to you an automatic pistol as the weapon used when only you and I and Doctor Redgrave knew that fact from the bullet that had been extracted. He tried to cover his slip neatly, but it was obvious he was covering up. Then he had a theory that the body had been dragged upstairs, based on the assumption that the murderer was trying to hide the place of execution. This was a ruse on the murderer's part to conceal the manner of entrance so as to hide the possession of missing keys. All this knowledge, Mr. Vereker, is not acquired by mere thinking; it can only be acquired by someone with long experience, a trained observation, and natural aptitude—ahem—like ourselves. I at once put it down as the astute criminal's usual bluff. I've met that kind of gent before and know him when he turns up again. From that moment I put him down as my chief suspect and though I was always open to change my mind, events only began to confirm me in my opinion. The method of firing the shot baffled me for a long while and then I remembered a very sordid case some years ago in which a young woman who lived in a west-end boarding house blinded one of the male lodgers by thrusting a knitting needle through the keyhole in her bedroom door. The young man was evidently a descendant of Peeping Tom and the girl had discovered his nasty habit of looking at her when he didn't oughter. This suggested to me that even a blind man could hit his mark if there was something to guide his pistol. The keyhole was the next deduction, and I was about to go and take that lock off the music room door to-day, when I found you'd struck the same solution. I must say you've had all the fat bits in this case; Redgrave's information about Miss Cornell; Miss Mayo's discovery of that damning note; and, finally, David Cornell's own pistol which you practically saw him stow away in the music room settee."

"I think it's the first time we've arrived at the same solution by the same line of reasoning, Heather. It all sounds so jolly convincing that I fear a snag somewhere," remarked Vereker with a smile.

"Yes, it's the first time we've solved a mystery on the same lines. Of course you've improved out of all recognition under my hand, but this time you've been masterly, Mr. Vereker. We must celebrate our success on our return to London. Again, it's the first time we've worked so closely together, which means you were almost bound to adopt the right course from the start. But there's something worrying you, laddie. Tell me what it is and I'll put you right."

"The clue of the ginger tabby doesn't quite fit in with all our beautiful deductions and intuitions, Heather. Cornell had nothing to do with Lister's cat. How did the hair get on the settee?"

"In a thousand different ways, Mr. Vereker. One of the men employed by the Vacuum Cleaning Company probably breeds ginger tabbies for profit, but I refuse to discuss any kind of cat at this hour. I must get a move on. With furious driving I can get to London with that lock, do my business, and be back here by, say, eight or nine o'clock to-night."

"Good. I'll await your return with impatience. I've got an appointment with Cornell at eight and if things turn out as we expect them to, I daresay you'll also call at the bungalow on getting back to Marston."

"If you're not here when I turn up, I'll follow on, Mr. Vereker. What are you going to do in the meantime?"

"Kick my heels. By the way, is there any news of Miss Stella Cornell's whereabouts, Heather?"

"You want an excuse to go and see the auburn-haired beauty at the Manor, eh? I must disappoint you. There's no news whatever beyond the fact that Miss Cornell caught a train to London from Bury early that afternoon. She's doubtless in London, and I don't see much use in worrying her in her present trouble. *Au revoir.*"

*

On Heather's departure Vereker went up to his room and to pass the time took out his case-book and began to write a full account of the tragedy at Marston Manor and a detailed précis of his own work on the case. Having completed this, he sat down in an easy chair, took out a volume of Emerson from his suitcase and fell fast asleep over it. He awoke at five o'clock and was just about to descend to the inn's private room for tea, when a loud knock sounded on his door and made him jump to his feet. He opened the door to find the landlord standing outside.

"Doctor Redgrave would like to see you at once," said Abner Borham. "He wanted to see the inspector but I told him Mr. Heather had gone to London and wouldn't be back till nine o'clock. He then asked if he might see you."

"I'll come down right away," replied Vereker and following the landlord was shown into the private room in which Heather and he had taken their meals during their stay at the "Dog and Partridge."

"Good afternoon, Vereker," said the doctor as soon as Borham had closed the door. "I've got rather serious news for you. I wanted to see Inspector Heather, but as soon as he arrives you can pass it on to him. David Cornell has committed suicide, cut his throat from ear to ear with a razor, one of the old pattern which we now call a cut-throat. Young Mary Lister went to his study to tell him his tea was ready and found the man dead in his armchair. She kept her head and 'phoned for me, but, of course, I could do nothing. He must have been dead before Lister discovered him."

"Terrible business. I'm sorry for his friends and relatives," replied Vereker recovering swiftly from the shock the news had given him.

"Yes, but this open letter which he typed and left with the superscription 'To those whom it may concern,' makes the whole affair infinitely more terrible. You'd better read it and hand it along to the inspector. It will interest you both. I must now get back at once to the Manor. Mrs. Cornell is in a state of collapse and I must attend to her. I'll possibly see you and the inspector later. I'll be at the Manor till about ten o'clock to-night. So long."

With these words the doctor hurried away and Vereker, after ordering tea, sat down and read the letter which Doctor Redgrave had left with him. It ran:

TO THOSE WHOM IT MAY CONCERN

I, David Cornell of the Bungalow, Marston-le-Willows, am about to commit what is usually termed *felo de se*. I'm not insane and I hope the coroner won't pass the usual kindly but erroneous verdict that I committed suicide during temporary insanity. The reason for my act is that I feel that the investigation now being carried out by Inspector Heather of Scotland Yard is drawing to a close and that I shall be hanged for shooting my nephew, Frank Cornell. I hereby frankly admit I was the person who shot him and confess I don't in the least regret having done so. The man was an unprincipled and heartless libertine who has ruined the life of my only daughter. My daughter loved him and taking advantage of her weakness he seduced her. Even if he had made reparation by marriage, I couldn't have forgiven him, for he was the last man on earth I would have chosen for her husband. He had, however, no intention of marrying her and when she pressed him to do so to cover her shame, for she is going to be a mother, he simply informed her he was engaged to another woman. As there is no redress at law for this kind of thing which, to my mind, is worse than murder, I took the law into my own hands. For the satisfaction of the inspector who has charge of the case, I state that I made a secret appointment with Frank Cornell in the music room of Marston Manor. He arrived at the appointed hour of twelve o'clock. I chose this rendezvous because he and my daughter used to meet there secretly when they were lovers, but principally because the only plan I could devise for shooting the man in a vital spot was through some aperture to which I could induce him to place his eye. This I managed to do by not answering the prearranged signal which he and my daughter employed when they were in the habit of trysting in the music room. To ascertain what was happening in the room he naturally put his eye to the keyhole. I heard his movements and judging the time accurately, I fired. He simply groaned and fell and I knew I'd accomplished what I had set out to do. Prior to killing Frank Cornell, I had thought out matters and had no intention of paying the penalty fixed by law for such. I intended to drag the man upstairs into his own room and leave him there so as to hide the fact that he had been shot through the keyhole of the music room door. I had partially effected this when I heard movements in one of the bedrooms on the first floor corridor and hastily made my departure. This miscarriage of my plan, however, was immaterial. Other factors such as bloodstains, the finding of the weapon, the tracing of its purchase, and so forth, were bound to enter into the business, and as I was prepared to kill myself rather than be tried and hanged, I did not carry out measures for escape from suspicion with any degree of thoroughness. I had a sporting chance of escape, and as long as the method of the shooting was undiscovered, my blindness was to a great extent a safeguard against my being suspected. This morning, however, I found out that I was discovered by Mr. Vereker who works in collaboration with his friend, Inspector Heather. I had just had an interview with Mrs. Cornell, and was leaving the Manor by the music room. Knowing that that room had been thoroughly searched by the police, I had just hidden the automatic with which I had committed the crime with the intention of recovering it at a later date, when I heard someone pass heavily on the half-landing. I guessed it was Mr. Vereker because he had an appointment with my sister-in-law, but feeling fairly certain that he hadn't looked into the music room, I quietly let myself out into the garden. There, to my surprise, I was overtaken by Mr. Vereker who made an appointment to meet me at eight in my bungalow. I had just thrown the secret set of keys to the music room, which I possessed, into the lily pool and I began to fear that he had seen me. After Mr. Vereker had left me, I had an impulse to return and recover my automatic, but by this time I was seized with panic and lost my head. I was fairly certain that before long Inspector Heather would make a surprise search of my bungalow so that it would have been foolish to take the weapon back with me. Again, Mr. Vereker might wait in the music room and catch me red-handed in the act of recovering it from the settee, should I attempt to do so. I decided to leave it there. During the afternoon I made some excuse to my sister-in-law for calling on her again and when passing through the music room, I took the opportunity of satisfying myself that my pistol was still where I had hidden it. To my horror, I discovered that it was gone and also that the lock had been removed from the door leading on to the half-landing. This was definite proof to me that the agents of the law knew that I had shot Frank Cornell and that my arrest was only a matter of hours.

At this point, without any of the usual expressions of regret to family, relatives and friends for the pain he would inflict on them by his suicide, the letter came to an end. Vereker with a sigh of relief folded it up, returned it to its covering envelope and thrust it in his pocket. There was nothing to do now but await Inspector Heather's return from London. As far as he himself was concerned, Vereker felt no further interest in the case. That portion of the investigation which always held such a fascination for him was ended, and as he sat smoking and alone in the private room of the inn, a depressing reaction to his days of keen excitement set in. He had a strong distaste for the ceremony of inquests and that function was before him and unavoidable. He looked forward to the next few days with a sense of dreary resignation. There was, he felt, one antidote to this feeling of dejection and that was exercise. Rising quickly to his feet, he left the room, thrust on his hat and, taking his stick, set forth.

As he walked along his thoughts reverted to the tragedy which had followed tragedy in the Marston Manor case and turned especially to the unhappy figure of David Cornell who had played so important a role in it. This was no sordid crime for gain like so many of the murders which he had investigated. It was not a crime of passion though human passion had been the seed from which it had sprung. It arose from the sense of frustrated justice of an intelligent and rather estimable man. He had loved his only child and that child had, in his opinion, been betrayed by a libertine. He had failed through his deep affection for her to view the matter in a judicial light. After all, she was a mature woman, competent to look after herself. She must have been a consenting party to her own downfall. In these days of equality of the sexes her position would be viewed from a different angle to that of past and more sentimental times when a woman was regarded as a weak and helpless creature, incapable of safeguarding her own interests and at the mercy of any designing and unscrupulous male. Yet Vereker could not help feeling sorry for both the girl and her father. Human beings were still creatures of instinct and emotion and they acted on those instincts and emotions rather than on reason. Reason was generally employed very efficiently by those who assessed their fellows' conduct from a detached and aloof point of view. It had to be employed officially by a judge in spite of all his understanding of the weakness of mankind and the irrationality of action based on strong emotion.

After an hour's walking the texture of Vereker's thoughts changed quietly, almost imperceptibly. His eyes, which had been flitting from one object to another without conscious observation or had been fixed blandly on the broad, well-kept road which he traversed, now began to take an interest in the beautiful Suffolk landscape round him. This was the Constable country and was still utterly unchanged and unspoilt. In this district of Marston there were no electric pylons to point out the march of time and change of manner of a people's living. Suffolk was, as someone had so aptly called it, "The Unknown County." Progress in life, if it could be called progress, had been so rapid that the artist's eye had only in very recent years begun to detach visual beauty from associated ideas bearing on a hundred other basic emotions. Only recently had the artist turned to industrial scenes, to smoke and chimneys and machinery to catch their beauty and express it as part of the beauty of contemporary life, of another era in history. To Vereker, at this moment, there came a violent reaction to an older school of painting, and the wide sweep of sweet agricultural landscape, its placidity and charm appealed with the sudden thrill of a new discovery. A windmill on a rise caught his eye, the intersecting lines of hill and dale adjusted themselves into a pattern. Above the landscape the cloud masses swung in sympathy with the general scheme. He drew a sketch-book from his pocket and began to make a rough outline of his composition. The detective's craze for investigation had vanished; he had returned to his life-long passion for painting. His one desire now was to see the close of the Marston case, to get his artist's gear together and forget that such a thing as crime existed.

It was dark when he returned to the "Dog and Partridge," physically tired but mentally refreshed. He found Heather in the little room just about to sit down to his evening meal.

"Well, Heather," he said, "I suppose you've heard the news. It's all over."

"Yes," replied the inspector in his matter-of-fact way, "it's all over, as you say, but it's not the kind of finish I like to see to a case. Most disappointing!"

"You came back with handcuffs ready for use, I presume. What happened about the music room lock?"

"Turned out according to plan. We were right; the shot had been fired through the large keyhole and the expert was amazed that it had been so effective. Still, it was, and an unlucky shot for Mr. Frank Cornell. But I like a case where you can finish up with a dramatic arrest, a sensational trial and a healthy hanging. There's always a sense of satisfaction in putting the darbies on your man. It would have been a most unpleasant job for me to arrest the blind man, though, of course, I'd have had to do it. It's not for me to go into the rights and wrongs of the affair, but I had a sneaking regard for Mr. David Cornell. Put yourself in his shoes and try to think how you'd have felt."

"I've been doing that all afternoon, Heather, and I'm not going to think about it any more. When all's said and done his suicide has saved a lot of trouble and another famous trial. There are several points in this amazing case that still bother me, but it's hardly worth discussing them now."

"I agree," said Heather. "The man was extremely intelligent, but he did some of the most foolish things a man can do if he wants to dodge the police."

"For instance?" asked Vereker.

"Why on earth did he write a note making an appointment with Frank Cornell? Unless he could retrieve the note subsequently it was almost bound to be discovered."

"That struck me, too," said Vereker. "It rather amazed me at the time that he could write a note at all, but that was only my ignorance. I tried it out myself with eyes shut and my note was perfectly legible. As he himself says in his final confession, he felt that discovery was almost certain and didn't trouble over much to guard against it. He knew that modern methods of detection make a murderer's escape more difficult every day and he was prepared to die by his own hand should Fate go against him. The concealment of the pistol in the music room also seemed to me to be too bold a move to be safe, and his discussion of the whole case looked like the procedure of a man deliberately trying to sail as near the wind as possible for the fun of running risks."

"When I first guessed the nature of Miss Cornell's trouble, I nearly swung off the track by considering Carstairs a likely," said Heather. "His motive was a strong one, for a man, madly in love with a girl— but there, it's no use discussing the matter farther. It's all over now."

"I'm rather glad it ended as it has. As soon as the inquests are over and the whole business finished with, I'm going back to London to get my painting gear and then return to Marston-le-Willows. This country appeals to me; there's magic in it."

"Yes," agreed Heather, "there are worse places in the world. When I retire I wouldn't mind settling down here. Then I could get down to chicken farming seriously. Murders distract a man when he's busy with an incubator in the spring. But it's getting late and there's a lot to be done. I'm going to the bungalow and then on to Marston Manor. Perhaps you'd like to come with me?"

"Right ho!" said Vereker. "I may as well see the business through to the bitter end. Besides, I can keep you from wandering into things and places that don't concern you."

"What about a pint before we start?" asked Heather brightly, as if the idea was a flash of inspiration.

"We'll have that when we come back. We'll possibly need it after what we've got to go through," replied Vereker firmly and together the two men left the "Dog and Partridge" and walked briskly up the main road.

Chapter Fifteen
The Last Word

It was a lovely morning in May of the following year. Anthony Vereker had walked down Bond Street into Piccadilly and had turned into the Green Park. London under the magical, generative touch of early summer was to him the most beautiful and romantic place in the world. As he had gazed at the sumptuous shops in Bond Street and noted the flicker and dazzle and colour of the tarmac in the brilliant sunshine, he had wished that he could see a historical panorama of that street going back year by year into the past on such an enchanting morning. He was feeling in a mood of strange exaltation, a mood which London never failed to rouse in him at this season. This sense of being thrilled was not altogether caused by its beauty but by a thousand resplendent associations— the glamour of its wealth, its social functions and cosmopolitan society, its importance as the centre of all that was worth while in the history of his own race. This sense was sharpened, too, by a strange acknowledgment of the city's actual unimportance when viewed in the light of even terrestrial vastness and the seething millions of humanity that lived and strove and laughed and wept, were pompously magnificent or meanly ludicrous in a thousand other cities on the earth's surface. How small was the scope of vision of one human mind! It was an exasperation to be able to grasp so little at one moment when one longed to visualize comprehensively and understand all! In the Green Park the foliage was fluttering lightly in the breeze as if symbolizing the joyous frivolity of existence and the futility of taking anything too seriously. Vereker's step unconsciously quickened to his light-hearted mood and the freedom of the Park. Lost in his own thoughts, he did not observe the approach of a man who, on coming closer to him, almost halted and then hurried eagerly forward to greet him.

"By Jove, Vereker, what a pleasure to meet you!" said Roland Carstairs as he held out a hand and shook Vereker's in a hearty grasp. "I thought you'd turn up at my place long ago and was beginning to think you'd forgotten all about me."

"No, Carstairs," said Vereker looking as if he had been suddenly wakened from a dream, "I hadn't forgotten my promise to look you up. I've just returned to London from a long stay in the country, and as soon as I'd settled down in my flat in Fenton Street, I was going to dig you out. Ah, well, here we are. If you're at a loose end, why not lunch with me somewhere. There's a whole lot of things I want to talk to you about."

"Can you spare the time?"

"My time's my own and I was just idling the morning away. You must come and lunch with me. I'll introduce you to my favourite restaurant—Jacques. Do you know it?"

"I can't say I do."

"Then you must get to know the place. This lunch is on me, as they say in America."

"We've got plenty of time," remarked Carstairs glancing at his watch, "and if you don't mind we'll have a rest on one of the seats. It's pleasant to be out of doors on such a day as this and we can talk without the interruption of eating. I've got a lot to tell you and I'm dying to get it off my mind."

Carstairs led the way to a neighbouring seat and sat down with an air of weariness. Vereker noted the expression of sadness and resignation on his sharp-featured face; he had the look of a man who had temporarily lost faith in himself and the world, whose courage to face adversity was at its lowest ebb and almost willing to let circumstances take their course and do their worst.

"You don't look any too well, Carstairs," said Vereker sympathetically. "Have you been ill?"

"No, not physically ill. I've passed through a bad mental crisis and I daresay it has left its mark on me. Still, I'm on the up-grade again and will soon be my old self," he replied.

Vereker saw that the man had something on his mind, something that he was eager to confide in a friend, and let him talk without interruption.

"Of course you know all about the end of the Marston Manor affair, Vereker, and I won't waste time going over all that again. Inspector Heather and you settled that to your own satisfaction and there was an end to it."

"I don't know about the satisfaction," remarked Vereker. "I've always felt that it was one of my most unsatisfactory cases. There were so many incongruous pieces in the puzzle that I never quite fitted in to please my sense of finality. On the quiet, I believe Heather felt the same but wouldn't admit it. Detection's his trade and he looks at things from a slightly different point of view to mine. However, I won't interrupt you. I see you've got something you want to talk about and it'll do you good to let yourself go."

"As you know, towards the close of your investigation, Miss Stella Cornell disappeared. You doubtless also knew the cause of her disappearance. It all came out subsequently. She went to the south of France to some friends of hers in whom she'd confided her trouble. They asked her to come and stay with them until she'd given birth to her child and made some definite arrangements for her future. She afterwards wrote to me and gave me her address and I immediately crossed to France. She was staying with some very charming people in a little village near Pau. I made one last bid to save the situation and begged her to let me marry her and legitimize the child. Of course it wasn't mine, but I loved her and would have done anything in the world to save her pain and humiliation."

"It was very fine of you, Carstairs, and you have my sincere admiration," said Vereker feelingly.

"She absolutely refused though she said she appreciated what she called 'my heroic spirit' in making such an offer. However, it wasn't to be, and in the end it didn't really matter. She became very ill prior to the crisis and both she and the infant died. I was with her to the last. But this is not the point I wish to tell you about. After her death, among her papers was found a letter addressed to me. She had left that letter in case anything happened to her, and she evidently had some premonition she wouldn't get over her trouble. In it, strangely enough, she mentioned your name and said it was one of the regrets of her life that she was unable to know you better. She said that in her brief meeting with you she instinctively felt that if circumstances had been different she could have found a friend whom she could implicitly trust. I read the letter on my way home from France and it gave me a terrible shock, for in it she confessed that she had shot her cousin Frank in a moment of anger akin to madness."

"Good Lord!" exclaimed Vereker with genuine consternation.

"You may well say so," said Carstairs quietly. "It was the last thing in the world that I thought she would have done. Of course she had sufficient reason for terrible anger, and in a way there was a lot to excuse her for having lost her head and given way to a desire for revenge. But her father's bogus confession took me in completely. I knew the old man pretty well, and such an act as shooting the betrayer of his daughter was more consonant with his fiery nature. She admits that when she knew Frank Cornell had left her for Valerie Mayo, though terribly hurt, she almost resigned herself to the inevitable. It was a cruel humiliation, but such things occur in life and one has to meet them with as much courage as one can summon. Later she made the terrible discovery that she was going to become a mother. On that fatal night, Doctor Redgrave had confirmed her in her fears. She had made a secret appointment to meet Frank in their old trysting place and discuss the new trend affairs had taken. In an insane moment, for sometimes women in such a state are quite abnormal, she decided, if he refused to break off his engagement with Valerie Mayo and marry her, she would commit suicide. She went armed with an automatic pistol that had been for years in the bungalow. Her father had bought it for her at a time when there was a minor

Ripper scare in the Marston district. Frank Cornell kept the appointment and definitely refused to fall in with her suggestion about marriage. She pleaded with him, pointed out the terrible trouble she was in, but he was adamant. In a cynical mood he asked her how could he be certain he was the father of the child. This was the last straw and, as she confesses, she lost all sense of proportion and was temporarily insane. She then told him if he refused to comply with her request she'd immediately commit suicide. He thought this was only bluff on her part and decided to call her bluff. Without further discussion he bade her good night and, leaving the music room, closed the door behind him. For some moments she stood hesitant with the muzzle of the pistol pressed against her temple. She knew Frank was on the other side of the door and hadn't gone up the stairs to his room. She instinctively guessed that he had his eye to the keyhole to see if she would leave the music room by the door into the garden. Against the light of the far window, even at night, it's easy to see what's going on in the music room.

"'I know you're looking at me, Frank,' she said to make sure of his action. His only reply was to laugh and in a paroxysm of rage she put the muzzle of the pistol to the keyhole and fired. The whole thing was done on the spur of the moment, and even then she had some kind of conviction that the lock would prevent the shot proving fatal if Frank was actually looking through the aperture. On learning what had happened, she at once recovered her senses and seeing that she would be arrested for murder, tried to cover up her tracks. She searched and found the empty cartridge case, locked up the music room, and pulling off Frank's shoes tried to drag the body up to his bedroom. She was going to leave it there, wipe the pistol to remove finger-prints and place it in his hand. It was the hasty improvisation of the moment and was, of course, hopelessly weak, for she had overlooked all idea of bloodstains on the staircase. Anyhow, after managing to drag the body very silently to the corridor landing, she heard movements in

Mrs. Cornell's bedroom and leaving everything to take its course slipped into Frank's bedroom and dropped from the open window into the garden. In doing so, her right heel caught one of the jambs of the window and she fell headlong to the ground. To her astonishment she found she was unhurt and, picking herself up, fled through the garden to the bungalow."

"I had a suspicion that the person who had fired the shot had made his or her escape through that bedroom window," remarked Vereker reflectively. "I found three tiny scratches on the jamb of the window and was sure they had been made by the small nails in the sole or heel of a shoe. As they might have been done by one of the maids in cleaning the window, I didn't follow up the clue in my subsequent investigation. But go on, Carstairs."

"On returning to the bungalow, Stella at once went to her father and told him everything that had occurred. He quietened her down at length and told her not to worry. He assured her that if she left the matter in his hands he'd do his best to cover up her deed. He cautioned her to say nothing that could possibly lead the investigators to suspect that hers was the hand that had fired the fatal shot. I think she succeeded in this to a surprising degree. She had a tremendous faith in her father's astuteness, and he took charge of the whole affair. He concealed the pistol on his own person for the time being and gradually formed his plans to save his daughter's life at any cost. On the day of his own suicide he wrote to her telling her that he had gradually led the detectives round to suspecting him of Frank Cornell's murder. He had planted a note making a bogus appointment with the dead man among Cornell's correspondence, which he had learned from his sister-in-law Miss Mayo was destroying. This note, he felt sure, she would hand over to the police. He then secreted the pistol in the music room and flung a secret set of keys into the lily pool. This was done on the spur of the moment and was a bright inspiration, for he knew that Mr. Vereker was standing at the door of the music room. He had heard him coming upstairs and distinctly heard him come to a halt on the half-landing. He declares he felt an impish sense of delight in thoroughly deceiving the detectives into the idea that they were making startling discoveries. You see from all this, Vereker, that David Cornell, on first learning that his daughter had shot Frank Cornell, must have decided at once on sacrificing his own life to save his daughter's. He concludes his letter to Stella by saying so and urging her not to let the past trouble her in making the best of the future. He, himself, he admits rather pathetically, had been a failure in life. Even his terrible affliction of blindness, he confesses, had hardly contributed to his failure in the one thing in which he had desired success above all things, namely his music. He had lost all hope of getting known in that sphere and winning the recognition he thought earlier he might have won. He digresses in his letter into a long disquisition on the art of composition and feels that his whole attitude to it was utterly divorced from modern conceptions as shown in the works of the present-day composers. Poor fellow, in spite of his extraordinary courage and resolution, he was extremely sensitive and was subject to fits of intense depression. In those moments of dejection he would complain that he was out of date, an anachronism in art and outlook, and would be better out of the hurly-burly. Then he would recover and commence work with renewed ardour and none of us thought he would ever take his own life. If this tragedy of his daughter's hadn't occurred, he'd probably have lived to a ripe old age and died peacefully, but it came as the fatal urge to carry out an idea that had always lurked in his mind. Not only that, but it lent the act the colour of a heroic sacrifice. To me it was heroic. Other people may think it was the act of a lunatic, but I cannot agree. I had a great admiration for David Cornell and his last deed on earth, to my mind, touches the borders of the sublime. 'Greater love hath no man,' says the Bible, and I shall always think of David Cornell with great respect. Other men in other and better causes have done the same and we call them heroes. David Cornell will only be called a suicide! But that's the end of my story, Vereker. Let's go."

The two men rose, walked through the Park back to Piccadilly and were soon busy discussing other matters in the way men do.

Some days later, Vereker called on his old friend Detective-Inspector Heather and told him the true story of the Marston Manor case as he had heard it from Roland Carstairs. The inspector listened to it with serious attention and on the conclusion of Vereker's narration remarked:

"Ah, well, that ought to take the conceit out of both of us, Mr. Vereker. We seldom go astray so badly in our efforts. An occasional setback only gives our methods a keener edge by showing us where it's possible to go wrong. We must profit by it. Now that I can look back without fear of being discovered I'm rather glad on the whole that we did go wrong."

"So am I, Heather," replied Vereker with a chastened smile. "In fact, I'm glad we didn't make full use of the clue of the ginger tabby!"

THE END